The Lonely Desert

Sarah
CHALLIS

The Lonely Desert

headline

First published in Great Britain in 2012
by HEADLINE PUBLISHING GROUP

1

Cataloguing in Publication Data is available from the British Library

Hardback 978 0 7553 5679 9
Trade paperback 978 0 7553 5680 5

Typeset in Bembo by Palimpsest Book Production Limited,
Falkirk, Stirlingshire

Printed and bound in Great Britain by
CPI Group (UK) Ltd, Croydon CR0 4YY

Headline's policy is to use papers that are natural, renewable and recyclable
products and made from wood grown in sustainable forests. The logging
and manufacturing processes are expected to conform to the
environmental regulations of the country of origin.

For my father

Emily

AT MIDDAY ON a bright, chilly Saturday in April, I tucked my cold and trembling hand through the crook of my father's arm and prepared to walk down the aisle of the little grey stone church in the Dorset village of Over Crompton where I grew up. We paused, the pair of us, just inside the open porch door and I could smell the lilies that my mother and Aunt Sadie had arranged on the altar, and the icy, intoxicating scent of narcissi and hyacinth at the end of every pew. A blur of pale faces turned towards me and there was a shifting of silk-clad bottoms on the wooden pews as a little murmur of excited expectation rippled to and fro amongst the congregation.

There was no turning back, not that I wanted to. This was it. My wedding day. The organ struck up, and at the front of the church I could see Hugh getting to his feet and stepping out into the aisle to greet me, a huge and unceremonial smile on his face. He looked uncharacteristically smart in a suit I had made him buy in the January sales. Unfortunately he had had a drastic haircut and his trademark floppy brown hair had all gone. It made him look very young and a bit raw – like a boy soldier, a new recruit.

Although Hugh is an anthropologist and spends his time studying the exotic ceremonies of remote tribes, he has a dread of any such events in his own life, and it was just as well I didn't yearn to be driven to the church from my parents' farm in a horse-drawn carriage bedecked with flowers, or to be attended by a pack of tiny bridesmaids and pageboys, or to walk under an arch of raised pitchforks. I wanted our wedding to be simple, too. I had the shortest guest list I could get away with, and wore an unadorned cream shift dress and woollen jacket, with my dark hair loose on my shoulders.

We could, I suppose, have got married in a registry office in London, with no ceremony at all, but I am a Kingsley, one of a far-reaching tribe of Dorset farmers, and I felt it right that I should make my vows in the little church where the bones of my ancestors lie in the churchyard. This is within a stone's throw of the low farmhouse where I grew up and where Clemmie, my cousin, and I had so often played at getting married, using a lace tablecloth as a dress and the ringpull from a soft drink can to plight our troth.

I am an only child, but there in the front pews of the church were ranged my six boy cousins, Clemmie's brothers, all tall, all shock-headed with the famous Kingsley thatch of golden hair, all turning amused faces to me, their podgy (as I was, once) little cousin Emily, traipsing up the aisle to get married. 'Here she comes! Here's Em! Can you believe it! Does the poor sod know what he's in for?' I could almost hear them whispering as they nudged and jostled.

In front of them was my mother, in a saucer hat and bright make-up, outclassing the Kingsley women in their unfashionable get-ups – all better judges of a dairy cow or a working hunter than what to wear at a wedding. Sitting beside her, beaming and serene, was Aunt Ellen, and next to her Uncle Peter, my father's brother. He'd been on the whisky since breakfast. Having a little stiffener, he called it, and now he swayed to his feet as the organ thundered my progress up the aisle.

Parked tidily in the space near the pulpit steps was Miss Timmis in her wheelchair, a tiny crooked figure,

3

her head on her breast like a little bird, her hands clasped under her chin. It was impossible to tell whether she knew that I had arrived on my father's arm to take my place by my future husband. A series of little strokes had left her largely adrift from what was going on around her, and yet she was a key figure in my recent history. It was through her, in a way, that I had first met Hugh.

On the other side of the church, Hugh's small family made little impression on the Kingsley mass gathering. His mother and father, one tall, one short, both timid and self-effacing, stood side by side, looking straight ahead, as if our marriage ceremony was an ordeal that had to be got through. It was a mystery how such a meek couple could have produced brilliant and eccentric Hugh, and Erica, his fierce eco-warrior sister, who sat next to them with her cowed husband, Neil, who worked for the BBC, and their dreadful child, Matthias, each of them with Joan of Arc haircuts and dressed in androgynous organic hemp clothing and vegetarian shoes. Later, at the reception, they would have to square up to all the beef farmers and fox-hunting maniacs on my side of the family.

Why did I feel so nervous as we arrived at the altar steps? My hands shook and a tremor in my left knee set the hem of my dress trembling. My father gently released his arm from my grasp and Hugh came to stand beside me. I must remember to look at him and smile and not spoil the moment by concentrating on his disastrous hair. How had it got past me — that unscheduled visit to a sheep shearer? Everything else about this wedding I had organised down to the last detail. I am used to bossing people around because I am a London primary school teacher, and I tackled the arrangements for my Big Day as I would a school project for my class of thirty-six seven-year-olds. My mother had complained about it. 'For goodness' sake, Emily! I'm here to help, but do stop addressing me in that teacher's tone of voice.'

Hugh and I suit each other in that way, because I discovered early on in our relationship that he needs organising, which I am naturally good at. He loses and forgets things and appears to have only half his mind on whatever is going on around him, but it is a mistake to underestimate his tenacity of purpose when he needs or wants to get something done. Like wanting to marry me, for instance.

We met just over a year ago in bizarre circumstances. I was nursing a broken heart after a long relationship had come to an end. I'm not going to call it a love affair, because although I had certainly loved Ted for a while when we were at school and then university together, the later years were miserable, and I know now that I was hanging on to an unobtainable dream. Meeting Hugh helped me to see that, and gradually I fell in love with the man with the awful haircut who was now waiting to marry me.

All the dreadful romantic yearning and emotional pain that I had suffered at the hands of Ted seemed to gather and swell and then burst like waters from a broken dam and sweep me towards Hugh, my rescuer. Gentle, decent, kind, clever, unselfish Hugh. Although I describe it as 'sweeping', it took time, of course, and Hugh was sometimes away on field trips or giving lectures in far-flung places, and I was busy and tired as London teachers always are, but once we had found each other, we were like homing pigeons coming back to roost side by side and exchange loving murmurs . . . well, sort of. Hugh is vague in the extreme, and often seems to forget my existence, and he is hopeless at conventional romance. No chocolates and champagne or loving text messages or heart-shaped anything comes my way – all the stuff that faithless Ted had been rather good at.

And then the service started, and hand in hand we

sang the first hymn, 'Glorious Things of Thee are Spoken', and I was surprised to hear that Hugh had a lovely bass voice – how was it I had never heard him singing before? A year isn't long enough to know anyone completely. Behind us swelled the sound of Kingsley baying, like a tuneful pack of hounds. They love outclassing the opposition in any sphere, and competitive congregational singing is one of them. I caught Hugh's eye and we exchanged a loving smile, and he squeezed my hand in his. I love his hands – so long and elegant and sensitive-looking, unlike the bunched, reddened sausage fingers of my forebears.

Our lady vicar – the Vicarene, my father calls her, whose name is Debbie, invited us to pray, and I told myself to concentrate on the words, not to miss a single one, and when she talked about our families and friends gathered to witness our union, it was Clemmie I thought of, and regretted that she wasn't there, in the pew with her row of towering brothers. Clemmie is my best friend and always has been, and her absence was the only sadness of the day.

I was thinking of her because, by not being in the church with us, she left a space that couldn't be filled by anyone else. Of all people, she should have been there, sharing this day with me. She was the missing piece of the jigsaw of my life. She should have been there at the beginning to tell me I was doing the right thing in marrying Hugh. She should have got drunk with me on my hen night. She should have helped me choose my dress and decide how to do my hair. Clemmie is the other half of who I am, closer than a cousin or a best friend. Hadn't we, at nine years old, scratched our wrists and mixed our blood in a ceremony of sisterhood, and pledged to be true to each other as long as we lived?

There's something special about Clemmie. When people first meet her, they are struck by her unusual beauty. There's a rare and exotic thread running through the Kingsley bloodline that surfaces from time to time to produce a throwback to a Viking king or a Saxon warlord. Clemmie is one such, as is my father, both possessed of a glacial golden beauty and mesmerising charm. In my father's case, his romantic good looks earned him the hand of my mother, an outsider, a city girl, and also the attention of countless other women with whom he fell regularly and disastrously in love.

With Clemmie it is different. When we were growing up, local boys, neighbouring farmers' sons and others, admired her from a distance while they messed about with the jolly, plump girls who were glad of their attention. Clemmie was too remote and unobtainable. She was too cool and vague. Her level blue gaze was too disturbing, and worst of all, she never fell in love with them. She was never groped in the back of borrowed cars or snogged in horseboxes at gymkhanas. She didn't shriek and flirt and squeal when she was teased and manhandled in the way that passed for lovemaking amongst country lads. No boy would have dared to muck about with Clemmie. She grew up like a medieval princess, distant and chaste, as if she lived in a castle protected by an impregnable thorn hedge.

It was our Great-Aunt Mary who years ago, when we were teenagers and Clemmie was complaining that she hadn't got a boyfriend, advised her that she was a girl born out of time and place. 'You should be loved by a man who lives to bear arms and love women,' she had said, her beady dark eyes shining with a wicked knowledge that she wasn't about to share. I remember the words because they annoyed me at the time. They made me feel left out and ordinary. I also remember them because they were prophetic.

My parents' farmhouse is close enough to the church to allow Hugh and me to link arms and lead our guests through the little churchyard with its sloping mossy headstones and brightly nodding daffodils, to our wedding reception in a small marquee in the garden. I would have been happy to have our party in the village hall, but my mother wasn't going to be done out of seeing her only daughter sent off in proper style. 'I've been waiting years for this,' she said, adding slyly, 'and sometimes gave up hope altogether!' She had been married at twenty-two, and any bride older than twenty-five she considered a dangerously late starter. To wait until my late twenties was to stare disaster in the face. 'I don't want a big lump of an unmarried daughter round my neck,' she used to tell me, tactful as ever. 'Your father and I want to be free of responsibility for a few years before we need walking frames and stair lifts.'

Someone had given the churchyard grass its first cut of the year and it gleamed a damp emerald green and wet clumps stuck to the shoes of anyone who stepped off the little gravel path where dog violets peeped between the cracked edging stones. Above the noisy chatter of the guests there was the constant babble of water from along the length of the valley, where the spring rain of yesterday had run off the hills to replenish the stream that followed the village main street. Banks of pungent wild garlic marked its path.

Above that sound, and drifting up to fill the dome of tender April sky, was the clamour of the sheep and lambs newly released on to the fresh hillsides.

We hurried as the sky darkened and ominous grey clouds bustled across the sun. It was splashy, unpredictable weather, sun one minute and vicious slanting rain the next. We took off down the lane, laughing, and peering anxiously up at the sky. Behind us people were opening umbrellas as the first fat drops fell, but now we were turning into the farm drive, across the yard, standing gloomily silent since my father had given up the milking herd a year ago, and up the two old grey stone steps to the garden gate and the shelter of the pretty little striped marquee.

'Lucky us!' said Hugh, catching me to him and kissing the top of my head. 'Lucky rain!'

'Happy the bride the sun shines on!' I reminded him, ever the pessimist.

'Not in Africa,' he said. 'Quite the opposite! Rain means a fertile wife and a full granary.'

'A bun in the oven!' shouted one of my cousins.

'Here comes Miss Timmis! Make way!' cried Pete, the youngest, who was in charge of the wheelchair. He and Tom manhandled it up the steps and charged into the shelter of the tent. Miss Timmis, dressed for

11

the occasion in a navy suit that hung about her shrunken shape and a jaunty green beret that had once belonged to Great-Aunt Mary, looked surprised at this pitching race. In the nursing home where she now lived, a trip down the corridor to the drawing room was an event. Stephen handed her a glass of champagne and I knelt beside her chair.

'Miss Timmis! It's me, Emily!'

'Of course, my dear.' Her voice was uncertain and her speech a little slurred. 'Your wedding day!'

'Yes! I've married Hugh, who I met in Mali, in Africa. You remember, Miss Timmis, where Clemmie and I went to scatter Great-Aunt Mary's ashes.'

I thought there was a moment of understanding in the faded brown eyes, but Miss Timmis answered vaguely, 'I'm afraid I don't remember that, my dear. Was that before the war?'

'No, Miss Timmis. Great-Aunt Mary died just over a year ago. You lived with her here in the village, in Jasmine Cottage. Do you remember? It was after she died that you moved into The Willows. Before we went to Mali you told Clemmie and me a lot about when you and Mary were girls. You were the only person who knew that she had spent time in French Colonial Africa when she was young. You were the person who helped us to understand why she wanted her ashes taken back there.' You told us a lot, I thought, but you missed out the most important thing; the truth that you had buried for years.

'Did I? I don't remember, I'm afraid. My silly old memory!'

'Her father was in colonial administration and she had gone out to Africa to visit him. She fell in love there.'

Miss Timmis' hand shook and champagne slopped on to the front of her blouse.

Hugh touched my arm. 'Don't, Emily,' he said gently. 'There's no need. You can see she's upset.'

'She should know about Clemmie,' I told him over my shoulder. 'She always loved Clemmie.'

'And guess what, Miss Timmis,' I persisted although she had shrunk away from me into the corner of her chair. 'Hugh and I are going to Africa on our honeymoon. We're going back to Mali. Hugh has some work to do, and I am going to find Clemmie!'

Miss Timmis looked up, her expression suddenly alert. 'Clemmie? Clemmie is there? In that dreadful desert?'

'Yes, she is! She stayed. You must remember, I told you all about it. She fell in love, like Mary did, but she decided to stay. She's there now, and I am going to meet her, I hope.'

'In love? In love with that man? That tribal man?' Miss Timmis was genuinely confused now, and her thin old spinster's voice rattled on, following her own jumbled thoughts. 'I never met him, of course. He wasn't there in that camp with the women. That terrible tent! The sand! The heat! My dear, you can have no idea! She was so very ill. I thought she would die.' Her voice grew stronger in her agitation.

'No, no, Miss Timmis. *That* wasn't Clemmie. That was *Mary*. That *was* just before the war. Years and years ago. Clemmie is there *now*. Clemmie is well. Clemmie's fine.'

This, of course, was a lie. I had no idea how Clemmie was. I hadn't spoken to her for three weeks, and the last e-mail she had sent me had left me anxious on her behalf. She talked of 'difficulties' and 'problems'. She said she was well but that things were 'not easy'. Sometimes, she said, she felt very alone.

When I showed her message to Hugh, he had shrugged. 'You can't be surprised,' he said. 'You knew this would happen. It's what you predicted when she decided to stay. The honeymoon is over, I would say.' He wasn't exactly reassuring.

'It was called French Sudan, Emily,' Miss Timmis

was rabbiting on. 'Her father was governor, you know. He was a most distinguished man. Colonel Barthelot. That was Mary's maiden name.'

'Yes, Miss Timmis, but it's *Clemmie* I'm talking about. It's Clemmie I am going to see.'

'I brought her back, entirely on my own. She was terribly ill. They were so grateful to me. It wasn't easy; a dreadful journey. Travelling was so difficult. We were two young women – alone. War had been declared.'

I gave up. Miss Timmis was working backwards through her life, and had reached a place where the long-distant past was more real and vivid than the present. I patted her hand and steered the champagne glass to her mouth, then signalled to Stephen to come and kneel beside her and listen to the flow. I had heard it before – this sanitised version of what had happened. It was a version that Beryl Timmis had concocted to ease the burden of her conscience.

'I know,' I said, soothingly, although that was the one thing I could never do. What she talked of was lost for ever in the passage of years. Deeds committed in a country as remote as any on earth, where the relentless sun and sand erased the trace of footsteps past and present, were never going to be understood or explained. Now we could only piece together the shreds of inaccurate and biased memory. 'You did your best!' I added comfortingly. 'You brought Mary home.' That I knew was true, and I didn't doubt that Miss Timmis had acted unselfishly and with Mary's best interests at heart.

'Oh yes! I did! I brought her home! They said I had saved her. Her father was so grateful. He was such a charming man. A gentleman in every sense, despite being French. It was later, of course, when she was better, that she married Timothy Kingsley.' Great-Uncle Timothy, the dullest man in Dorset if my father is to be believed.

'Miss Timmis, Hugh and I are going back. We are going on Monday.'

'Oh I shouldn't do that, my dear!' Miss Timmis looked alarmed. 'It's a cruel place, a hard place. Mary never wanted to go back, you know.'

Of course she didn't, I thought. She believed her lover had deserted her and her baby was dead. What was there to go back for? She gave herself up to a life of disappointment, to grey London streets, rain, a colourless sky and a boring English husband. Twenty years of widowhood found her buried alive in Over Crompton with Miss Timmis as her companion, but despite all this, and without her ever betraying her true feelings, the desert never relinquished its hold on her heart. Her request to have her ashes scattered there had astonished us all, particularly Clemmie and me, who were asked to carry out her wishes.

It was Clemmie who had insisted that we go. I was more than reluctant. It was a wild goose chase, an old woman's mad fancy. It was inconvenient and difficult; Mali was too far to go, too remote to get to easily, it was impossible to pinpoint the exact place, which no one had ever heard of and was not to be found on any map. Clemmie virtually frogmarched me all the way. And on the way home, mission accomplished and Great-Aunt Mary's ashes dusting the sand in her chosen place, fate had intervened and our paths had divided. I returned to England with Hugh, and on the wildest and most romantic whim, Clemmie stayed in the desert to follow her heart.

Does anybody remember much about their wedding? It seems odd that my conversation with Miss Timmis remains clear in my mind while the rest of the day passed in a blur, like a fast-forwarded film that occasionally pauses for a moment, before racing on. Lunch over, the rain stopped and the sun shone splashily, and our guests emerged from the marquee and stepped gingerly over the lawn to admire the view down the valley. This was apart, of course, from the Kingsley relatives, who knew the country like the backs of their roughened hands and would never bother to stand and take in a view unless it was to admire a covert that always held a fox, or have a look at livestock, or see how the seed was coming along. They sat on at the lunch tables, leaning back and overspilling their little gilt chairs, heartened by free drink and gladdened to think that my father was paying for it. Rumours of how well he had done when he sold off the herd and leased out the grazing provided an endless diversion.

Our own guests, of our generation and mostly from London, stood in groups and eyed one another speculatively. Hugh and I hadn't known each other for long enough to have shared friends, and this was the first time most of them had met. I saw Merry, with whom I work, laughing with Jem from Hugh's department, and other unlikely combinations and pairings. There was laughter and jokes and later there would be dancing. My cousins were everywhere, entertaining themselves and everyone else. Someone was pushed in the stream, and someone else got on my father's old horse and rode him bareback round the field.

I saw Erica deep in conversation with Divinity, my

cousin Will's partner. Divinity is black and feisty and they appeared to be getting on like a house on fire. Erica liked an ethnic minority if she could get hold of one. Neil appeared to have had much more to drink than was permitted under the health regime imposed by Erica. For once, he looked less repressed, and had taken off his tie and was flirting with my most glamorous friend, Tabitha. Erica wouldn't like that. Good old Tab represented everything she loathed, being white and well-bred, educated expensively, and utterly frivolous. Of the ghastly child, Matthias, there was no sign. With any luck it was he who had fallen into the stream.

My parents sat with Hugh's father and mother, and I could see that my father had worked his charm on my mother-in-law and her nervous, twitchy little face had relaxed and she was looking into his faded blue eyes and smiling. Aunt Ellen was talking to Hugh's father about the first early potatoes. They were getting on tremendously well, which allowed my mother to chain-smoke and taunt the Kingsley relations, which was her favourite blood sport, and Uncle Peter to get quietly sozzled. Everyone was having a lovely time.

These little tableaux are fixed in my memory, but I can't remember much else. Someone from The Willows came to collect Miss Timmis and her wheelchair, and while she was being loaded up, like a horse being taken home from a show, I had a moment to kiss her whiskery cheek and apologise if I had upset her.

'I'll come and see you when I get back,' I promised. 'I'll bring photographs for you to look at, and I'll give your love to Clemmie!' She nodded brightly and held my hand. She had forgotten all about our earlier conversation.

If there was one person who felt lonely that afternoon, it was me. Has anyone else in the world felt lonely on their wedding day? I didn't act it, and I made sure that no one could have possibly guessed, but Hugh, that day, seemed distant and preoccupied. He was worried about his parents and his friends, concerned about their bed and breakfast accommodation and their taxis and their trains back to London. He was worried about making a speech – just a short one to thank my parents – and there was a crease of tension between his eyes. We cut the cake, made so beautifully by Aunt Ellen, and he stood beside me, his hand over my hand which held the knife, but I felt no connection between us. He could have been a helpful stranger at my shoulder.

It was a lovely day, a perfect country wedding, but there was a tiny thorn of disappointment in my heart, a stab of pain as from a little sharp stone trapped in a shoe. You know how the smallest stone can hurt way beyond what is merited by its size. Although I never doubted Hugh's love, I knew that he wasn't entirely mine. He kept back something of himself.

I wished Clemmie had been there, I really did. I could have told her how I felt, and she would have understood. She could have told me that loving someone is not about possessing them and that wedding days are notoriously stressful and are often disappointing. Although Clemmie appears fanciful and über-romantic at times, she talks a lot of sense.

The decision to go to Mali for our honeymoon was obvious. We would have gone back anyway, even if we hadn't decided to get married. Hugh wanted to combine our time away with some field work amongst the Dogon people, because his long-term academic project is a study of animism, which attributes a soul to natural objects. It was through this field work that I had met him in the first place.

When Clemmie and I were roped in by a clause in Great-Aunt Mary's will requesting us to scatter her ashes in a country we had barely heard of, we found that the best way to get ourselves out there was to join a small group of travellers organised from London by Jimbo Trott of Trotts Travel.

It was the first time that Jimbo had organised such a trip to Mali, and the others in our group of six turned out to have particular reasons for wanting to go there. Two of the party were East African safari types – Clemmie and I loathed them – who were keen to track the elusive elephants of Gourma that appear at certain times of the year like dusty shadows out of the desert to find water. They were accompanied by a trendy young photographer whose work was subsequently exhibited in London.

Hugh's interest took him in the opposite direction, to the great Bandiagara escarpment, the home of the Dogon people, whose ancient rituals and unique belief system were threatened by encroaching tourism. He spent his time blissfully happy and high as a kite on maize beer and other home-produced narcotics and, in his more sober moments, collecting vital data for his research.

Now, eighteen months later, we both wanted to return. Hugh needed more time with his Dogons, working out the five known distinct dialects and trying to record some of the oral history that was so rich in strange mythology. I was happy to help him with all of this, but most of all I wanted the opportunity to find Clemmie, whom I had left behind with such apprehension and about whom I was growing so concerned.

This time we were travelling independently, using the driver and guide who had looked after us on our first trip, and we were going in the company of Will, my eldest and favourite cousin, and his girlfriend, Divinity. It might seem odd to be taking other people along on our honeymoon, but I was glad they were coming. It meant that I didn't have to travel into the desert on my own while Hugh was working in Dogon country, and Will was just as keen as I was to re-establish contact with his sister. It was an adventure we were going on and I was glad of their company. There is safety in numbers, it seemed to me, and Will is a special sort of person.

When we were growing up, he was the leader of the pack and we deferred to his judgement. It was a sort of hero-worship, because he is one of those rare, effortlessly perfect people. He is tall and good-looking and athletic and clever. When he was a boy, he won a scholarship to Bryanston and was a bit of star there too. He got heavily into music and drama, and even had a play he had written broadcast on Radio 4 when he was still at school.

It was obvious from early on that he wouldn't go into farming, and it can't have surprised Uncle Peter and Aunt Ellen that after university he started work as a humble runner in a documentary film company. So far he had worked on a touching exposé of homesick European field workers, sitting in their bedsits in Peterborough, missing their forests and mushrooms and mothers with their pans of soup, and another about how greyhounds are chucked out when they are finished with racing. He arranged special screenings in Dorchester and there wasn't a dry eye among the Kingsleys who flocked to see what one of their tribe who had strayed off the land had got up to now. They could relate to homesickness, being so attached to their bit of Dorset and feeling ill at ease and foreign if they strayed into the next county.

The dog film was right up their street, too. Traditionally they exchanged Christmas cards to benefit dog rescue trusts, and they rarely felt as charitable about the plight of humans unless they were Injured Jump Jockeys.

Going back to Mali with Will was almost as good as going the first time with Clemmie. We were made of the same timber, my dad would say, and cut from the same cloth. He would be a great travelling companion, with his interest in people and how they lived their lives, in a quite different way from Hugh, who thought of people in terms of scientific data. Divinity would be fun as well. She was the sort of girl who had her own original take on most things. We would get on like a house on fire.

Divinity

I SOMETIMES ASK MYSELF how I got involved with the Kingsley lot. They're, like, as far removed from my own family as it's possible to be, and going down to their Dorset stronghold is like visiting a foreign country.

I met Will when we were both students in London. He was doing an MA in English at university, and I was at art school – the first person in my family ever to go on to further education. Because I liked clothes and fashion, my mum had assumed I'd be happy to leave school and get a job in a shop on Oxford Street. She wanted me to be out there earning money. She wasn't keen on the student thing. Where's it going to lead? she used to ask me. Show me white girls who want to wear black fashion? She's the most racist person I know, my mum.

I came across Will when we both worked in a bar in the evenings. I was in my final year and had started making bespoke handbags that featured in my friends' end-of-year shows, and at London Fashion Week. He lent me money and helped me launch my business and we've been together ever since.

In London our differences aren't so obvious. Will comes to visit my mum in Mile End, where I grew up. The block of council flats isn't anything special. It's not on a sink estate; if anything, the area has gone up in the world lately, and intends to go into orbit with the Olympics round the corner, but you still notice the litter, the broken lifts, the boarded-up doors, the metal screens across shop windows. It's poor London, that's all.

My mum's family are from Jamaica. My dad came from Senegal. He left not long after I was born and Mum brought me up on her own. Later she found a new man or two, or three, and my half-brother, Giraldo, was born. He's sixteen now and causes us a lot of worry. Mum works as a care assistant in a hospital and does long hours and night shifts, and God only knows what Gira is up to.

My mum loves Will. She can't get enough of him, because he's tall and white and has a posh voice. He makes her scream with laughter. She likes his old-fashioned manners and she loves him for loving the food she makes. He rings her up and says, 'Eloise, I'm dreaming of salt fish and butter beans!' and she says, 'You just get your butt over here and your dream come true!'

The Dorset scene came as a bit of a shock to me. I'm not from a background of landowners. A scrubby patch in Jamaica with a goat on it and a couple of growbags on a strip of balcony is more my thing, although Mum's put her name down for an allotment. I can't get my head round standing at the window of Will's old bedroom at his dad's farm and knowing that everything I can see belongs to his family.

His dad still farms it, too. He goes to bed drunk every night but gets up in the morning cold sober. He doesn't sit in an office all day working out subsidy payouts; he gets out there in his rubber boots and his overalls and does the work, as hard as my ancestors worked on the plantations. 'He works like a black,' someone in the family once told me, and blushed when they realised what they'd said. 'Believe me, he works a bloody sight harder,' I said, no offence taken. He has one young guy to help him and an old bloke called Ivan who has lived in the cottage by the church all his life. They talk about the old days all day long and then go down to the pub together in the evening.

Will's brother, Jake, is champing at the bit to take over, but he's still at agricultural college, learning how to do everything the modern way and leaning towards organic methods, which his dad calls mumbo-jumbo. Remembering me, he corrects this to muck and magic. Jake's future is mapped out, and this makes me think, sadly, of Gira, who has no future that I can see, unless he kicks himself up his own arse, like I had to do.

Emily and Hugh's wedding was okay. I was the only black person there, but I'm used to that in Dorset. I'm treated quite politely, like an exotic specimen, and Will gets his ribs nudged by his male relatives, who are as randy as old billy goats. They think I'm hot because I have a typical African figure with large boobs and a jutting bum you could stand a teapot on. Next to their horse-faced women, I can see what they mean. One of them told me his wife was so hard and thin it was like going to bed with an iron railing.

Emily looked lovely, considering she doesn't care much about clothes, and isn't really interested in fashion. She's the sort of girl who puts comfort before anything else. She had chosen a plain wool dress and jacket, with her lovely dark glossy hair loose and natural. I had made her bag — a little heart-shaped clutch in raspberry-pink leather with a pale green leaf on the front. It was a spring bag for a spring wedding, and in my view it lifted her whole outfit and made it special.

Hugh's a nice guy. I like Hugh. He's tall and thin and looks a bit intense and serious, but he's good fun when you get to know him. He's quite shy and quiet and I guess the whole wedding thing was an ordeal for him. Afterwards, at the reception, he looked distracted, as if he wished he wasn't there. Socially, he's not very at ease. In a big, loud group he looks trapped, as if he's turned up at the wrong party and can't find the way out. Emily fusses about him like a mother hen, watching him with anxious eyes. It's at quiet moments, when they are away from other people, that you can see they love each other.

It was cool to be going to Mali with them. Will loves West African music and was researching for a documentary film about the rise of Islamic schools in Britain. Some of the oldest madrasas are in Mali, apparently, and he wanted to take a look at them. I wanted to discover the fabulous textiles and jewellery. There was a lot to interest us. We would give Emily and Hugh plenty of space. We wouldn't get in their way.

Clemmie was going to be the problem, I could see that. Will and Emily were worried about her. They seemed to think she was in trouble. Frankly, I wasn't surprised that this business she'd got herself into was turning sour. Running off with a Tuareg tribesman is a typical Clemmie stunt. She's been indulged all her life. Maybe she had discovered for the first time what real life is all about.

There might be a touch of jealousy here, I am honest enough to admit. Clemmie grew up adored by her band of brothers. They all talk about her like she is a princess. I've never had any of that. I grew up on my own, and learned to be tough. No one told me I was wonderful, and although Mum has three sisters who live round the corner on the same estate, my cousins were more likely to kick my face in than play with me. Everything I did, I did on my own. Staying on to do A levels set me further apart, and going to college was a struggle for me. Even my mum told me I had airs and graces. There was a lot of 'Who do you think you are, madam?' Oh, yes, she was proud when I made it, and everyone was congratulating her on having a successful daughter, but there wasn't much encouragement on the way. There wasn't much belief in me.

Clemmie, on the other hand, didn't *do* much that I could see, despite all the advantages she had been given. She drifted about doing crap jobs, trying to decide what she wanted to be when she grew up. I don't have any patience with that.

What gets to me about her is that she's effortlessly good at things in a vague sort of way. I noticed at once that she has a real eye for clothes and fashion, for instance. She roots about in a charity shop and emerges looking right on, in her own style. She can draw and paint but has never bothered to make anything of it. I'm not saying she's lazy, but she's never applied herself to anything worthwhile.

To be fair, I don't know her that well. Before she went off to Africa, our paths didn't cross much, and when they did, she was lovely to me, in that special way she has, when she makes you feel as if you are the only person who matters to her in the whole world. I was resistant to her charm. I don't fall for that kind of thing. I don't do sweet. Will loves her, though, so I keep my mouth shut.

Will and I had a few days in Paris in February getting the visas sorted out. I had never been there before and it was exciting for me – an overdue visit to the fashion capital of the world. We stayed at a two-star hotel on the Left Bank and wandered around the cold streets for two days while the Malian Embassy sat on our passports. Fog hung over the Seine and crept under the beautiful bridges. The city was lit with hundreds of white lights. It was very beautiful, but I felt uncomfortable there.

I missed the noise and clamour of dirty old London, and there were few black people in the cafés and restaurants, although there were plenty pushing brooms down the streets in the early mornings or changing the linen in our hotel.

It was the same in the art galleries Will took me to. Hardly a coloured person to be seen. 'Where are they all?' I asked him. 'Where is France's colonial past?'

'Well, not in this part of Paris,' he told me. 'It would be like walking down New Bond Street or going to the Tate and wondering where people like your mum and her sisters were. People stay in their neighbourhoods, don't they? They stay where they feel comfortable.' Yeah, well, I could see this was true, but it didn't make me feel that Paris was a welcoming place.

'Paris doesn't welcome anybody,' said Will. 'It's not that sort of city. It doesn't have to. It's beautiful enough not to have to bother.'

The embassy was weird. We walked all the way there, right under the Eiffel Tower, to an expensive-looking neighbourhood where there was nobody about on the streets at all. Everything seemed to go on behind high courtyard doors that looked as if great horse carriages had once swept through with bewigged and powdered aristocrats off to the ball, while the peasants starved. The embassy had such a door, which was firmly closed without a knocker or a bell or even a handle on the outside. There was a handwritten notice pinned to it saying 'Closed'. Will had looked up opening hours, and it should have been open, so he telephoned the embassy number and eventually a dozy voice answered and said we should come back at three o'clock.

We found somewhere to have lunch, and I watched amazed as stick-thin girls, with their little silk scarves tied round their necks and their neat little handbags at their feet, ate plates of stuff like braised kidneys, and fat steaming sausages on heaps of potatoes.

When we went back to the closed door at three o'clock, one side of it was open, and we stepped through into a courtyard at the far end of which was another open door into an office. Two large black women sat behind a desk, arguing quietly about something, not in French. They didn't look at us, even when we were standing right in front of them, waiting to be noticed. They were both magnificent in their way, big-boned, fleshy, with haughty faces and wearing fabulous printed dresses and matching turbans.

'Excuse me!' said Will, laying our four passports on the desk. The women hardly gave us a glance. Evidently we had to wait until they were ready. Then one of them looked across at me and said something to her colleague. She glanced at me with sudden interest and then idly picked through our passports until she found mine. They studied my photo and the personal information on the back pages.

'American?' said one of them.

'No! British! Look, UK.'

'West African,' they agreed, nodding their turbaned heads together.

'Yeah, well maybe, somewhere in the past.' I wasn't going to tell them about my dad. I didn't know anything about him anyway, the bastard.

Through an open door behind where they sat, on which there was a tattered poster for Air Afrique, I could see an inner room with eighteenth-century panelling, long shuttered windows, a high moulded ceiling and a beautiful tiled floor. It looked as if at any moment bewigged gentlemen and ladies might appear to dance a quadrille, but instead there was a cane chair with a broken seat and an electric kettle sitting on the tiles and an upturned child's stroller. The place had a makeshift and temporary air, as if squatters had moved in.

One of the women turned to search slowly through a cardboard box behind her, and produced some fuzzily printed forms.

'Fill in here. You have photographs? You pay fee now.'

'Yes, yes, we do. We will!' said Will, glad to be making progress. By their offhand manner, these two made it seem that getting into Mali was at their behest.

It took ages to fill in the forms for four of us, and when we had finished, the two grandes dames weren't to be hurried either. Languorously, with long-fingered, slender hands, they shifted through the paperwork and counted out our pile of euro notes, then said, 'Tomorrow. You come back tomorrow. Same time.'

'Ten o'clock,' said Will, emphatically, 'You open at ten.' He flicked open his guidebook at the appropriate page. They shook their heads.

'Tomorrow. Same time.' There was no arguing with them. It would mean we would be cutting it fine to catch our Eurostar train back to London. We would have to bring our bags with us and take a taxi straight to the Gare du Nord.

The women had now lapsed into their own language again and were looking across at me and Will and laughing quietly. Whatever they were saying, there was something mocking or suggestive in their interest in us.

'Heh!' I said. 'What's so funny?' Will looked embarrassed. He thought I was going to make a scene.

They shrugged, and rolled their shoulders, pretending they didn't understand English. Maybe they didn't, I don't know, but the whole experience was weird and made me uncomfortable. I was glad to walk away and out of the courtyard to the street.

'What was it with *them*?' I asked Will. 'It didn't feel exactly like welcome to Mali!'

'Embassies always seem to employ the most congenitally unhelpful people to staff their visa counters. I've come across it loads of times. It's rarely a reflection of the friendliness of the country itself, thank goodness.'

'Hmm. Let's hope not.'

When we went back the next day, our passports lay on the table ready for us, held together by a thick rubber band. Behind the counter, very black and handsome, sat a beaming man, with a rumbling voice and a booming laugh. He jumped up to shake our hands. 'Welcome to Mali!' he greeted us. There was no sign of the women, and the atmosphere today was brisk and professional. Our taxi was waiting for us outside and we were on our way in a matter of minutes.

I checked the visas when we were safely on the train. They were beautifully written in curly writing in green ink and accompanied by a fine, imposing stamp. I noticed that Hugh's passport was almost full. He had travelled all over the world as far as I could see. Emily's was empty apart from her Malian visa for her last trip, when she and Clemmie had been accompanied by their great-aunt Mary's ashes.

As flat northern France swept past the window, I thought of how I had made a little bag in the shape of a pug dog in which to transport the dusty remains. It was quite an inspiration, because pugs were Great-Aunt Mary's favourite dogs, and they come pretty much bag-shaped.

Great-Aunt Mary had left two pugs behind when she died, and they had gone to Emily's parents' farm and were both dead within a few months, the girl dog of natural causes and Pugsy, the rather disgusting, wheezy boy, knocked over by a car in the lane when he was taking himself out for a walk.

He'd set off on his bandy legs in search of a farm collie bitch on heat, according to Emily's mother. 'Serves him right!' she said. She can be tough, Emily's mum. I sometimes think that Emily can't have had that much of an easy time when she was growing up. I can identify with her in that way.

The ashes scattered, the dogs' going should have

been like the end of the story, given that Great-Aunt Mary wasn't even a blood relative; but it wasn't, or we wouldn't have been on our way back to Africa. What had seemed like the end was really a beginning.

Clemmie

TODAY IS EM'S wedding day, and from the moment I woke up, I thought about her. I lay still with my eyes closed and tried to imagine the wet greenness of Dorset, but I couldn't do it. I haven't been able to for months. My eyes see nothing but sand and the burning red of rock, and bleached sky and white sun, and I can't conjure green any more. Even at the oasis, where there are date palms and rows of vegetables springing through the red earth to remind me of a kinder landscape, I can't remember what a field of spring grass would look like, or hear the sound of the running water of the stream that threads its way down our valley.

It's getting hotter than ever as the seasons turn. It's wrong to think that the desert is just hot. It is hot, hot and very hot. The promised rains will start soon, so I have been told, but they come violently and wash

40

away the sand roads and run off the parched ground. They will be followed by a sudden greening of the dirt, and the bony cattle and goats will be pastured outside the town and will fill out and look sleek and glossy again. But first we have to endure this heat.

I am here in Kidal, sleeping on the roof of the house of Chamba's cousin, and tomorrow I will start the journey south to meet Emily and Hugh and Will and Divinity. I last spoke to Ems about three weeks ago, when Chamba's satellite phone was working. It was a wonderful clear line, as if she was calling me from a few miles away, and I was able to ask her all about the wedding so that I would not feel so left out. She wanted to know about me too – about my life – and I found it hard to tell her anything but the barest details. There is not much I can say that she would understand. I told her I was well, and Chamba too, and that I will tell her everything else when I see her. *When I see her.* I can hardly believe that it's true and that I will start on the journey tomorrow.

I'm alone here on the roof – lying on a thin stained mattress and wrapped in a cotton sheet against the biting flies. The other women won't sleep outside unless the men are at home. They lie in the stifling, window-less room downstairs where the children call out in their sleep and the old women snore. I don't know what they're frightened of, although the nightwatchman is fast asleep on the outside stairs. I stepped over his inert body twice to go down to the loo. He was so well wrapped against the hot night that I couldn't tell which end of him was which.

The women think I am strange in every way, but I am used to that now. They stare and laugh at how I look. They think I am peculiar because I am happy to sleep up here alone. To be alone is something completely alien to them. They do everything together; grandmothers, mothers, mothers-in-law, sisters, cousins, daughters. To begin with, I tried to be one of them. It seemed to be the most comfortable place to be, but it didn't work like that. I didn't understand their language, or how they cooked or did the simplest domestic chores. I couldn't even draw water from the well without the bucket tipping and spilling. I was better with the animals – I'm a farmer's daughter – and they screamed with laughter and cheered when I yanked up my long skirt and headed off a ewe or caught a darting kid, and I could milk as well as any of them.

When I decided to stay with Chamba – nearly eighteen months ago – and left Emily to go back to

London on her own, I was so in love that I hardly thought of the consequences. I was following my heart, and even though times have often been difficult, I have never regretted it. I climbed on the back of his great camel, and accompanied by his uncle, Sidi, we rode three days back to his tribal lands, a remote place in the shelter of the mountains of Adrar des Ifoghas where his family were living in their traditional goatskin tents.

I had a romantic idea of what life would be like. My head had been turned by our adventure in this magical and strange country, and I had fallen in love not only with Chamba, but with the glamour of the Tuaregs themselves. I told Emily that there was an affinity between us, the daughters of Dorset dairy farmers brought up in a rural community, and the nomadic way of life centred round herding camels and sheep and goats.

That was bollocks, of course. I had a bit of understanding about animal husbandry, but there is nothing and nowhere like the Sahara, or its people, who survive the hardest life imaginable. I couldn't be one of them however hard I tried. For weeks at a time when the heat was unendurable, Chamba left me in the town of Tamanrasset in a shady house belonging to his family, while he disappeared back into the desert.

I hated it. The house was crowded with two families of women and children, but the loneliness was dreadful and the food disgusting. I suffered from heat rashes and blinding headaches and the appalling idleness sapped my energy so that everything was an effort. I took to hanging about round the few tourist hotels and hostels, longing for someone to talk to, and begging paperback books to alleviate the terrible, suffocating boredom.

I would have jacked it in and booked a flight to Algiers and gone home had it not been for Chamba and the love I felt for him. I hung on because he might turn up today, tomorrow, next week – I never knew. He would arrive with the dust of the desert on his clothes, his eyes bloodshot and weary, and I would help him bathe and fetch him a clean robe, and the women would bring us tea and sweetmeats and close the door discreetly on our lovemaking.

As I lay in his arms, he would stroke my hair and say, 'I thought you would have deserted me. I thought you would have left. It is so hard for you, so far from your home. You are like a little white dove lost in the desert.'

Now the sky is turning rosy pink and gold and the first cocks are beginning to crow. Soon the dogs will start to bark and the donkeys to bray and I will not be able to lie here much longer and think about England. If I stand up and lean my elbows on the wall that surrounds the flat roof, I can look over the muddle of mud-brick houses out to the desert. The sand creeps in between the lowly buildings and banks up against the walls. It sifts along the streets and is swept out of the houses twenty times a day.

To get here on the first leg of my journey, I have travelled across the Sahara from a village called Tin-Zaouaten, a tiny speck on Mali's north-eastern border with Algeria. When Chamba is not out in the desert, he lives in this lonely place where his family have a house like the one in which I have woken this morning. There is water just below the surface of the gritty soil and the village is full of gardens growing vegetables, and date palms. It lies up against black, rocky hills, surrounded by the never-ending desert. It is hard for me to think of it as home.

One of Chamba's brothers brought me here in his beaten-up truck. Bazet is not particularly friendly towards me and I would rather not have travelled with him, but I had no choice. It was a hard journey, and a dangerous one. We drove only at night and early morning because of the terrible heat. Bazet has smuggled goods on this route for years and knows every yard of the way. He drove without headlights and he could see as well in the moonlight as he can in the day. Chamba says he is known by all the other smugglers and bandits who hang out in the burning sands looking for easy pickings. God only knows what he smuggles back and forth. Alcohol? Arms? Cigarettes? Drugs? People? There is so much I didn't understand that went on between the men of the family, and Chamba never told me. He said there was no need for me to know.

There were army checkpoints on the way, and our papers were examined by nervous young soldiers slung about with machine guns. They wore dark glasses and big gold watches. They looked at my passport with no particular interest. I am a tourist. My tourist visa has been extended and approved in Tamanrasset. I am perfectly legal.

Bazet sat impassively while the young soldiers flicked through his papers. He wore his traditional blue chech pulled high on the bridge of his nose. His dark eyes glittered. His long brown hands lay completely still on the steering wheel. These soldiers were not Tuareg. They came from the south of the country. There is long-standing hostility between them and the Tuareg.

Kidal is considered a rebel town. Anyone going there is suspect, but on the other hand it is the first place you reach when you cross the desert. It is a natural stopping place for water and other supplies.

Bazet answered their questions in a quiet, monosyllabic voice. His eyes were averted. It reminded me of the way we were taught to handle a difficult animal on the farm at home; a maddened cow or a bellowing, stamping bull. You must move quietly, avoiding eye contact, poised and alert but presenting no challenge. The soldiers were inexperienced recruits who fear the Tuareg. The tension in the cab of the truck was suffocating. I hardly dared to breathe. I looked straight ahead, my headscarf pulled forward to hide my face and hair. It is best not to attract any attention. Sometimes Bazet was asked to get out and stand by the vehicle. Once he was taken for questioning to a makeshift shack beside the road where soldiers lolled in the shade of a tin awning. Two of the men came over to the truck and leaned on the window, their elbows resting on the roof. They stared at me impassively and I looked down, unsmiling, at my hands resting in my lap. I studied the ring that Chamba gave me. It is smooth Tuareg silver and is marked by the symbols I have come to understand, the crosses and arrows that represent the desert and camels, the sun and the moon, the stars and wind, journeys taken away from one's love, and back again to his arms. I wear it on the third finger of my right hand. It is my wedding ring.

Mostly there was no road to follow. Bazet's eyes searched the horizon and his sense of direction was unerring. We met no one on the way. Not until we neared Kidal did we pass some empty date lorries heading back to Algeria, and a convoy of army vehicles. Bazet knows how to avoid company. Chamba says that his nickname is 'Fox'.

To begin with, we moved through high sand dunes where progress was slow but not once did our truck get stuck. Chamba was right to trust Bazet. At other times we raced across gravelly plains, the hot wind whipping through the window and snatching my scarf off my head. Bazet decided the best place to sleep and threw the bedrolls from the back of the truck. The first day we stopped beside a dried-up gulley where acacia trees were black and twisted in the rocky bottom, and we loaded the pick-up with enough wood for the trip. When we stopped to rest, Bazet ignored my attempts to be useful. He nurtured a little flame within minutes, and soon the kettle was boiling and he started to make the hot, sweet tea that fortifies desert nomads.

We didn't talk, Bazet and I. He has some French but he didn't want to speak to me. He was not exactly rude, but withdrawn, uncommunicative and unsmiling. I know he disapproves of Chamba's love for me. He has seen French women take up with Tuareg lovers in Tamanrasset, and he knows the trouble that results. European women are rich and spoiled. They soon got tired of the humdrum life in the hot, sand-filled towns and can't adapt to the deprivations of the desert camps. They promise their men new lives, new opportunities. They open a hotel, a café, a tour agency, and then, after a few months, or years if things go well, they become worn down by the hardships of frontier life and disappear back to civilisation, taking what is left of their money with them.

Bazet is disapproving that Chamba, the Lion of Temesna and leader of his tribe, has acted so foolishly in forming an alliance with me. There are many beautiful Tuareg girls available and family ties to be strengthened, and he chose me, who knew nothing about anything. I was just a useless piece of decoration.

Bazet has a Tuareg wife, Dianni, and two small children. Dianni cooks and sews and looks after the animals, and her hands are hard like cracked leather and her bare feet blackened and dusty. She is as useful a partner as any Tuareg man could hope for. She is hard-working and good natured. I have swum with her in an oasis pool, and her body is stocky, with full breasts and hips. She was bred for the life she leads. She and the other girls stared in amazement at my white skin and laughed at my small tits and the blonde hair between my legs. They were used to the blonde hair on my head, but this was a hilarious discovery. They laughed about it for days, looking slyly at one another before bursting into giggles behind their hands.

Every evening when Bazet had the fire going and the tea made, he prepared his own food – a pot of macaroni and sheep fat, a few onions and some flaps of flat bread we brought with us from the town. I usually had a boiled egg and some rice and some dates. I had to make myself eat because I had got thin, too thin. Chamba ran his hands over my sides and said it was no good – that women should have fat on their ribs. He said that if I was a camel, he would not buy me, because I would not last the lean months. He made me drink bowls of milk to fatten me up.

Bazet and I travelled three days and nights before we arrived at Kidal and he delivered me here to this house where I was received by the women. I was stiff and tired and there was warm water and a functioning shower, which was the most welcome sight that I could think of. I washed my long hair and let it dry in the sun sitting in the yard outside the two-storey mud house while news of my arrival spread through the narrow streets. All day people came to the yard gate to peer in at me. Young women slunk in to sit on their haunches next to me and touch my hair as it spread on my shoulders. They were amused by my clothing, which was an adapted version of their own. I had found a tailor in a back street of Tinza, who was the proud owner of an old treadle Singer sewing machine, and he had made me long cotton skirts and loose tunic tops. I wore a coloured sash round my middle and a load of the lovely silver jewellery that Chamba had given me. My old riding boots had stood up well to life in the desert and I was glad of the protection they gave against snakes and scorpions. I rubbed them with fat and soap to keep them supple. I could understand that I looked a bit weird. These girls wouldn't have seen Europeans for some time, if ever. In the last year or so, tourism has dried up here in Kidal – not that there were ever many adventurous enough to come this far off the beaten track.

Recently the government in the south have prevented

tourists coming further north than the river town of Mopti, three days' drive away. It is too dangerous; there are kidnappings and murders, we were told. They are blamed on the Tuareg, and here outside Kidal there is now a big army base and it is rumoured that the Americans are here. I think it must be true because last night I heard the sound of helicopters overhead and saw the beam of a searchlight in the sky.

Chamba got so angry when the Tuareg were branded as Islamic terrorists. He and the men of his tribe sometimes sat about talking all day long, their voices raised. It always sounded as if they were in great disagreement and that there would soon be a fight. Many of the men wore long knives tucked into their belts and to begin with I got very nervous, but Chamba laughed and said that no, they were just discussing 'the situation' and that largely they were in agreement. Just before I left, a Tuareg policeman was attacked and killed by five government soldiers in Gao. The president of Mali himself had had to travel to Gao to try and calm things down.

The women took little part in these discussions. They ran daily life and made all the everyday decisions while the men argued about politics. What's new in that?

What I did know was that something very big was going on here that I didn't really understand. I knew that my Lion was involved. It made me rigid with fear for him and his safety. When I rode away with him on the back of his camel, I had no idea, *I knew nothing* of what I was getting into. In so many ways I was a willing lamb to the slaughter.

Emily

W E SPENT OUR wedding night in a Dorset country house hotel. I hadn't wanted to waste the money on unnecessary luxury, but Hugh had insisted and I'm glad he did. The dancing at the reception finished at midnight – we couldn't keep the village awake any later than that. Bob, our local taxi man, took us and our suitcase through the tiny lanes to the old manor and we found ourselves alone at last, looking at one another, perched on the end of an enormous chintz-draped four-poster bed.

Some thoughtful person had put a bottle of champagne in our case and Hugh sent the cork flying across the room, and filled our glasses. This would have been the first drink I could enjoy of the entire day, just as the excruciating shoes that I now kicked off were the first real high heels of my life.

'Thank God that's all over!' I said.

'Didn't you enjoy any of it?'

'Not really. I felt like someone completely unlike me, as if I was an actress playing someone getting married. It's just not me, that sort of fuss. I felt silly most of the time, to be honest.'

'When asked about her wedding day, the bride replied, "I felt silly most of the time . . ." Just as well we didn't invite *Hello!* magazine.'

'You know what I mean! It's not a reflection of how I feel about being married to you. Did *you* enjoy any of it?'

'I only did it for you. The wedding bit, I mean. I would have been just as happy to elope and cut out all the crap – although I understand the importance of ceremony.'

'I know. And I did it for my mother.'

'Aaah! So she's to blame!'

'And for the Kingsley tribe. Family pride and all that bollocks.'

'Well, let's hope we'll never have to do it again.'

'I don't intend to, do you?'

'Never! Let's drink to that! I tell you what, though. It was worth it. I like being married. It feels very good already. I like you being my wife and not just my girlfriend, or my *partner.*'

'Partner is the worst. It's the opposite of "lover". It cuts out all romantic love and sounds as if you spend your whole life together exactly dividing bills, and have a rota for putting out the bin and argue about who has spilt Fairtrade coffee on the *Guardian*.'

Hugh walked round the room picking up objects and studying them with interest. He was never off duty as an anthropologist. The style of the decor was Edwardian country house party. There was even a pair of antique hunting boots under the window and pictures of shooting parties on the walls.

'Sex and the chase,' he observed. 'They are very definitely related in the English pysche.'

'Come to bed and stop theorising,' I said. My wedding dress was now a heap on the floor and I climbed into the great expanse of snowy white linen. 'Look how huge and historic it is. As the actress said to the bishop! Queen Victoria probably slept in it.'

Hugh had by now discovered an electric kettle. 'Would you like a cup of tea? There's the full kit here, and a tin of biscuits. I'd quite like a cup of tea with my wife.'

'Go on then. Throw me a biscuit! Are you hungry? I'm ravenous. Brides always starve themselves, you know.'

'In most communities they get nice and fat. You were lucky not to be locked up and force-fed for a few months.'

I lay back on the lacy pillows and unwrapped and ate both the heart-shaped chocolates from the bedside tables. I felt incredibly happy and as if the best time of my life was about to begin. It seemed as if all the years of growing up, my happy childhood, my awkward teenage years, my miserable time with Ted, were just steps on the road leading me to this room and this man.

Hugh padded carefully across the plush carpet with a flowered bone-china tea cup in each hand and the tin of biscuits wedged under his chin, like a domesticated version of a St Bernard dog. Even with the haircut he looked incredibly desirable in his white shirt, unbuttoned, and his tie under his left ear.

'Here you are, missus,' he said, putting the cups down on the bedside table, getting out of his clothes, and climbing in beside me. He reached out to take me in his arms. 'God!' he said. 'I'm happy!' I could feel, through his skin on mine, that he meant it, and it was a very wonderful thing indeed.

On Monday, early in the morning, we met up with Will and Divinity at Heathrow and our proper honeymoon trip began. It was a horrid, cold, grey morning. Spring seemed to have forgotten that it had arrived, and winter seized the opportunity to slink back like a cold slap in the face. I couldn't help but think of the first time I had made this trip, with Clemmie, full of apprehension, and with Great-Aunt Mary in the pug bag round Clemmie's neck. I had been so desperately unhappy, travelling with my heart full of the misery of the end of a relationship that I had been in since I was eighteen. It was amazing how one's life could change in such a short time, and that here I was with my new husband and with the same heart, mended now and full of love.

Hugh and I had packed very carefully. It always helps if you have been to a country before and know the sort of gear that works, and leave behind all the wrong stuff that travel guides suggest you'll need. The whole bottom part of my backpack was taken up with things for Clemmie. It wasn't too hard to work out what she would be short of by now, although she told me she was able to buy some jeans and underwear in Algeria. I'd taken her a suspicious number of good old Brooke Bond tea bags, de-boxed into plastic bags. It looked as if I was a major pusher. You know how something peculiar happens to tea bags in other countries and English tea never tastes like it does at home? Two large pots of Marmite were rolled into Hugh's spare trousers and shortbread biscuits in mine. I'd bought a load of face stuff – high-factor sun creams and moisturisers. God knows how Clemmie's pale skin had suffered after months of exposure to desert sun. We had also taken some broad-spectrum antibiotics and a lot of painkillers. We were like a travelling chemist, because can you imagine having a cracking headache or toothache and no paracetamol? These things, which we take for granted, are hard to find and very expensive in the desert towns.

This time everything at the airport was much more relaxed and easy. Heathrow seemed to have sorted itself out, and the queues for check-in and security were not so slow-moving. We had to fly first to Paris, and then on to Bamako. As we passed the final security check and collected our hand luggage, Divinity and I grinned at each other. It was fun to be travelling together. I don't think she's been abroad much, and although I've been around Europe, Africa is an altogether more exciting continent and I really wanted her and Will to enjoy it. Shared experiences are always value added.

We had left plenty of time, and while we waited

for our departure gate to be announced, we sat in a row and talked about the trip. Thank goodness neither my mother nor Aunt Ellen are fussers, or they would have created a lot of bother over us going to what is ranked as a dangerous country.

'Foreign Office advice is no travel to northern provinces at all. They say there is a high threat of terrorism, kidnapping and murder,' said Hugh cheerfully, 'but if you look at the stats, there haven't been *that* many incidents, and those that have been reported are where tourists have behaved stupidly and made themselves targets. It sounds as if Niger is more dangerous.'

'We'll be fine travelling with Tuaregs,' I said to Divinity, who was looking anxious. 'There were dire warnings when Clemmie and I went to Mali last time, but really, the country couldn't have felt more safe and peaceful.'

'Who are these kidnappers? Do they just want money, like those Somali pirates, or is it political or something?'

'Apparently al-Qaeda has moved into the Sahara,' said Will. 'It's called al-Qaeda in the Islamic Maghreb, or AQIM. Rogue Tuareg are blamed for the kidnappings, and it's claimed that they sell the victims on to AQIM, who ask for a ransom. If that isn't forthcoming, they bump them off.'

'Holy shit! We're not going anywhere near those parts, are we?'

'Hugh isn't,' I said. 'I don't think there is any danger where his Dogons live, apart from mass tourism spoiling everything, but we'll be going much further north to meet up with Clemmie, and that is where the trouble is supposed to be. But, you know, the Foreign Office posted this same stuff last time, and our Tuareg drivers and guides told us there was no problem; that we were completely safe travelling with them. You'll see when we get there – you won't feel in danger at all.'

'It's a bit like London, which is always on high terrorist alert, isn't it? I mean, you'd never go out of the house if you took any notice of it,' said Divinity.

'Exactly! Londoners are used to threats after years of the IRA bombings. They just get on with life. But on the other hand,' I said, 'you have to be responsible and use basic common sense. Last time, Clemmie and I saw some really stupid Europeans who were travelling on their own in four-by-fours – or in a little convoy, without guides. That's really asking for trouble. Our Tuareg driver shook his head over them because they stand out like sore thumbs and are sitting ducks; if you can *be* both thumbs and ducks.'

'Or dumbs and thucks,' said Will. 'Or dickheads, if

you prefer. What does that thing – "Maghreb" mean?' he asked Hugh.

'It's actually an Arabic word for "west occident", and it used to denote the westernmost territories that fell to Islamic conquests in the seventh century. Now, used with the definitive article "al", it loosely means the five modern states of North Africa and the areas of adjoining countries that border the southern Sahara.'

'You see,' I said to Divinity and Will. 'He knows everything! He ought to be a tour guide.'

'It has an interesting history,' said Hugh. 'The Arabs reached the Maghreb in early Umayyad times, and encouraged the development of trans-Saharan trade, which was hugely profitable. They traded salt, gold, spices and, in particular, slaves. The Arabs were actually the first slave masters. Later the Tuaregs dominated the route and demanded payment for safe conduct. So you see, the Sahara has always been a dangerous place to cross, quite apart from being one of the harshest environments in the world. If you avoided dying of thirst and exhaustion, you ran the real risk of being taken prisoner by tribesmen and sold off as a slave.'

'What the hell is your sister doing mixed up in a place like that?' said Divinity to Will in an exasperated voice, throwing her hands up in the air. 'Isn't Dorset exciting enough? Couldn't she have stayed in Piddletrenthide or Up Cerne or somewhere and married a nice farmer, and milked cows and listened to *Farming Today*, rather than running off with a nomad and herding camels in the desert?'

Will just shrugged. He and I were both aware of some hostility in Divinity's attitude to Clem. I knew where it came from. She thought Clem was spoiled and princessy, which isn't true at all. She hardly knows her. She is not in a position to judge.

'I mean, what the hell does she think she's *doing* out there? What's the point of it all?'

'Actually, Divinity, she's been doing quite a lot,' I said, a touch stiffly. 'She's been teaching, for one thing. Tuareg children get very little education if they are out in the desert. There are no schools for nomads. We actually visited a new one that was built as part of a government concession to the Tuareg, but it was completely deserted – an empty breeze-block shell – because there were no teachers.

'Clem's been teaching English to older children. It's virtually the only way out for them, you see. If they can speak English, they can work as tourist guides or interpreters for mining companies, or banks, or for NGOs or anything. Suddenly their horizons broaden beyond the desert. She has set up a little class at the oasis where Chamba's family live most of the time, and organised a proper system. She teaches a selected group of older children and then they pass on what they have learned to another, younger group – a sort of pyramid teaching system. It's working really well, apparently. When they have no paper or pencils, which is most of the time, they write in the sand.'

Divinity pulled down her bottom lip. She is very good at looking disparaging. 'Yeah, okay. It all sounds a bit colonial to me – like as if she's a missionary or something. More to do with making *her* feel useful than being effective. Anyway, how are we going to meet up with her and this man she's with?'

'We've got Serufi meeting us at the airport in Bamako and generally looking after us. He was the man who drove us last time. He'll deliver Hugh to his Dogons – which is a couple of days' driving – and then he'll take us on up towards the north, to the crossroads where were handed over to the desert men last time – a sort of halfway house – and Clemmie will arrive there from the other direction. The place is like a simple café and hostel. We can stay there for a few days, and then go back to pick up Hugh so that you guys can see Dogon country.

'Clemmie will have started on her way down from the north now, from the opposite direction, but her man can't come with her, apparently – there's some sort of crisis with his people. He's like a prince, a sort of hereditary leader. He's called the Lion of Temesna. Wonderful, isn't it?'

Divinity sighed deeply and raised her eyes. This news would fit in with her view of Clemmie.

'So, anyway, she's travelling with one of his brothers, she said. By now she should have crossed the greater part of the Sahara and have reached Kidal, which is where we started our camel trek from – you know, with Great-Aunt Mary's ashes. It's a Tuareg town – their sort of home base in Mali. In the nineties, it was the centre of the various rebellions against the government in the south.'

'Will there be anything interesting on our way up to meet her?'

'Of course there will! Just wait till you see what the road going north is like! There are stalls and markets along the way and masses of wonderful stuff to buy. The people are incredible craftsmen. You'll love it all; the wood carvings, the jewellery, the textiles, even the plastic buckets are more colourful than ours, in pink and white stripes. It won't be a long, boring journey at all and we are stopping a night in Djenne, which is a World Heritage Site.'

Divinity smiled and patted my hand. She has the best and widest and whitest smile I know. 'It'll be great! Don't worry about us, darling,' she said. 'This is your honeymoon, remember. Even though it looks as if you're choosing to spend it apart from your husband!'

Meanwhile, Hugh and Will had maps and itineraries spread over their knees, and ours, and Hugh was busy telling Will about his research and where he intended to spend the days we were apart. He was going to trek into the heart of the Dogon country, far off the tourist trail, where he knew from his last trip that medicine men and soothsayers still held sway.

'Right!' I said, standing up. 'I'm going to duty-free to buy Clemmie some scent. Are you coming, Divinity?'

'Yeah, I'll come. I could do with some more sun cream and some lip balm. Do you want anything, Will?'

'Get a bottle of whisky. Medicinal purposes, of course.'

'Good idea,' said Hugh. 'Make that two.'

Divinity

THINGS WERE DIFFERENT when we reached Paris. The weather was just as grey and dismal, and we had to get on an airport bus and change terminals, but when we arrived at the departure gate for our onward flight, there was a marked change in the atmosphere. Most of the passengers bound for Bamako were black, and now it was Will, Hugh and Emily who were in the minority.

These were my people, I suppose. I looked around me at the women who were dressed up like for a tribal wedding or something with turbans, the lot, in one-shouldered long dresses worn over a T-shirt. The prints were fabulous, bold and bright, and most of these dames were substantial ladies. They wore a lot of sparkly jewellery and high heels and dark red lipstick and walked with a slow, hip-rolling gait. Some of the men were traditionally dressed, but a lot of them wore flash business suits and favoured massed gold rings and watches and dark glasses.

To be truthful, they appeared like ridiculous caricatures to me, and I felt embarrassed for them. Couldn't they see that with their well-appointed wives, they looked like corrupt fat-cat businessmen, from a black African country that was one of the poorest on the planet?

I slunk down into my hooded jacket. I was dressed like any London girl in tight jeans and trainers and my straightened hair was tied up in a knot on my head. I have never felt the need to parade a black identity with ethnic stuff.

The others had gone quiet, sitting in a row taking in our fellow passengers and marvelling at the enormity of their luggage, all plastic-wrapped and taped up and the size of an average fridge freezer. These were people going home with a whole lot of booty.

The next thing I noticed was the noise they made – a happy hum that rose to a crescendo of laughing and chattering. Europeans don't talk and laugh like that in public unless they are drunk. These were happy people and they weren't worried about showing it.

Hugh pointed out a group of middle-aged Westerners dressed in a uniform of khaki combat trousers, green polo shirts and Velcro sandals. They had an earnest, inoffensive air about them and were in a fussy state, patting their numerous pockets looking for lost items, or handing each other antibacterial hand gel. When I got up to visit the ladies', I stood next to one of them at the mirror while she combed her grey bobbed hair and was able to read 'Saviour, Sanctifier, Healer, Coming King' emblazoned on her bosom, along with a wine glass, crown and cross. She saw me looking and explained that they were a Protestant Christian group on a fourteen-day missionary trip from Miami. Her breath smelled of peppermints and her pale eyes shone with the joyful expectation of lost souls to bring to Jesus.

God, they are still at it – these Christians, I thought. Emily had told me they met up with missionaries the last trip they made. As if there wasn't enough religion in the world. My mum, who grew up in Jamaica, is a-moving and a-shaking Pentecostal Christian, thanks to her upbringing but I won't touch it, thank you very much. As soon as I was old enough, I said I wasn't going to church with her any more. That caused a lot of weeping and wailing, I can tell you, and they prayed for me, so my mum told me, that I would be turned back to the path of righteousness. But I wasn't budging.

The more I learned about the world, the easier it was to see that the white man's faith had been used to keep the blacks under control, courtesy of missionaries.

When I got back and told the others, Hugh said the logo sounded as if it should represent the Christian Wine Growers' Association, which sounded an altogether better idea.

I slept most of the way on the plane, despite the horrible child sitting behind me kicking my seat non-stop. His father, one of the over-important men in suits, was up and down the whole flight and dropped something hard on my head from the locker above, with no apology. Then we were bumping along a runway and I looked out of the scratched plastic of the cabin window and saw Africa for the first time. Well, it was pitch black, actually, but I saw African darkness.

There was a stampede to get off that made me furious. I'm so British about things like that. Just wait, can't you, I muttered under my breath, but nobody could or did, and there was a lot of shoving and elbowing. The Christians all got up and trooped off together in their sandals, like a little herd of pale, nervous animals, frightened of the dark night, bunched together for comfort.

'Oh, Will!' said Emily, all shiny-eyed. 'Isn't it just great to think we are in the same country as Clem? We'll see her soon. She'll be thinking of us arriving tonight! I might have a message from her on my phone. I'll switch it on when we are off the plane.'

The first thing that hit me as we came down the aircraft steps was the terrific and wonderful steamy heat and the high-pitched thrumming of insect noise that was in the background but deafening at the same time. Crickets, I supposed, but it seemed weird that there should be so many in the middle of a capital city.

We were herded across the tarmac towards a brightly lit building, where we were all pressed in together. The heat was overwhelming and the excitement and noise and clamour quite unlike anything I had ever experienced. My God, these people knew how to push. The Christians had disappeared in the throng. There seemed to be just as many people pushing the other way, crowded against the rope that divided the arriving passengers from those who had come to meet them. It was almost scary, because it seemed to lack any organisation, but then I saw that we were being moved towards passport control. Suddenly I was singled out and directed by an official to a different queue, the one that was massed with all the home-going Africans. 'No!' I said. 'I'm British! British! Look!' and I shoved my passport under his nose. Please don't think I'm one of that lot, I thought.

Before too long we arrived at the front of the queue and were through with no problem. Our luggage was waiting, heaped on carts in the arrivals hall, and it was really quite efficient. Emily was getting bossy because she had done it all before; 'This way!' she cried, 'Come on, keep together!' She kept checking that Hugh had got everything.

'Hugh,' she said, 'where did you put your passport? Here, give it to me. Where are your glasses? Don't put them in that pocket. You'll sit on them!' She couldn't stop being a primary school teacher, and if she went on like this the whole trip, I was going to get very sick of it.

We fought through the crowd and got to the outside of the building, which was equally congested with taxi drivers and hotel touts and pathetic-looking cripples with outstretched hands, the most dis-abled being hauled about on handcarts. I took Will's arm because I felt I needed protecting from this sudden introduction to the Third World. I didn't know how to behave. I wanted to get out my purse and empty it into these yellow-palmed hands stretched towards me on stick-thin arms. I wanted to make a fuss, to accost the policeman who was lazily directing taxis and demand why these people weren't being taken care of, but as I hesitated, I was besieged by other hands reaching out and pulling my sleeve, and then a second policeman appeared and drove them all away and they melted into the dark to reassemble across the road in the car park.

'Oh my God!' I said to Will. 'It's dreadful, shocking, to see people like that!'

'I'm afraid you'll get used to it,' he said. 'You just do. After a while you almost stop noticing.'

'There's Serufi!' cried Emily, and a small, squat figure appeared from across the road, dressed in what I recognised as Tuareg clothing, a long cotton shift and trousers in dirty white and a huge length of bitter-ochre-coloured cloth wound round his head and across the lower part of his face. He wasn't exactly an impressive figure, but he was a welcoming one, waving, and then shaking our hands and seizing armfuls of our luggage, and indicating that we should cross the road to a battered 4x4 vehicle.

As soon as we reached the truck and put down our bags, Hugh embraced him warmly. He didn't seem embarrassed to really hug him.

'Serufi!' he cried. 'The last time we saw you, we left you with a crashed vehicle in a field by the road, in the middle of nowhere. I've felt guilty ever since.' Serufi beamed, not understanding a word, and so Hugh said the whole thing again in another language, and Serufi laughed and clasped him back just as warmly.

'It's Bambara he's speaking!' said Emily proudly. 'The majority language of Mali. Hugh is one of the very few Westerners who can speak it. He speaks some Tamashek, too, which is the Tuareg's own language. Right! Hop in! We're booked into a hotel in Bamako for the night, and Serufi suggests we go out later to a club. He's very keen that we should see the sights.'

'Sounds good!' said Will and we climbed in.

It was equally mind-blowing to take in the general chaos on the roads as we got nearer the main part of the city. Very ancient and ramshackle lorries, packed with goats or cows, or rubbish, or people, or bulging sacks, lumbered along beside battered minibuses crammed with more people. Sleek Mercedes and Range Rovers changed lanes, with horns blaring, while all along the side of the road were bicycles and handcarts and stalls selling piles of fruit, and sack-covered shacks and throngs of people, children, donkeys and dogs, under an explosion of vivid green banana trees. The women were amazing – sinuous and graceful and dressed in the most wonderful one-shouldered dresses – usually with a matching turban – in vibrant patterns of red and yellow and orange. They looked like queens emerging from a midden of poverty.

'Wow! Wow!' was all I could say, until Emily dug me in the ribs and said, 'I told you you would love it, and this is just the beginning!'

Serufi took as a large modern hotel which could have been anywhere. The air conditioning was icy, and in the reception area a lot of aircrews were sitting about in that killing-time way. There was a Moroccan-themed evening in full swing in the dining room, and a fat belly dancer undulated half-heartedly while a group of overweight white businessmen lounged in armchairs watching.

Our rooms were fine – air-conditioned and comfort-able – and after a quick shower we changed and went back down to meet the others. I was looking forward to seeing a bit of nightlife and was getting hungry. Serufi was waiting for us, and took us off to an entirely empty restaurant – when we saw the prices, we knew why. It was dominated by a huge plasma television screen showing *Lord of the Rings* with Arabic subtitles. It was altogether a bit unreal, like a dream when you watch yourself watching yourself watching, and so on. The waiters and bar staff leaned round the walls, gazing at the screen with a sort of hypnotised intensity. It was hard to stir anyone to come and take our orders from a menu that was in French, and then the food took hours to arrive. Will had rabbit and mashed potatoes, as if he was in Dorset in the winter, and we had very dried-up pizzas. The beer was good, though, and Will and Hugh had one of those blokes' conversations about beer drunk round the world and which was good and which wasn't.

Serufi then took us off to a crowded bar with a Wild West theme – Wild West in steaming Africa? Who dreamed up that idea? There was a long rough-hewn wooden bar behind which were ranged about twenty amazing-looking long-haired blonde girls in extremely scanty outfits.

'What's all this about?' I asked Will, who was just as bemused. It turned out that you were expected to buy yourself and one of these girls a drink from a price list that included favours ranging from a quick, flirtatious conversation to what I imagined was the full works. The clientele were black businessmen of the type we had seen on the plane, and seedy-looking European men. Emily and I were the only women on our side of the bar. Will bought us all beers and talked to the girl who served him. When he came back with our drinks he said, 'She's Ukrainian. She's only been here six days and says her life is "work, sleep, work, sleep, work, sleep". She wasn't even sure what country she was in. She thought she was going to work in a hotel in Paris.'

Emily started to get very agitated and wanted to speak to the girls herself. 'It's a form of slavery!' she cried. 'I've read about how this happens! These girls are recruited in eastern European countries by gangsters and then subjected to slavelike conditions and forced into the sex trade. They take away their passports and get them hooked on drugs!'

We all felt uncomfortable by now, and I watched the girls' vacant painted faces as they slid full glasses across the bar or leaned forward to flirt with sweaty, unattractive men. At the far end one of the girls sat slumped with her head on her arms in an attitude of exhaustion or despair, and we saw her woken and moved away by a slightly older woman who appeared to be the boss.

Emily went up to the bar and indicated that she wanted to talk to her. The woman came over and had a few brief words, and Emily returned looking angry. 'She's Russian. She only speaks a bit of English. The bar is owned by a Russian and an Australian. That's all she would say.'

'It's a dirty old world, Em,' said Will. 'You can't fight it all.'

'We can absolutely NOT drink here!' she said, standing up. 'I'm going to take details of this place and report it to the Russian and Australian embassies. It's appalling. You can see what's going on!'

Personally, I couldn't get too worked up. To me, the girls looked as though they knew what they were doing. Maybe it was a better life than back in a Ukrainian village where the most exciting thing to eat was a potato, and the bad news was that the cow was ill. I knew so many eastern European girls on the game in London that I thought Emily could start her crusade at home if she cared that much. Still, I didn't want to stay there any longer and we trooped out into the night, where Serufi was waiting for us.

Hugh spoke to him, and Serufi explained that he thought we would enjoy the club – that most Europeans wanted to go there. 'Girls for Go Go!' he said in

English. 'Very good!' He could tell from our glum faces that we didn't think so. We had let him down by not being enthusiastic. Shrugging sadly, he drove us back to our hotel.

Clemmie

I T WAS NOT unusual for me to have no idea what was going on. It had become my default setting – this sense of bewilderment, when I couldn't communicate with anyone and plans seemed to be constantly changing. I hadn't seen Bazet since he left me here in this house of women two days ago, and yesterday I was up early expecting him to come to collect me to take me on the next stage of my journey, but he didn't turn up.

'*Où est Bazet?*' I asked of anyone who came into the courtyard, but nobody seemed to know.

The head of the household was a middle-aged woman called Mariam. She was some sort of relative of Chamba's – what the Tuareg loosely call 'cousin'. She spoke a little French – very little, a few words only – but when I asked her '*Quand?*' she shrugged and smiled and patted my hand in a sisterly way and said, '*Bientôt! Bientôt!*'

Soon. But how soon? I was getting very jittery about the plan to meet Emily. There had been no electricity here since I arrived – nothing unusual – and I couldn't recharge my mobile telephone. I had enough juice left for the moment but I didn't want to waste it. I sent her text messages, but since I had been here they had come back with 'delivery failure' against them and I didn't know why. I asked to borrow a phone from the women in this household, but the messages failed from that mobile too. They shook their heads and tried different ways to put in Emily's number, arguing about the code – but nothing worked. I knew she would be waiting anxiously to hear from me when she arrived in Bamako, and the next day she would start on the long drive north to our meeting place, without knowing for sure that I would be there.

I needed and missed Chamba. I hated to be away from him, and in this instance he was the only person who could have explained to me what was happening. He had planned that Bazet and I would stop here overnight and that the next morning we would set off again for the crossroads at Homberi, two days' driving from here, across the Niger river at Gao, and deep into the country known as sahel – the semi-desert no-man's-land of nomadic herders and poverty-stricken villages. When we reached Homberi, where there was a little guest house, I would wait for Emily and Will. I knew that I had time in hand, but I was anxious to get there. Many things can cause delays on desert journeys, and if I arrived early, I didn't mind waiting for them. I had grown good at waiting. So much time in the desert was spent in a state of suspended animation. Too hot to move, we rested long hours in the shade until it was bearable to move about again. Nothing happened very fast. There was no urgency. Everything could wait.

But now I couldn't bear the unexplained delay. There was nothing for me to do, nothing to distract me. The women wouldn't let me help in the kitchen. They smiled and laughed and bustled me out, indicating that I should sit on the floor cushions in the stuffy reception room with no windows and a dusty carpet and they would bring me tea and pastries. They wouldn't let me sweep the sand from the downstairs rooms but took the brush from my hands and suggested I should move to a plastic chair in the shade of the tree that sheltered the yard.

They were set on making me feel an honoured guest, but not at home, and definitely not one of them. Mariam sent two of the teenage girls out to buy me cans of cold drinks and a bag of hard green oranges.

I played with the children and sat on the plastic chair, with my bag packed, and kept an eye on the gate, trying to be patient.

While I waited, it was evident there was something going on, a lot of talk and discussion, and I guessed it was about me. Men came into the yard, veiled and silent, dressed in the traditional Tuareg style. They greeted the women formally, exchanged sal'aams with me, and then got into a huddle with Mariam while someone went to prepare tea. The ceremony went on and on, pouring the tea from the silver pot into tiny cups and then tipping it back in the pot to pour again and again. There was a sense of occasion, and not until the first two cups had been drunk did the heated discussion in Tamashek begin, with glances thrown in my direction. My understanding was so minimal and they talked so fast that I could only pick up the odd word and I was none the wiser. What the fuck was going on?

This was the worst of life here – the sense of isolation and apartness that only left me when I was with my Lion. We spoke in French together but we also understood one another in a way that needed no spoken language. He knew what I was feeling before I knew it myself. It was when I was apart from him that I felt so alone and far away from anything that was familiar, although I'd like to think that I had made friends amongst his family. I loved his sister Amadou, for instance, and we giggled and gossiped and she tried to help me with my Tamashek, but there was no escaping that I was an outsider. When I was not with Chamba, the other women didn't bother to try and talk with me, or include me in anything. Their early curiosity and interest in me had worn off, and yet I had the uncomfortable feeling that I was always under observation and a subject of discussion.

When Chamba was away, I often took his horse, a bright chestnut stallion whose name means Evening Star, and went riding out of the village on my own, keeping to the tracks that were worn flat by the feet of animals, always anxious that I might get lost. The landscape was still featureless to my eyes, one dune like another, one parched wadi of acacia bushes like the next. Coming from a farming family, I grew up knowing every field, every tree, every rise and fall of the land. You could have left me blindfolded somewhere on the farm and I could have found my way home. When we were children, Emily and I used to do this sometimes on our ponies. We would ride with our eyes shut for the fun of it – a bit of a cheat because her Tom and my Blazer would take care of us – but we knew from the sound of the ground under their hooves, from the incline of the track, from the smooth wood of a gate, exactly where we were. But here, I was blind with my eyes wide open.

When I turned the horse's head, I usually saw that I was being followed by a distant truck, a single camelman, another lone horseman or a couple of boys perched on the back of a donkey. There was always someone watching me. When I said this to Chamba, he shrugged and repeated a Tuareg proverb – something about the desert having eyes and ears. 'You are precious, you see,' he said, 'with your hair of gold! We look after what is so valuable.'

The happiest times I have had with him were when we were living in the family tents in the desert in the traditional way, tending the herds and riding out each day to look for new grazing. We took camels and rode together, side by side, and he was proud of how I rode, and I loved his praise. He had given me a pure white camel with an unpronounceable Tuareg name, whom I called Orion. He was gentle and obedient and beautifully trained, like a dressage horse. I had my own camel saddle with a high decorated back and a tall Tuareg cross on the front, and Orion wore a rein strung with brilliantly coloured tassels and a saddle cloth of red and green. I felt like a medieval princess out with my prince. Being alone in the desert with Chamba was the most romantic thing in the world. It was what I thought of when I was away from him. I carried the memories of these times, like sparkling jewels, in my mind.

It was hard to reconcile ordinary life, the humdrum stuff, with what I had experienced at these times with my man. When I was away from him, I had a terrible fear that I would never have it again – that something would happen that would prevent us from being together in that extraordinary way, our hearts and souls and bodies, under the glittering canopy of stars. I thought often of my Great-Aunt Mary, who had loved like I did, and who suffered appalling loss from which she never really recovered, and I felt overcome with a sense of dread.

Part of this fear must have come from knowing how impossible our love affair was. It broke all the bounds of family and culture and it put me in this alien and unforgiving land where I had no friends or family and no means of supporting myself or making independent decisions. I still had money in my London bank account, and whenever I had the chance I drew out enough to

buy sugar and flour and millet and the bottled water
I had to drink, but I was acutely aware that times were
hard for Chamba's people and I was an extra mouth
to feed. I was entirely at the mercy of the man I loved
with all my heart, and I felt helpless in a way that I
hated.

The enforced delay in Mariam's house sent galloping
horses of fear through my head. I wanted Chamba
terribly and wished that I could speak to him, but I
didn't know where he was. I had tried his satellite
telephone, but he didn't answer. The day I left, he was
himself setting off somewhere in the desert, as he often
did. He went with men of his tribe and no women
accompanied them. He called it 'tribal business' and
opened his hands in an expressive way to suggest that
there was much to be seen to. Maybe it was to check
on the herds of goats and sheep belonging to his family
that were out beyond the town, but I thought it was
more likely that he had to settle a problem with a young
relative, a hothead, he called him, who had got into
trouble with the police. There was always something for
him to worry about.

I realised that I could be overreacting to the hold-up
because I was so excited at the thought of seeing Emily
and Will, and because of a sort of nervous exhaustion

I knew I suffered from. I felt a raging restlessness to be on my way to meet them, instead of wasting time in this airless yard, not understanding what was happening.

I half suspected that Bazet was doing this on purpose. He was being awkward to bring me in line, show me who was in charge. We would set off when he was ready and not before. I wished I knew where he was staying. If I knew, I would have gone to find him and made him tell me what was going on.

There was a sudden commotion in the yard. One of the children had fallen over a kitten and was crying. Her mother rose from the shade of the tree where she and the other young women had been squatting, watching me impassively, and at the same moment Mariam appeared from out of the house. She had her head covered with a brilliant yellow scarf and her big flat brown feet were shoved into a pair of silver plastic flip-flops. She had her purse in her hand and I guessed she was going shopping. On an impulse, I got up and reached for my old leather bag. I would go with her. Maybe I would meet someone who spoke some French who could translate and explain to me why I was being kept waiting like this.

Mariam turned to look at me and smiled. She was

quite happy for me to go with her. Kidal was a large town by desert standards and there was a big market and a lot of small shops. It was natural that I would want to look round. It was like the chance to go up Oxford Street if you normally lived in the country. She pushed open the metal gate and we stepped out on to the wide sandy road and into the battering force of the sun. I pulled my scarf further forward to protect my face. I had long since learned not to wear open sandals because the sand burned my feet. Mariam didn't seem to notice and slid her bare toes through the scorching silky white drifts as we walked towards the shops. From the street, Mariam's house appeared bigger and more imposing than its neighbours, which were mostly unfinished mud-brick dwellings — one storey, with flat roofs and open windows and doors. In the strip of shade along the roadway, people, mostly Tuareg, stood or squatted on the sand, talking, or silently watching passers-by. Loose donkeys and sheep wandered freely, and dogs nosed about in the piles of rubbish that were heaped indiscriminately here and there. Amongst the rubbish the very poorest lived, black people originating from further south, in shacks created out of thrown-away plastic sacks and whatever else came to hand. Their little fires smoked, and pots and pans were set in the dirt, where the babies and older children, dressed in rags, sat idly.

Mariam marched past purposefully. Tuaregs have a natural dignity and air of superiority, but she was positively regal. She was an important person, there was no doubt of that, and she evidently enjoyed having me in tow and causing a bit of a stir.

We stopped first of all to buy sugar in a big sparkling block wrapped in blue paper. I reached for my purse and offered to pay, and Mariam accepted graciously. She told the shop owner to send a boy to deliver the sugar to the house. Next stop was the butcher, where bloody carcasses hung from hooks in the sun and the butcher's assistant idly swiped at the clustering flies with an old-fashioned basket-weave fly swat. Mariam selected a lump of dark red meat, chopped roughly with shards of bone splintering the flesh. Again I paid and she nodded her acceptance. Vegetables were next, and she picked through the piles of onions and potatoes and beans until she found what she wanted; then to the baker to buy some long loaves. There had been a French fort here in Kidal until independence, and the legacy was the surviving expertise in making delicious baguettes. I selected a bag of sugar biscuits for the children.

So far I had seen no one who could possibly help me. These were simple desert people who spoke a little rudimentary French but not much else. We passed the school but there was no one about and I didn't feel I could march in in search of a teacher.

We turned off into a side street and moved amongst market stalls selling clothes and sandals and cheap jewellery and mobile telephones from China and hideous synthetic blankets.

Whenever Mariam stopped I asked, 'Bazet?' looking about me, and she would laugh and shake her head. '*Non! Non!*' She waved her hand into the distance as if to tell me that he was far away. She chose herself a pair of red rubber flip-flops and indicated that I should pay. I started to feel that I was being made a fool of, but I nodded and opened my purse. I shook my head when she started sorting through bottles of shampoo, and she looked at me and laughed in my face.

Laden with parcels, we began to make our way back, trudging through the sand while the sun beat on our heads and backs. A dusty police truck cruised past us, a young Tuareg man at the wheel. He looked at us curiously and Mariam waved back. 'Son!' she cried. 'Son! *Mon fils!*'

'*Your* son?' I asked, pointing at her. She wagged her

head. The truck had drawn to a stop and the young man got out and came back to us. The bottoms of his loose cotton trousers were grey with dirt. He wore a khaki police jacket over his robe, despite the heat. He greeted his mother formally with a stream of polite enquiries and she introduced me with a torrent of Tamashek. He turned to me and put out his hand to me as a Westerner.

'Welcome,' he said, in English. 'I am Ibrahim. Welcome to my town. Is there anything I can do to help you?'

I could have kissed him in relief. He was very handsome, actually. It would have been no hardship.

'Oh, yes!' I cried. 'I am trying to find out what has happened to my arrangements to go on to meet my cousin beyond Gao, across the river. Chamba's brother, Bazet, is supposed to take me, but he has disappeared. We should have gone yesterday, but he hasn't shown up and I don't know where to find him. My mobile doesn't work for some reason so I can't contact my cousin, and I don't know what's holding us up and I am getting very anxious.'

Ibrahim turned to his mother and they began another stream of talk, Mariam warming to her theme and shouting in answer to his questions. It sounded more like a stand-up row than a conversation. Eventually he turned back to me.

'Permission has to be given to travel the road from here to Gao. These are difficult times and my mother tells me Bazet has some problem with his papers which must be cleared with the army. There is also a difficulty with his vehicle. There is a leaking of brake fluid. He tries to get this mended, but do not worry – all this will be arranged and he will come for you as soon as possible. I will take you back now to the house of my mother and then I will go to Bazet and tell him to explain to you his progress. Meanwhile you may use my satellite telephone to contact your cousin. Sometimes reception is difficult here in Kidal. The mountains, you see . . . No, no, this is my pleasure . . . you are welcome.'

I did kiss him then – I couldn't help myself – and Mariam shrieked with delight. We climbed into the front of the police truck with the shopping on our knees while I took his telephone and tried to call Emily, and then Will. There was no answer from either, but I left Em a text message. Mariam sat next to me with her scarf pulled over her face. I understood that she didn't want to be seen, even with her own son. The police were still unpopular here in Kidal, a rebel town by reputation, and even though Tuareg were now permitted to join the force, there was still a stigma attached.

When we got back, Ibrahim helped us unload and then shook my hand again. 'Do not worry,' he assured me. 'I go now to find Bazet. I will send him to you.' Oh God, I thought. He won't thank me for that.

Mariam bustled inside with the shopping and indicated that I should sit again in the plastic chair under the tree. A few minutes later one of the girls appeared with another can of sugary drink for me. I didn't want it, but I smiled and accepted. I felt so much calmer now that I had sent Emily a text and she knew where I was and that I would be on my way as soon as possible. I took my notebook from my bag and found my pencil. I would amuse myself by writing – but my thoughts kept wandering. I thought how annoyed Bazet would be by Ibrahim telling him to come to me. I wondered where he was staying and with whom. I wondered how Ibrahim knew where to find him.

An hour later there was an angry tooting from outside and a boy darted into the yard and indicated I should go with him. I got up and looked through the gate. Bazet's battered truck was parked outside and he was sitting at the wheel with a face like thunder.

'*Allez! Allez!*' he shouted at me, banging his hands against the steering wheel. 'We go!'

'Okay!' I shouted back. 'I'm ready! I won't be a minute!' I ran back and collected my bag, calling for Mariam, who came to the door holding a kitchen knife in her hand. 'Thank you, thank you!' I said. 'I am going! Bazet is here! Please thank Ibrahim.'

The other women and girls got up from where they had been resting in the shade and gathered round clucking like a flock of chickens. I kissed them all and gave Mariam a hug. She had sent one of the other women inside, and now she ran out with a kitchen pot covered by a cloth, which she shoved through the window to Bazet.

'*Belle!*' Mariam said to me, touching my hair. '*Belle! Mais dangereuse! Très dangereuse! Allez! Allez!*' and she made a throat-slitting gesture with the knife

I laughed. She was joking, obviously, but when I climbed into the truck and slammed the battered door and looked at Bazet's furious profile, I wasn't so sure.

I didn't dare speak as we slewed through the blistering, empty streets, Bazet using the horn to scatter a herd of goats out of the way. The teenage boy tending them threw his stick at the windscreen. It bounced off, but I ducked and banged my head. Bazet began to shout, but at me and not the boy.

'Speak in French!' I shouted back. 'How can I know why you are angry if you don't tell me?'

'You go to police to speak of me!' he yelled back, slamming his hand against his thigh as though he would like to hit me. 'We are here in Kidal very quietly, and you speak to police! You are mad! Mad Englishwoman who understands nothing!'

'I *didn't* speak to the police. He's Mariam's son, for God's sake. He's your family! Stop shouting at me and tell me what the problem is!'

'YOU! You are the problem!'

'Why? You must tell me *why*!' I was fed up now with tiptoeing around, being anxious not to offend. I had been on my best behaviour for too long. I had been so keen to please, to be accepted, but I wasn't going to allow this guy to bully me – no way. I have six brothers, remember.

I was furiously silent for a moment, trying to work out a strategy to cope with this bitter, hate-filled man, when he looked across at me and spat, 'Go home! Go home with your cousin! I take you to meet her, and then you go.'

I took a deep breath and spoke vehemently. 'Listen,

Bazet, and understand what I'm saying. I'm not leaving. I love Chamba. I'm not leaving!'

'If you love him, you go!' he yelled. 'You are trouble for him. Big trouble. He needs Tuareg wife who understands his life.'

'That's for him to decide. That's his choice. You can't tell him who to love!'

'We will see,' he said. 'We will see,' and from then on he wouldn't say another word to me in French.

Emily

OUR FIRST EVENING in Bamako got us off to a bad start. We were tired and I can see I may have been feeling a bit flat and post-wedding, but the horrible Bar really got me down and I was angry with the others for not sharing my indignation. Surely Divinity, with her cultural background, should have recognised entrapment and slavery when it stared her in the face, but she didn't seem to care, and the guys, they were just like, 'Okay, Ems, calm down, there's nothing you can do, just accept that this sort of thing exists.'

I have to admit that Hugh disappointed me in that he didn't feel like I did – didn't even support me that much. When we got back to the hotel, a terrible weariness set in and I felt irritated when he couldn't get our door open with the keycard thing. 'Here, let me try!' I said and snatched it out of his hand, turned it round and opened the fucking thing with no trouble. Sometimes Hugh's hopelessness with the simplest technology is not endearing.

I went straight to the bathroom and cleaned my teeth and got into bed, ignoring Hugh, who was trying to open the window. I lay there tense with irritation because I knew it wouldn't open. It was sealed shut – that was obvious. You were supposed to use the aircon in the place of hot, humid fresh air from outside, but Hugh fiddled around with blinds and curtains and thumped at the window frame.

'Oh, leave it and come to bed!'

'But we must have some air! I think I'll ring down to reception and find out how to open this thing.'

I turned over and pulled the pillow round my ears. It was filled with something peculiar and lumpy – like cold mashed potato. I didn't want to make love even though it was only the third night of our marriage. I just wanted to sleep. This fact, on its own, made me feel depressed.

After a bit, Hugh gave up with the window and began to mess about with the temperature control on the wall by the bathroom. He evidently couldn't get that to work either, because I heard him sighing and then getting into bed beside me.

After a moment he said into the dark, 'Don't be angry, Em. I love it, you know, that you care about things so much,' and he slid his arm round me so that my head could rest on his shoulder and we lay like that, side by side, like an old married couple. 'I'm a trained observer, you see,' he said, 'which means I have had to learn not to intervene; but you are the opposite. You are a natural-born intervener, a warrior, a crusader, a protester, and I am very glad you are.'

'Hmm!' The stubborn and grouchy person inside me didn't give way so easily.

'Come on, Em. Don't be cross.'

'I'm not exactly cross, but I hated that place,' I said into his shoulder. 'I found it really offensive. But it's not only that. I'm very tired, actually, but most of all I'm upset that I haven't heard from Clemmie. I have sent her texts and tried to ring her but her phone seems to be switched off. It's weird that she must know that we have arrived in Bamako and she hasn't been in touch.'

'Look, Em,' said Hugh kindly. 'Please don't worry about her. She's been living out here for quite a long time. She knows what's what, and she is a born survivor with the well-developed knack of making people do what she wants. She'll be there — at the crossroads.

Don't worry.' Although Hugh has only the briefest of acquaintance with Clemmie, he has the impression that despite her appearance she is a tough cookie and can look after herself. In a way, he is right. What he said made sense.

I sighed. 'Well, maybe I'll hear from her tomorrow.' Hugh is so sensible and rational, unlike my family, who are driven by wild and arbitrary opinions which they defend to the death without quite remembering why.

I must have gone straight to sleep, because when I woke, the sun through the plate-glass window was like a smack in the face but the aircon blast had made the room like a fridge. I tottered out of bed and turned it off. Hugh was already in the bathroom – I could hear the shower running – and in what seemed like only a few moments the room was steamy hot. I checked my telephone – still nothing from Clemmie – and put it on to recharge, then spent some time repacking my case, putting the warmer clothes I had travelled in to the bottom and rearranging everything else on the top.

I felt better this morning – more cheerful and optimistic. The gloom of last night had gone and I was excited that the day's journey would take me towards Clemmie. I was looking forward to the drive.

It was going to be fun to share Divinity's reaction to what we would see en route. I remembered how wonderfully exotic it all had appeared to Clemmie and me, how the colour and the smell and the heat of West Africa had blown us away.

Hugh came out of the bathroom, blinking into the light. He had put his glasses down somewhere and couldn't find them. I slid my arms round his waist and kissed him.

'Better this morning?' he asked, kissing the top of my head.

'Much!' I said. 'And you?'

'Great. Ready to go. I slept really well.'

'Like on the polar ice cap. I woke up freezing.'

'In a few days' time you won't be able to remember what it feels like to be cold.'

'I know. Is the shower hot?'

'Yes. But as the water runs away, it bubbles up out of a drain in the middle of the bathroom floor, so I'm afraid you'll have to paddle.'

I nearly said that Bamako could do with some eastern European plumbers but decided not to. It would be a bit too much of a reminder of the experiences of last night.

'Look! You *can* open these windows!' said Hugh,

fighting with yards of net curtain and finding a catch on the frame. The floor-length glass swung open to reveal a sheer drop to a concrete patio five floors below. 'Christ! That's a bit suicidal! Thank goodness I didn't do that last night!'

'Hugh! Don't even *say* it!' I went to stand beside him, looking down. 'It really would have been "tragically, on honeymoon", and everyone would suspect I had pushed you out to get your life insurance, or that I'd realised it was all a terrible mistake.'

'Better not for life insurance. You would have been disappointed. I don't have any.'

In the hotel grounds, two ragged young men were very slowly chipping away at baked earth with Stone Age-looking hoes. A riot of tropical vegetation pressed against a high wire fence beyond which some donkeys were tethered on a scrubby patch. Immediately below, the paved terrace skirted a bright blue, irregularly shaped swimming pool, up and down which a very impressive and gleaming young black man was swimming the crawl. On the other side of the pool there was a thatched building that looked like a club house. Two or three young men in white jackets and bow ties lounged in chairs in the shade of its overhanging roof.

'It looks as if breakfast is in there.' I pointed. The

swimmer had now got out of the pool and was doing some strenuous and showing-off exercises involving a lot of springing about. The line-up of waiters watched impassively. He then wrapped a small and inadequate towel round his waist and went to sit, muscular legs spread, on a sunlounger. He clicked his fingers at the watching boys and one of them brought over a jacket, out of which he took a mobile telephone, which he consulted and then pressed to his ear.

'Go and have your shower,' said Hugh. 'I'll wait for you, but get a move on. I'm starving!' But my eye had been caught by the sight of Divinity crossing the terrace towards the breakfast room. She was wearing very tight white jeans, high-heeled sandals and an off-the-shoulder orange top. She looked sensational. The sunlounger man was galvanised. He sprang up and evidently said something to her, because she paused and laughed and shook her head and he tried again, but she wasn't having any of it, and he sat back down, disappointed. The waiters watched. The approach of a breakfast customer had no effect on them. Divinity went into the building and then a moment later came out again and said something to the nearest one, who heaved himself up – he was a fat young man – and trailed in behind her. It all looked a huge effort.

By the time I turned on the shower, there was no water at all in the taps, although there was plenty still lapping about on the floor, so I gave up for the moment and got dressed in a much more prosaic outfit than that chosen by Divinity, and Hugh and I went down. Outside our bedroom door the humid heat enveloped us again. On each flight of stairs there was a woman on her hands mopping at the treads, which were extremely slippery. I clung to the wall to avoid my feet skidding from under me.

'If you don't fall out of the window, you fall down the stairs,' said Hugh. 'They get you one way or another.'

Outside on the terrace, the young man by the pool took no notice of us. We were much too dull compared to Divinity. He hardly looked up from his mobile phone. Inside the breakfast room we found Will and Divinity eating large cheese omelettes with a basket of French bread in front of them.

'It took a bit of a battle to get it,' said Will, pointing at their plates, 'but worth it. I think you would call the pace leisurely.' There were no other guests in the whole place. 'We're waiting for coffee. There's no sign of it yet.'

'We're still on European setting. We need to chill,' said Hugh, and ambled off to see what he could do.

I asked Divinity what the guy by the pool had said. She laughed. 'He's a personal trainer. He wanted me to join him for a work-out. He couldn't know that my idea of exercise is window-shopping.'

'Is it just women on their own he offers his services to, do you think? He took no notice of us.'

We looked out of the window to see a plump young blonde woman in a bikini preparing to enter the pool, very gingerly, via the steps. Mr Personal Trainer was already in the water and holding out his hand to encourage her, his white smile flashing. He looked as if he might eat her.

'It's a dream job, isn't it?' I said. 'No wonder all the waiters sit out there looking envious. Better than making omelettes.'

'Serufi is coming for us at eleven,' said Hugh. 'He'll take us to the embassy to drop off our travel itinerary, and then we can be away. We've got a whole day to look round Bamako at the end of our trip. We'll be at Ségou in time for a late lunch at the Independence Hotel.'

'That sounds very well organised,' said Will, coming to the end of his omelette. 'I like to finish one meal and have the next one already on the horizon.'

After we had eaten, we trailed back to our rooms to

pack our bags and met in the foyer a few minutes before eleven o'clock. Divinity was outside looking at the stalls selling tat to tourists, and had already found a brown leather purse on a long plaited string that she liked, and a length of tie-dyed bright pink cotton which she had draped round her head, turban style. It was amazing with her orange top – she looked like one of those rocket-shaped ice lollies. I was relieved to see that the unsuitable high-heeled sandals had been replaced by her usual trainers. Will went to join her with a wad of West African pounds. I've noticed that he pays for everything. He acts like Divinity's lady-in-waiting. She always says, 'No, I mustn't! I love it, but I don't need it!' and then Will buys whatever it is for her. Her wanting something, but going through the motions of denying herself, always has a result. It annoys me a bit. I would never expect Hugh to follow me around buying me things. He doesn't get the acquisition thing, anyway. He can't see why you should want endless stuff.

Serufi appeared then, wearing his black leather jacket over his grubby robe as if it was a chilly day. He was beaming and smiling and shook Hugh's hand and then put his arm round him in a close embrace. Hugh has a special place in his heart because he speaks Bambara, which is pretty amazing for a foreigner.

Divinity completed her purchases – she had bought a carved wooden hippopotamus as well – and we all piled into the truck. Our bags went on top of Serufi's provisions. There was a crate of bottled water and oil drums and mattresses and string bags of onions and sacks of flour and who knows what else. Evidently you didn't come into town without stocking up.

'Come on!' said Hugh, being quite dynamic for once. 'Let's go! It's too hot to stand out here in the sun.'

As we pulled away from the hotel and made to inch our way into the nose-to-tail stream of traffic into town, I heard my mobile phone signal that a message had arrived. I scrabbled about to pull it out of my bag. I didn't recognise the number, but when I opened it, it was from Clemmie and my heart soared.

'It's from Clem! Everything is fine! She has been a bit delayed in Kidal but she will be on her way soon. Everything is fine! Phew! What a relief!'

Hugh leaned across to squeeze my hand.

'I know,' I said. 'You told me so. It's one of my shortcomings – foreseeing disasters that will never happen!'

Clemmie

SITTING ENCLOSED IN the sweltering cab of a pick-up, in the company of someone who deeply resents you, isn't the best experience in the world. It's especially unsettling when you are driving through a remote desert landscape in which, should you get dumped, you wouldn't have much chance of survival. As I had been aware since the beginning of this journey – I was in Bazet's hands.

Actually, that's a bit of an exaggeration, because we were still on the outskirts of the town and there were people about if I looked hard enough – a little group of women beneath the shade of a lone tree, two boys riding double on a donkey, a lone veiled man on a tall white camel in the distance.

I sat and looked out of the window. I couldn't see the point of trying to talk. Bazet slewed the vehicle from left to right through the sand, trying to frighten me, but he didn't know that it would take more than that to make me shriek and beg for mercy.

We went on like this for a while, until we had left all trace of Kidal far behind us and were in an empty landscape, rocky and difficult to cross, with no track to follow. Bazet drove with narrowed eyes, just visible above his veil. I had done this journey from Kidal to Gao a few times over the past months, but in no way could I recognise the route, and yet I had an uneasy feeling that we were going in a different direction. Surely by now we should have wound through the high rocks shaped like red tin loaves, where Emily and I had seen a jackal? We should have passed the little cliff with 'Kidal' painted on its side where there was usually an army roadblock. The thought occurred to me that Bazet was not taking me to Gao at all.

Why was he so against me? It was a question I had thought about a lot on this journey. I didn't really believe it was anything personal. It wasn't that he didn't like me as a woman. I don't think that came into it, although I had seen him looking at me almost jealously on occasions when Chamba was paying me loving attention or when he told his family that we were going alone into the desert because we wanted time together away from the rest of them. Perhaps he felt that I was taking his place in the hierarchy of Chamba's affection?

Bazet was the next brother down from Chamba, and I wondered at first whether he was jealous of his position as the leader of the family, but I didn't think that was the case either. It was easy to see the love and respect Bazet had for him. Anyone could read it in the way they threw their arms round each other, the way they laughed together – they were close; as close as brothers can be.

I think the cold, sideways looks were because he resented Chamba's affection for me, not because it left him in the cold, but because I was a distraction in the way that a Tuareg girl would not be. I demanded more – I knew that. I loved riding out with Chamba, by camel or horse, while the women stayed behind in camp. Chamba was proud of the way I rode, and it marked me out from the other women. I also liked going with him in the truck to buy supplies or to meet men of his tribe far out in the most remote desert areas, or in the mountains, where there were chains of caves full of God knows what – smuggled goods, I suspected, but did not ask.

Possibly Bazet thought I knew too much, that I was unreliable, and that if Chamba and I fell out of love,

I might grass on him – go to the police and report what I knew. My recent conversation with Ibrahim would have reinforced this view, and maybe that was why he was so angry.

He couldn't be more wrong. My sympathies were so totally with the plight of the Tuareg in their struggle for existence that I would take up arms to defend them – I really would – and I didn't care how much smuggling they did in order to survive. Maybe, though, Bazet didn't, or couldn't, believe that to be the case. I was a foreigner, an outsider, and not to be trusted in a community where family and tribe matter more than anything.

I had earned some respect generally, because the work I did, teaching English, was appreciated. The children were so keen to learn, and some had made real progress and could manage basic conversation and write simple sentences. It made me feel that I had something to give in return for Chamba's love and his family's hospitality. In fact, one of Bazet's children, his daughter, Amou, was one of my pupils. She could sing 'Twinkle, Twinkle, Little Star' and count to twenty, and was learning the alphabet. She was only eight. Her warm hand, the skin already dry and brown, yet still childishly plump, would creep into mine as we sang, and her dark eyes sparkled with the fun of learning something new. I admit I tried especially hard with her because I wanted to earn Bazet's goodwill – with no success.

I intended to build up the teaching. It was the one thing that made me feel I could have a useful future here in Mali. Emily was bringing me out books and flashcards and pens. I was going to try and organise a sort of twinning with her London school. I was working on raising money for materials by applying to various NGOs for support. Although none of them were willing to send field workers into the north of the country, I couldn't see why they couldn't sponsor my efforts. It was sponsors I was after, and I was determined to network amongst my friends back home and any influential person I could rope in. With a little backing, I could set up a proper school, a nomadic school, and buy materials and get my pupils up to scratch in French and English so that they stood a chance of improving their lot.

As things were, when the rains failed and the desert was gripped by terrible drought and famine and the animals died and the people starved and young Tuareg men migrated to the towns to search for work, there was nothing, nothing at all, for them. They might feel they were proud Tuareg tribesmen, but in the cities they were lowly, penniless herdsmen. Looking after animals was all they knew. They found that they had to pay for shelter and water and food and firewood and they were worse off than in their homelands. At least at home there was water in some of the far-off wells and firewood to be found amongst the tamarisk trees, and they could eat their fallen stock and look after each other until the rains came.

With a little learning there were so many more opportunities to find work, and there was also the important matter of respect. You weren't looked down on as an illiterate, worthless nomad if you could read and write in English and French.

So all in all, I couldn't see why I was such a bad thing in Bazet's eyes. Or why Mariam had done that peculiar throat-slitting action when I said goodbye to her. Was it me who was dangerous, or was I in danger? I couldn't work it out.

As for my personal safety, I have never felt safer than I have in Mali, protected by Chamba and his family. Knocking about London was far scarier. Muggings and violence are part of life there. Late-night buses, walking home through empty streets after closing time and deserted tube stations were far more dangerous than anything here in the desert. For instance, there was real gang warfare where I lived in east London, near where Divinity comes from. Young black boys get hold of guns and murder one another, and anyone who gets in their way, on a fairly regular basis.

In Mali, I have witnessed no violence at all. I have never heard the terrifying drunken shouting of late-night London, or seen junkies with their minds blown away by drugs, or the psychotic behaviour of people turfed out of mental hospitals to roam the streets.

Here, the violence was the violence of poverty and hopelessness, and the anger the anger of the dispossessed. I'm not naïve, so don't think I don't understand that the smuggling and banditry that some of the Tuareg go in for isn't violent – of course it is – but that's not Chamba's life. He is a man of peace and a negotiator between his people and the police and the army. He was away even now on a mission to calm a situation where frustration had caused a young relative to get into trouble and be taken into custody.

So I didn't understand what all this was about, this outburst against me. I glanced again at Bazet. He seemed to have calmed down a bit and was driving less aggressively. Every few seconds he glanced in his rear-view mirror as if he was searching the empty distances for something or someone following us.

115

As we drove, I became more and more convinced that we were not taking our normal route. We were passing through flat desert plains and not the range of hills I expected. Well, there was no point in even questioning Bazet's decision to come this way. I really was too ignorant – as much of a passenger as the mattress rolls and blankets thrown in the back.

I sat and looked out of the window, the hot wind scorching my face, and thought of Ems. At least by now she would have picked up my message and be assured that I was on my way to meet her.

I thought then of my mother, Ellen, knowing that she would be longing to hear first-hand news of me. I missed her terribly and knew that by taking this path and following my heart, I had caused her and Dad a lot of anxiety and the sadness of separation. I thought of Mum a lot. In my head, I often asked her for help and advice, and waited to hear her voice giving me an answer. I wished I had a recording of her voice. Thinking about sitting in the kitchen at the farm, as I so often did, watching her cook – her comfortable figure, her smooth grey hair, her deft, efficient hands peeling vegetables, or rolling pastry – brought tears brimming to my eyes. I loved her so much, and yet I had chosen to live so far away that I couldn't see her, and communication was obviously difficult. My cell phone often wouldn't, or didn't, work, but I tried to speak to her at least once every two weeks using Chamba's satellite telephone. The connection was excellent and she felt as close to me as if I was in the next village, calling her to tell her I would soon be home.

I had been desperately lonely and homesick in Mali. Chamba lived within a large extended family, as I did, and there was always noise and laughter and talking – just like there was at home – but there was no one to whom I could say, 'What do you think about such and such?' or 'What would you most like to eat right now and who with?' These were the sort of silly things Em and I said to each other all the time. We amused and distracted each other, shared everything, understood one another inside out. Ems and I could exchange looks and know exactly what we meant by them. We could share a joke without opening our mouths. There was no one who could take her place.

Sitting in that hot cab, the atmosphere buzzing with hatred, and thinking of home made me want to cry, but I damn well wasn't going to weaken. Bazet *wanted* me to feel demoralised. It was part of his plan to get me to go home with Emily, to get rid of me. I was made of sterner stuff. Ems and I often said that our upbringing had made us tough. It was nothing to be turfed out from the fire in filthy, freezing weather to bring in sheep from the hill, or stay out hunting all day, soaked to the skin and shuddering with cold. We weren't pampered children. We were expected to stick at things and not complain. Whingeing and whining was not allowed. Kingsley women were tough like that. My female relatives were dreaded in ladies' races at point-to-points all over the West Country. They thought nothing of swearing blue murder and riding the competition into the wings over three miles and eighteen fences.

Bazet didn't know what he was taking on. If he thought he could scare me off, he had another think coming.

Night drops like a curtain in the desert. There is a slight lessening of the heat from the metal-coloured sky, and a violet light creeps across the horizon and gradually glows gold and crimson as the sun sinks, and then bang, it's dark, and a delicious coolness comes with the night-time breeze. That evening, we drove only two or three hours out of Kidal and then Bazet swerved away across an area of hillocky sand and coarse dried grass. Goats scattered in front of us and a group of camels cantered lopsidedly across our track.

Bazet stopped and got out and went behind the truck. He squatted down, peering at the ground. I watched him in the broken wing mirror and wondered what he was doing. He stood up and got back in and then drove slowly and carefully for another mile or so before coming to a stop amongst a long line of rocks, like broken teeth in the sand. By now it was nearly dark. I scooped up the sleeping rolls and mattresses that Bazet threw down from the truck and he shouted at me that we should camp further away. He made a small fire and boiled a kettle for tea. We were still not talking more than was necessary, but the atmosphere was better and more relaxed. The calm of the silent, starlit night had reached us. We hunkered down behind the rocks and I sat with my back against them, feeling the warmth of the day for a second time. It was getting really cold now and I drew a blanket round me.

Mariam's pot contained vegetables and chicken in peanut sauce, and as we ate, my spirits were restored and I felt less angry and hurt by how I had been treated.

Bazet ate like all desert men who have often been hungry. He lifted his plate close to his mouth and wolfed down the contents and chewed the bones. I was just going to ask him if he wanted more when he paused, his spoon halfway to his mouth, and raised his hand to me, palm forward to silence me. Very carefully he laid down his plate and, getting on to all fours, crawled forward to peer between the rocks.

I felt a sudden nervousness. What the hell was it? Some sort of predator? Matching his stealth, I crept forward to try and discover what had alarmed him. I kept so close to him beneath the rocks that I could smell his sweat and hear his gentle breathing. I could see nothing out there in the darkness, hear nothing except the far-off bleat of a sheep. I watched Bazet's face for clues. He remained frozen and tense, listening. He knew there was something out there.

Divinity

I WAS FINDING EMILY a bit of a pain, to be honest. Don't get me wrong, I'm really fond of her and everything, but on this trip she couldn't stop being Chief Guide or Head Girl, or whatever. The heat was getting to me, too, which is odd, considering my heritage and all that. I felt sticky and sweaty and uncomfortable and I had swollen up so much that my trousers were tight. It was stifling in the jeep although hot wind blew through the open windows. The plastic seats were burning and I could feel sweat trickling down my back.

Emily was definitely disapproving of the stuff that I bought from the stall outside the hotel – although, frankly, what had it got to do with her? She was like – 'what do you want *that* for?' and looking down her nose at me. I wanted it because I wanted it, okay? I wanted to show these things to my mum and brother because they were exotic and different from anything I had seen before.

It was really hot when we got in the jeep, and when I asked if there was air conditioning, Emily gave me a lecture about fuel, and said to just keep the windows down, but we were stuck in solid traffic when we hit the main road into Bamako and it was fumes we were breathing. The little driver bloke knew short cuts through unmade-up back streets that were more like country roads, where animals were lying in the dust and children played in the dirt. My God, these people were poor, but what struck me most was the elegance of the women. How could they live in shacks with no running water and cook over open fires and look like queens?

They stopped and stared as we went by and they must have wondered at my black face amongst the whites. They must have thought I had got lucky to be riding through town. What would they make of my life and the fact that I was thirty and hadn't got a brood of kids to care for? I didn't see a girl past puberty who hadn't got a baby strapped about her person and another one hanging off her arm.

To be truthful, I didn't know what to make of it all. The women were the ones sitting at the stalls selling fruit, or herding goats, or filling empty cola bottles with petrol from jerrycans to sell by the litre at the side of the road, while the men sat beneath the trees, dozing in the shade. It was how my mother told me it was in Jamaica when she was growing up, but I'd never seen it first hand, this black male indolence and arrogance. Get off your arses, I wanted to yell at them. It made me feel ashamed to see it, as if my colour and culture was right there to be judged, and found wanting.

The British Embassy was an old building in a leafy road with greenery exploding through the metal rails that topped a high wall. Two sentries watched us from seats in the shade. Will got out and posted a copy of our proposed itinerary through the mail box and they stood up, only slightly curious. That was that – we could start our journey.

Emily, Will and I were squashed together in the back seat, with me in the middle, while Hugh sat in the front. This, Emily explained, was because Hugh was the tallest and needed more space for his legs, and also because he spoke the language and could chat to the driver. I didn't mind the arrangement because I could lean against Will's shoulder and close my eyes and have a little sleep – or I could have done had it not been for Emily, who wanted me to look out of the window at the dull countryside – nothing but dry grass and trees and then a straw and tin hut village flashing past. She was forever wanting to know things: 'Hugh! Ask Serufi the name of those trees. Hugh! Ask Serufi if the maize harvest has been good . . .' And so on. She was always the bloody teacher, and there's something stubborn in me that makes me resist if I am expected to do something. I was inclined not to pay attention to the endless boring scenery just because Emily was making such a thing of it.

So far, I didn't think it was wonderful to see gangs of donkeys and goats crossing the road herded by stick-thin children, or women pounding maize with great wooden bats that they raised above their heads. It was all primitive and poor and filthy, and when Emily went on about the strong communities, beautiful people and simple lives, I said, 'Yeah, well, Emily, you try living in a shack and see how much you like it!' To me it felt like taking a holiday amongst the poorest people in the world and feeling superior about it, as being more adventurous than going clubbing in Ibiza. It felt like being a poverty voyeur. Okay, I shouldn't have come to West Africa, then, I could see that, and I was beginning to wish that I hadn't been talked into it by Will.

I felt hot and sulky and at odds with everyone else in the jeep until, maybe a couple of hours on, we pulled up in a village with a long line of stalls beside the road. I had to wake up and take interest then, because the handiwork was amazing. There was silver jewellery and beautiful coloured glass beads which I was told were Venetian and had been used centuries ago as currency. There were wooden tribal carvings and some fabulous figures – nearly life-size – which I would have killed for, but how to get them back to London? Will is such a generous guy – he bought me some wonderful bracelets, roughly made with wire and beads but each one different and telling something of the hands that had made them.

The little black kids swarmed round us, screaming '*Cadeaux? Cadeaux?*' and Emily gave instructions about what we were and weren't to do. She had pocketfuls of sweets ready and pens for the older children. It seemed to make the situation worse, and they wouldn't leave us alone until our driver chased them off, shouting. They were barefoot and ragged but looked healthy and smiling. Emily asked Hugh to ask if they went to school, and apparently they did – for a few hours each day.

Hugh was in his element rootling about amongst

the stuff on the stalls. He said most of it was produced for tourists, but amongst it there were bits and pieces that were interesting to him. He picked up some little wooden figures with hugely extended stomachs and sexual organs. These, he said, were used in fertility ceremonies amongst the Dogon people, who are the ones he is studying.

I felt in a better mood after this. Our driver gave the kids some empty plastic water bottles, which the older ones reached out to grab over the heads of the little ones. God knows what they wanted them for. It made me think of how kids at home are so spoiled. Imagine them getting excited about an empty water bottle.

'We'll stop for lunch in about an hour,' said Emily, looking at her watch. 'Isn't that right, Hugh?' Hugh asked Serufi, and there was a long exchange between them. 'What's all that about?' asked Emily.

'He said yes, Ségou is about an hour's drive and we are going to the Independence Hotel where we went last time. Do you remember? It's run by Lebanese brothers. The food was really good. He was also asking me about Clemmie.'

'What was he saying?' said Emily, leaning forward eagerly.

'He was asking when we had heard from her. He wanted to know where she was travelling from. He said he had seen her a few months ago.'

'Oh my God! Really?' Emily was practically climbing over the seat. 'Where? Where did he see her? How was she?'

'He said she was well. It was up near the Algerian border, where he comes from, where his home village is. He said she was trying to start a school, as you know. She's been teaching the children English.' I could see Serufi's eyes using the driver's mirror to watch Emily's face. I didn't get the impression he was reporting something he was particularly pleased about. He had his scarf thing pulled up over his mouth, so it was hard to tell, but his eyes weren't smiling.

Emily was babbling away with further questions, which Hugh translated and Serufi answered. Yes, as far as he knew, all was well. Yes, she was living with Chamba's family. Yes, she travelled with them when they moved with their herds. Yes, sometimes she and Chamba crossed over into Algeria. Yes, she rode her camel very well. And so on.

Serufi said something else that Hugh didn't translate. Or chose not to.

'What? What did he say?'

'He said that Chamba needs a Tuareg wife,' said Hugh eventually and a bit reluctantly.

Well, of course, Emily couldn't leave *that* alone, although it made perfect sense to me. Anyone could understand why Serufi thought like that – it was obvious, living in the desert, that you'd need a wife who was used to it all. Like, I couldn't have survived half a day. I looked out of the window and saw only squalor and lack of modern facilities of any sort, and animals I was frightened of, and people who scared me.

'Why does he say that? Aren't things going well between them? Ask him what he means, Hugh!'

Hugh was trying to calm her down. 'He says it's a hard life, that's all, for a girl like Clemmie, who hasn't been brought up to it.'

Emily sank back, looking worried. 'She's never said that she doesn't like it!' she protested.

'She *has* said it's hard, though,' said Will. 'That's all Serufi means, Ems. It's got to be hellishly tough for an outsider, and especially a girl.'

'Well! It's her choice!' I said.

I had to shut my eyes then and clutch Will's arm, as a vast lorry bore down on us from the opposite direction at top speed, horn blasting. The way the trucks drove on this main road was terrifying, with vehicles swerving round stray animals and donkey carts, and men on wobbling bicycles. God, what a country! If you survived the poor diet, lack of sanitation and health care, you stood a good chance of getting slaughtered on the road.

I thought about what Serufi had said and guessed that he had meant something different. Will and Hugh were just trying to calm Emily down. Although I didn't understand a word, I felt sure that he had said that Clemmie was not good for Chamba. You can't mix oil and water. Clemmie, with all her beauty and charm, wouldn't cut it out here. I had seen enough already to know that.

Will perked up with the thought of a good lunch. He sat up in his seat and put his hand on my leg, where it burned through the thin cotton of my trousers. I put my hand on his hand. I knew what he wanted, and I wanted it too. How weird was Emily – on her honeymoon, with her husband sitting in the front seat of the truck and her in the back, worrying about her cousin? It takes all sorts, I suppose, but I call it weird.

When we stopped for lunch, we had a repeat performance, with kids swarming all over us. It's a pain and a hassle, and I was getting fed up with it. Emily knelt down amongst them and showed them a toy thing she had in her pocket – an electric mouse or something. She stopped the bigger ones from pushing the little ones out of the way. She always wants everything to be fair, does Emily. I suppose things were always fair and proper back home in the Dorset primary school in Piddletrenthide, or in the Pony Club or whatever it was that she and Clemmie went to with their *ponies*! She wasn't brought up on a rough housing estate like me. She doesn't know that her idea of justice doesn't exist on the streets.

We had teachers like her at my school. They thought they could teach the tough guys and the bullies that there was a different way, and oh boy, were they wrong! We just laughed in their faces and ran riot in their classes. The teachers that we respected were the ones who were tougher and rougher and meaner than the worst of the kids. We hated them, but we didn't mess them around. I remember one guy, Mr Simmonds, lifting a bully up by his sweater and holding him against the wall and saying, 'You do that again, and I'll make your life a misery. Got it?' He had a personal menace about him and he was six foot three and built like a brick shithouse, which helped.

Anyway, I left her to it, and went into the restaurant,

which was cool, and the ladies' toilets were more or less okay, and there was water and soap. When I came out, the guys behind the bar gave me long, insolent looks – like, who do you think you are? The only black women in the place were the cleaners. But I walked straight past them and out into a garden where I could see the others sitting at a table under the trees. It was shady and pretty and looked more like a holiday destination than anything we had seen so far.

The boys had already ordered cold beers. Hugh got up and went to look for Emily, who was still dealing with the kids out in the front of the hotel in the blazing sun. It was nice where we were, sitting in the dappled shade of flowering trees, watching lizards scuttling about and drinking iced beer. I felt really relaxed for the first time, as if I was properly away from everything. I didn't even bother to get out my iPhone and see if it was working, and if I had any messages from home. Will put out a lazy hand to stroke my neck.

'Enjoying it?' he asked. 'I knew you'd love Africa. It gets to you, you know. Gets under your skin.'

'It *is* my skin, in case you hadn't noticed,' I said, and he laughed and kissed my shoulder.

Clemmie

BAZET DIDN'T MOVE. My legs started to ache and I shifted my position, which made him glare at me. Without saying a word, he pointed his arm out across the desert the way we had come. I looked, but saw nothing but blackness under the brilliance of the stars. I strained my eyes, screwing them up, and then saw it – a pinprick of light far off, moving to and fro.

'What is it?' I whispered. 'What's going on?'

'We have been followed. It's as I thought. They are looking for our tracks. That is why I chose our path carefully over rocks and gravel that leave no clues.'

'Who are they? Why are they following us?'

He shrugged. 'Perhaps the police. Perhaps the military. Perhaps others.'

'Why? Why are they following us? We haven't done anything wrong.'

Bazet didn't answer. He crawled back to the shelter of the rocks, and I scuttled after him.

'Bazet! Tell me! What do they want?' I couldn't bear this hostile silence, this sense of being kept in the dark.

'They want to know where we are and what we are doing, who we are meeting, what we are carrying. It is in their interest to know. You are a valuable cargo because of Chamba, but also because you are foreign and therefore you are valuable. They cannot take you so easily.'

'Take me! What do you mean, *take me*?' I felt a shiver of fear and bit at the nail of my thumb. I remembered what Mariam had said, and her throat-cutting gesture. Bazet looked at me coldly.

'You have never heard of kidnapping, of ransom to be paid? You have never heard of hostage-taking? You have never heard of deportation? All these things are possible. It is for me to keep you safe and take you to your cousin. Then you must leave. Go home to your own people.'

I shook my head. 'You don't frighten me like that, Bazet.'

'Then you are a fool.'

Oh God! Were we to go round and round this

subject the whole journey? It was best to ignore what he said.

'What are we going to do now?'

'We will stay here for the night. At dawn we will move again. Then we will see who it is who follows us, and understand why. For the moment they have lost us and we are well ahead of them. It is safe for us to sleep now.' He went to the truck and got a rifle out of the back, to dramatic effect, loaded it with cartridges and laid it down by his bedroll.

You can guess how much I felt like sleeping. I crawled into my blankets fully clothed and lay listening to the wind keening through the rocks. I tried to make sense of what Bazet had told me. He was trying to make me think that this mysterious episode was all about me, but I couldn't see how it could be. I was legitimately in the country, so why should I be deported? Kidnapping was a possibility; I knew Europeans had been taken, and some even murdered, but hundreds of miles away in Niger. Chamba would never have allowed me to make this journey if it was too dangerous. The road from Kidal was a safe place for Tuareg, and because I was Chamba's woman, no Tuareg would threaten me. I wasn't a regular tourist, oblivious to danger, taking stupid risks.

A tiny nagging doubt crept into my mind. What if Chamba was tired of me? What if this was his way of getting rid of me? Maybe he had asked Bazet to scare me out of the country. But it was ridiculous to think like this. Chamba's love was like a steady light in my life. He would never deceive me. I never felt the slightest qualm about his feelings for me, and he had left me with so many loving words. Shit! I so wished that I could speak to him now, hear his lovely voice reassuring me.

Pointlessly, because I hadn't had a signal for days, I reached into my old leather saddle bag for my phone. Maybe I would have a message. Maybe, out here, there would be a signal. My hands searched for the familiar shape amongst the other stuff I carted about with me. I couldn't find it. I searched again and again, and then tipped everything out on to my blanket and searched through it on my hands and knees. My telephone wasn't there.

Feeling sick and panicky, I tried to remember when I had last used it – or tried to – back in Kidal. It was in Mariam's house – in the yard. I had had it then, I was sure. Shit, shit, shit. Losing my phone was losing my contact with everyone. But if it was at Mariam's, at least it wasn't lost and I could collect it on my way back north. She would keep it safe for me.

A mobile telephone that doesn't work is not much use anyway, but not having it made me feel incredibly isolated. It was like losing a lifeline. I really was alone, in the true meaning of the word. In it was stored photographs that were dear to me, and all my contact numbers. How could I have been so careless?

I shoved everything back in my bag and sat hugging my knees. It was a low moment but I had got to keep my spirits up. It wasn't the end of the world. Bazet had a working telephone and would have to let me use it. I had my key telephone numbers written in my trusty notebook as a safeguard against something like this happening. I had learned this the hard way, having lost or wrecked phones in the past – dropping at least two down the loo from the back pocket of my jeans, and losing all my contact details as a result. It was always a hell of a nuisance, but in the end the mobile was replaced, most of the numbers reassembled, a few irretrievably lost, and life went on.

Weary, I lay down and rolled myself in the blanket. I felt grubby and my mouth tasted foul. I hate not cleaning my teeth, but tonight it hadn't been possible. As soon as lay down I wanted to go to the loo, and I had to get back up and shuffle to a spot behind the rocks, away from the inert body of Bazet. He didn't stir, and it made me wonder how good a bodyguard he would be. If he was so concerned about who was following us, why wasn't he more alert? What use was the rifle, lying ostentatiously beside him, if he snored peacefully while I moved about so close by?

When I got back to my bed, I was cold and couldn't get my feet warm. I searched through my backpack for some socks. I lay down again, but sleep wouldn't come. A bird whistled somewhere in the darkness and I froze, my heart thumping. I looked across at Bazet, but he remained an unconscious mound of blankets. It called again, closer this time. Chamba had told me that there are many owls in the desert and I have heard them often, but this didn't sound like an owl. I hardly dared breathe. The bird called again, further away this time, and I relaxed a little, but I swear I was awake all night. I certainly saw the first glow of dawn in the sky.

I was up by the time Bazet stirred. I imagined that we would be on our way as quickly and silently as possible, but after saying his prayers, he set about making a fire for tea. He hardly bothered to scan the horizon for our pursuers. I cleaned my teeth and washed my face and then sat by the fire, still cold, and gratefully accepted the glass of hot, sweet black tea. We ate some bread and goat cheese that Mariam had given us, and I began to feel better. I was certain that last night had been an absurd charade. In the clear light of day, I realised how easily I had been demoralised. This morning I felt strong again.

'So what happens now?' I asked Bazet. 'I mean, about the people who you say are following us?' My tone was flippant and dismissive.

'They are still there,' he said coolly. 'They wait for us to show ourselves.'

'How do you know?'

'Because I have seen their fire.'

I looked at him closely. He had let his chech fall from his mouth and I could tell from his expression that he was not joking.

'I've been looking and I can't see anything at all out there,' I protested. He turned contemptuous eyes on me.

'Where you see only sand, a Tuareg can read many things.'

I stood up and searched the empty plain the way we had come. He was right. I could see nothing but rock and sand.

'We start when you are ready!' he said. 'Further on there is a place where we can conceal ourselves, and then we will see who it is that is so interested in us.'

I had to hand it to him. He knew how to pull his punches. I was determined not to appear rattled.

'Okay!' I said, and began to tidy up my stuff and chuck my blankets in the back of the pick-up. On the way, I examined the rifle. It was a familiar-looking old 16-bore, made in England. Once it had been used to pot game, I guessed, and I wondered how it had ended up in the Sahara. It was reassuring to see the same sort of firearm I was used to on the farm, and not a pump action, or a modern sort of gun I associated with criminality.

'By the way,' I said, looking over to where Bazet was kicking out the fire, 'I've lost my mobile. I know I had it at Mariam's. I must have left it there. It's a real pain because I need to keep in touch with Emily. I'd like to borrow your phone, if I may, and perhaps you would ring Mariam and check that it *is* there. They should have found it. I must have left it on my chair in the yard. I don't know how I could have been so stupid, but I can collect it on our way back.'

Bazet didn't answer. He completely ignored me as if I had never spoken and carried on packing up our camping stuff and loading the pick-up.

'Bazet!' I said, keeping my voice pleasant. 'Maybe you didn't hear. I was talking to you.'

'Allah protect us! We have other things to think about,' he said, adding with a definite menace, 'As you will see.'

Okay, Bazet, I thought to myself. I am as interested as you are in these pursuers, but I have a feeling they are not going to materialise. For the moment I would play along with him. How ridiculous and childish it was, this sort of point-scoring.

I wrapped my scarf round my head and climbed into the truck, my leather bag on my knees. Bazet leapt in and slid the gun, loaded, between us, and started the engine. I couldn't believe it. It was incredibly dangerous to drive like that. The gun could go off and blow a hole out of the roof or the windscreen. Seeing my horrified face, he moved it and stuck the barrel out of the window on his side.

The pale green daylight showed me that we had camped within a line of red rocks that stuck up dramatically on the edge of a sandy bowl across which vehicle tracks could just be seen. Now we slewed down through the sand and joined the main track, tearing along where the depth of the sand permitted. Bazet was driving like a maniac again, crouched over the wheel, his eyes searching the way ahead with deadly concentration. I had to hang on to the window frame to prevent myself from being hurled about. It was immensely uncomfortable. Every few moments he glanced into the driver's mirror to look behind us. The wing mirror on my side was splintered into fragments so I could see nothing. It was like looking into a kid's kaleidoscope. As usual, I felt useless and powerless.

We went on like this for a full half an hour. My ribs ached from being banged against the door or the gear stick, but it was a test of endurance that I was determined to sit out.

The route ahead looked even rockier and more impassable. We seemed to be skimming along the rim of a vast plateau. To my right, I could see the land dropping away steeply in sheer cliffs to a flat, dreary plain that spread out in all directions below us. Travelling along the edge, we ploughed through deep white sand that had drifted in waves against a ridge of rocks, each as big as a small house. It was a strange, desolate landscape, and even to my eyes, accustomed now to the desert wastes, it was a melancholy, sinister, glowering sort of place.

As suddenly as he did everything, Bazet threw the pick-up into a spin that brought us to a stop, nudging against a huge rock on one side and the cliff on the other. It was a tight place to be in every sense of the word, but I could see at once that it offered us cover, as well as a clear view of the way that we had come.

I felt not the slightest bit scared. I mean, who would ever follow us into a godforsaken place like this? The sun was well up now – a blazing white disc in a sky of hard cobalt blue. When Bazet stopped the engine, a great weight of silence dropped on us. I could hear my own breath and the slither of my skirt as I pulled it across my knees. It was incredibly hot. Sweat trickled down my back. I got out my water bottle and had a swig. I did not offer it to Bazet. I indicated that I was going to get out to find some shade on the other side of the rock, but he wagged his finger at me. No, I had to stay where I was. He got out with the gun and took up what looked like a firing position.

Then I heard it. The tiniest throb of an engine, far away and coming closer. Bazet came back to the truck and got a pair of old military field glasses and indicated that now I should get out. I went to stand beside him while he searched the landscape and then passed the glasses to me. To begin with I could see nothing, but he directed my sights and then I saw what he had spotted – two vehicles, moving in convoy. The first was a Land Cruiser type of vehicle and the second a pick-up, the back of which seemed to be packed with men – at least six of them. I could now see that some of them were holding what looked like rifles, pointing upwards.

'Who are they?' I whispered.

'Bad.'

What sort of bad? As far as I could see, they were not in police or army uniform. That probably meant the worst sort. If they were bandits or robbers, we had nothing of value to give them and they would shoot us and take the truck. If they were kidnappers, it would be me they wanted. It seemed a hopeless situation – me and Bazet in a battered pick-up with one old rifle between us. Maybe this was it. Maybe the date of my death, which has been travelling towards me since the day I was born, had arrived. I felt remarkably cool and calm. I thought of my mum and I thought of Chamba. I love you with all my heart, I said to them both, and I hope that I have told you and shown you this in the life that has been allowed me.

Bazet didn't need the glasses any more. Even I could see the vehicles quite clearly. They were travelling fast in a little cloud of dust and sand. What was he going to do now? Our position would remain hidden until they were nearly on us, when our pick-up would suddenly become visible. We had the advantage of surprise, but were so outnumbered and underarmed that we would be as good as helpless from that moment.

Maybe I should run? Perhaps I could scramble down the cliff face and hide until they had gone. Bazet would stand a better chance on his own. But if they killed him or took him away, then I would die alone, of thirst, in a few days.

Seconds passed. I didn't know what to do, and it was agony to do nothing. In a minute or two it would be too late; the engines were now loud, revving to move the laden trucks uphill through the sand.

I crouched behind the rock. I didn't want to see what was going to happen. Bazet raised the rifle to his shoulder, and as he did so, I saw that in the box of cartridges he had thrown at his feet was a mobile telephone. A glance told me it was mine.

Emily

A REALLY EXCITING AND unexpected thing happened when we stopped for lunch at the Independence Hotel in Ségou. I was outside with the clamouring children, trying to create some sort of order before I handed out the coloured pens I had got in my bag, when a huge and immaculate 4x4, with smoked-glass windows, drew up alongside Serufi's jeep and a black driver in a dazzling white shirt got out to open the passenger door. The attention of the children was immediately diverted away from me, but they hung back. They recognised instinctively that they would not be welcome crowding round such a princely vehicle.

The driver went to the rear passenger door and opened it with a bow of his head, and a white man got out, silver-haired, late-middle-aged, smartly dressed in cotton trousers with a crease down the front and a

145

crisp shirt. He looked across at me and half smiled an acknowledgement. The children stood back, watching.

He reached inside the vehicle and took out a brief-case, then said to the driver in an American accent, 'Shall we say two thirty, Jacob? Go get something to eat,' and passed some folded notes into the man's hand. The children watched, transfixed and open-mouthed, and I took the opportunity to hand out the pens, starting with the smallest and most shy.

This done, I followed the man into the hotel, where he was greeted effusively by the owner. I slipped past to the ladies' cloakroom for a wash before finding the others in the pretty, shady courtyard. Although we had asked him to join us, Serufi had disappeared to have lunch on his own somewhere. Maybe it was more restful for him like that.

'We've ordered for you,' said Will. 'We couldn't wait any longer. Where's Hugh got to? He went to find you. He hasn't wandered off somewhere, has he? Look, here's your beer. Bloody good it is too.'

'No, I'm here,' said Hugh from behind me. 'I was just looking at some fantastic old sepia photographs they have in the dining room. They must date from the 1890s, I would say. Amazing shots of the Niger river and the steamer that brought Europeans north into the interior. There are men crowding the decks in three-piece suits and bowler hats and ladies in crinolines holding parasols. It must have been so thrilling back then – teeming with crocodiles and hippos.'

'Here comes the food,' said Will, looking over Hugh's shoulder. 'God, it looks good!' The beaming waiters set down plates of tomato salad and baskets of bread, and platters of capitaine fish and thin-cut chips.

We all tucked in hungrily. This was evidently the sort of place that Divinity liked; she looked quite contented for once. She sat opposite Will and slipped her foot out of her sandal and rested it on his thigh. Every now and then he ran his hand over the arch of her foot. I couldn't help but notice and feel that they looked more like a honeymoon couple than Hugh and me. I smiled at Hugh across the table and held out my hand to him. He took it and gave it a squeeze, but I could tell that his mind was on the photograph collection. I knew that absorbed mood well by now. He was eating in an automatic sort of way, without tasting anything.

Will ordered another round of beers. It really was lovely, sitting there in the shade of the tree, listening to various highly coloured birds whistling and calling.

The air was as hot and thick as soup, but there was a fan set to stir a breeze in our direction. It was relaxing not to be worrying about Clemmie and to know that she was safely on her way to meet us.

We were chatting idly when the smart man from the big Land Cruiser came out into the garden and made a beeline for our table.

'Excuse me! But I believe that you are English and are travelling north? My driver has been talking to your driver. May I?' He indicated the spare chair drawn up to our table.

The others looked at him in polite surprise. 'Of course,' I said. 'I'm Emily, and this is my husband, Hugh.' It gave me so much pleasure to call him that. 'And this is my cousin Will, and his partner, Divinity.'

'Hi! My name is Alvin Brockenhurst. I'm out here as director of a UN children's project.' He turned to me. 'I noticed, Emily, that you are interested in children?'

'Well, yes,' I said. 'Particularly these children, who have so little and who need so much.'

He nodded. 'Please excuse me for interrupting your lunch. This is a pleasant spot, isn't it? I always try and arrange to stop here on my way to and from some of our projects run from Mopti.'

148

'Are you based here in Mali?'

'Lord, no. I have departments in Paris and Geneva, and I report to New York. I have a wider brief, you see. West Africa, in fact. I have to shout quite loud for Mali when there are crises of the first order in other parts of Africa.'

'Not loudly enough,' I said. 'The north of Mali gets nothing. All aid seems to stop at the river. The Tuareg, for instance, are starved of any sort of international interest. It seems to be purposely diverted away from them by the government.'

'You know these people?' said Alvin, looking a bit taken aback.

'Well, I've been up there, into the desert. I've travelled with them and I have friends in Kidal. My cousin, Will's sister, is still living up in the north, in the Sahara, with her Tuareg boyfriend.' It seemed inappropriate to call Chamba a 'boyfriend'. 'He's a tribal leader known as the Lion of Temesna.'

'Is that so?'

'Yes! She's been trying to get a number of projects off the ground, but she's found it hard to find the support she needs. She's teaching English to the local kids, but she can't access the most basic materials.'

149

'It sounds like she's the sort of useful local contact we are always looking for.'

'Really?' This was the best news. What an amazing piece of luck that we had bumped into this guy. What a gift for Clemmie!

'Yes, sure thing. We have no contacts on the ground up there, so it's hard to get an accurate assessment of the situation. Where are you people headed exactly?'

Alvin was wearing dark aviator glasses and it was hard to tell his age, but I reckoned he must be middle fifties. He was an insubstantial sort of man, quite thin and rather academic-looking. It was hard to imagine him knocking around this tough country, but then he appeared to travel in comfort, and I don't expect he roughed it much.

Hugh explained that we were going on to spend the night in Djenne, where there is an enormous mud mosque that has earned itself World Heritage status. He had always wanted to see it – it was the stuff of dreams in its strangeness – and we hadn't had time on our last visit.

'I'm heading that way myself. I have a meeting in Mopti with some Dutch medical field workers. There are some reasonable hotels there, on the river. I expect you're staying there?'

'No. We're staying in Djenne, at what is called, on the internet, an "encampment" for tourists. Apparently it's right next door to the mosque and the market,' I said. 'We'll look round tomorrow, and then Hugh's heading off to the Dogon country to do some research – he's an anthropologist – and we're going on north, to meet up with my cousin.'

'Is it really okay to travel up there? Any NGO workers going north of Mopti always fly in and work with army protection. It's a dangerous part of the world. I guess you guys are aware of the risks?'

'How about you telling us?' said Divinity, rolling her eyes. I could see where this was leading. Any moment she was going to say she didn't want to go on.

'Come on, guys!' said Alvin. 'You must know al-Qaeda is operating up there? There's a real risk of banditry and kidnapping. Surely your Foreign Office has warnings on its site? We don't put any aid workers into those desert tribal lands. We consider it's too dangerous.'

'Excuse me, but I think that could be an exaggeration,' said Will. 'If you look at the actual figures, there's almost no crime at all. I mean, I understand how careful your organisation has to be, but project workers are much higher-profile than three anonymous travellers like us.'

'Yeah, but there are real risks none the less.'

'We'll be fine,' I said, desperate for no more of this alarmist talk. 'We have an amazing Tuareg driver who comes from the north. We trust him one hundred per cent. He knows what's what and won't let us come to any harm. I think the most hassle we're going to get will actually be from the army – checkpoints and so on. Our driver has shown us the sheaf of papers he now has to carry.'

'Well, look, guys, I'm going to give you my sat phone number and you can call me any time.' He pushed a business card across the table. 'I have a few strings I can pull. I know the general who looks after security on the road towards Gao. I mean, I hope you understand where you're headed. It's tough country up there from every point of view.'

'We understand, and we won't take risks,' said Will. 'And thanks for the card.' He picked it up, showed it to us, and put it in his wallet.

'Now, tell me a bit more about your sister,' said Alvin, gesturing to the waiter to bring another round of beers. 'And what she's told you of the situation. Where is it she's been living?' We told him. 'Wow! That's really up country. I don't think I've heard of anyone working up there.'

'She's not *working*,' said Divinity. 'You can't call it *work*! She's just living up there with this man she met, and teaching a bit of English.'

'So who is this man?' said Alvin, taking in this information. 'When did you say she met him?'

'Oh, it's quite a story,' I said. 'My cousin and I were out here eighteen months ago. In accordance with the will of our Great-Aunt Mary, we were tasked with scattering her ashes in a certain place in the desert. It took a bit of finding, but we did it, and while we were travelling – by camel – we met this man, a Tuareg, who turned out to be a direct relative of our aunt – her grandson, in fact – but she didn't know he existed.'

'Hey! Whoa! Is this a film script you're telling me?'

'No, no – it's all true. It really happened like that. Amazing, isn't it? Anyway, Clemmie decided she wanted to stay.'

'I'd like to hear more about all of this. You're telling me your great-aunt was out here before the Second World War, right? Mali wasn't a country then. It still belonged to the French empire.'

'She was half French. Her father was with the French army. That's why she came out here, to visit him, and she met up with this Tuareg guy and they fell in love.

153

It's quite a story, and Clemmie seems to be following in her footsteps.'

'So where exactly are you meeting her? I guess she's coming home with you?'

'No, she's not. At least I don't think so. She wants to stay. She's committed herself to this man and to helping his people in whatever way she can,' said Will.

'Jesus! She's not had enough? I can never wait to get back to a hot shower and clean sheets.'

'Not that we know of,' I said. 'She loves him.'

'What did you say his name was?'

At this point, Hugh stood up and looked at his watch. 'Look, Mr, er . . . will you excuse us? We really should hit the road.'

'Not literally, I hope! The driving is hair-raising, isn't it?'

'Well, that is something we *do* know,' I said. 'We had an accident last time. In the middle of the night and in the middle of nowhere we were driven off the road. We were on our way to the airport to fly home.'

'And you've come back?' said Alvin in mock amazement, 'I guess you really must love this place.' He stood up and shook our hands. 'Now tell that cousin of yours – what's her name, by the way? – to get in touch with me on the number on that card. I'd sure like to arrange a meeting.'

'That would be wonderful. She's found it so hard to raise any interest in the area for various reasons – mostly political, I guess.'

'Look, I'm not promising anything, but the political side is the part I'm responsible for – the negotiations to get our teams into these difficult situations. I can tell you it's never easy, but I've got aid into some tight places before now.'

I got my notebook out of my pack and wrote down Clemmie's name and her mobile number. It was such a piece of luck to have met this man whom she would never have had access to in the normal way, and I felt pleased and excited.

Serufi was waiting patiently for us in the shade of the hotel lobby. We split the bill, paid, and piled out into the wall of white afternoon heat. In a second I could feel sweat trickling down my back. The little kids gathered under the trees at the front didn't bother us again. It was even too hot for them to stir, and they knew they weren't going to get anything else, but one or two waved their pens in the air and shouted something that I couldn't understand.

'They're thanking you,' said Hugh. 'They are actually saying, "Thank you, Mum!"'

Divinity snorted.

'It's a compliment in this country,' said Hugh, 'to call you Mother.'

Divinity snorted again. 'It must be the way you dress!' she said.

When we were in the tin oven of the jeep, bowling out of town, past the concrete football stadium and the parks of huge and overladen lorries destined for the Ivory Coast, Serufi began a diatribe to Hugh, waving his hand in the air as he spoke.

'What's all this about?' I asked when there was a break while he concentrated on overtaking a lorry.

'He didn't like that UN chap's driver. He said he was an arrogant city man from the Ivory Coast. He's being quite racist about him actually, calling him all sorts of names. He said he tells lies about the Tuareg.'

'I expect it's all to do with football. Mali have often played their national team in the African Cup of Nations.'

'How on earth do you know something like that?' asked Hugh, incredulously.

'I've got a boy from the Ivory Coast in my class. I even know that they are called Les Éléphants, and that they qualified for the World Cup in South Africa.'

'You never cease to amaze me, Emily.'

'I amaze myself sometimes!'

Divinity, full of beer, had fallen asleep all over Will, who also had his eyes closed. I had to content myself with stroking Hugh's arm where it lay along the back of his seat.

'It was fantastic, though, wasn't it, to have met Alvin like that,' I said to him. 'Clemmie will be so pleased with the contact.'

'Yes. It sounds as though he's the top man in UN aid out here. He was a bit unexpected, to be honest. He looked like a university professor, didn't he? Not robust enough for Africa. I guess he is a sort of career aid negotiator who doesn't get involved with actual projects on the ground. He must be responsible for an enormous budget and accountable for how it is spent. That's quite a big deal. Think how hard you find it to decide which child to give a pen to, knowing that you are turning others away. It would be easier to do that from a distance, on paper, and according to set criteria, wouldn't it?'

'Yes. I'd be hopeless. I'd find it an impossible responsibility. But the point is, Hugh, that *no* aid gets north to the Tuareg. Their leaders talk about it with the government, but it doesn't happen. That was the cause of all the unrest and the rebellions.'

'Well, maybe this guy can help.'

'He certainly seemed interested in Clemmie and the work she's doing.'

'Yes, he did.'

At that moment, the shiny black Land Cruiser overtook us with a blast of its horn. The smoked-glass windows revealed nothing of its occupants. Serufi had to swerve on to the loose stones and dust at the side of the road. He shook his fist and swore.

'Goodness! That was a bit of arrogant driving. No wonder Serufi's not impressed.'

Hugh half turned in his seat and saw the others sleeping. 'Hey!' he said quietly, reaching for my hand. 'I love you, missus . . . it's great being here in Mali with you again. The last time we drove this road, we had only just met.'

I smiled. 'You had to put up with me and Clem teasing you. You were so serious.'

'I thought you two were nutters – setting off into the Sahara with your great-aunt in a handbag – but I had to admire your courage. Especially you, Ems, who didn't want to be here at all.'

'No, I didn't. I thought it was mad. If I'd had my way, we wouldn't have come, and then I wouldn't have met you.'

'So we have Clemmie to thank for everything.'

'So we do. I wonder where she is now. It's wonderful to think we are travelling towards each other. I've been sending her texts but she hasn't responded. I'm not convinced that they are actually being sent. The signal seems very erratic.'

Out of the city, the drive seemed endless, through deserted villages baking in the afternoon sun. Donkeys trotted along beside the road – sometimes three of them to a single cart, like a troika. It wasn't a bit of the route I enjoyed. We passed through San – an ugly, sprawling concrete town where I saw several carts pulled by very lame, bony horses, belaboured with cudgels by their drivers. I glared at them through the window and thought they had brutal, surly faces.

After that, the road grew very quiet and empty and passed through a featureless plain. To the far left I kept thinking I could see the glint of water, and a distant fringe of green, and thought maybe it was the bank of the Bani river, a tributary of the mighty Niger. Serufi drove steadily on, and as the afternoon faded, the road turned into a violet ribbon laid against the flat ochre-coloured earth. There was nothing to interrupt the sky meeting the curve of the earth; not a tree, not a building. Will and Divinity slept on and missed it all. Hugh chatted away to Serufi, who every now and then held out his hand to him in a gesture of friendship and humour when they shared a joke.

The country became very dry. There were no more maize fields on either side and just the occasional Peul herder astride a donkey with a herd of goats browsing amongst the scrubby thorns. I started to feel the peace of lonely places. All the busyness of the past weeks leading up to the wedding receded and the knots of tension in my shoulders relaxed. I had felt this shedding of all the things I worry about the last time I travelled this road. The emptiness and the lack of any connection with my life at home seemed to free me from the little snags of anxiety that were always there, lodged in the back of my mind.

There was so much sky and earth and emptiness that I felt insignificant. All my scurrying about and frenzied activity seemed of no consequence. The Peul goatherder had a simple job to do and a simple goal in life – to find enough food and water for himself and his family. I almost wished I could live like that.

Divinity stirred beside me, yawned and sat up.

'Jesus, I need a pee!' she said. 'I've got beer bloat.'

'Do you want to stop?'

She looked out of the window. 'Where? It looks like there's nothing here.'

'What do you expect? A public lavatory? You'll just have to squat. The men will look the other way.'

Divinity pulled a face.

'Serufi wants to stop to pray, anyway,' said Hugh, as the truck veered off the road and came to a halt.

Will woke up and we all climbed out. As soon as the engine was cut, a deep silence fell. Serufi took out a dusty piece of carpet from the back and went off to kneel and begin his prayers. He looked a very small figure against all that emptiness and the vast blazing sky.

Divinity walked to the other side of the strip of road and marched about, looking for cover, the slightest scoop in the sand, which didn't exist. It was as flat as a pancake in every direction.

'You have to get used to it,' I said, following her. 'The lack of privacy. I'll hold up my scarf if you like, as a screen. You can go behind it.'

'There are millions of giant beetles marching about,' she complained, staring at the ground. 'They might bite my fanny.'

161

I had to laugh. 'Get on with it! If you want to go, go! They're dung beetles. They won't hurt you.'

She really had no option, and I held up my scarf to provide cover from the road.

She squatted down, but only for a moment. 'Oh my God!' she screamed, leaping about. 'They're attacking me. They have great big pincers!' No one can make more noise than Divinity when she lets rip. The men over by the truck jumped to attention and shouted out 'Are you all right?' I waved back to reassure them while Divinity yanked up her trousers. I noticed she wore a very tiny G-string. I wondered whether Hugh would like stuff like that. I'm afraid in the knicker department I wasn't very adventurous, even on my honeymoon.

'You've got the beetles excited now,' I said, 'Look at them! They think it's started to rain.'

Divinity laughed and linked arms with me, and we started to walk back to the jeep.

'Listen, Emily,' she said. 'This whole thing is great, you know. Fabulous. But I'm finding it hard to get my head round it all.'

'I know. It's overwhelming. Everyone who has been to Africa says that.'

'Yeah, but it's different for me.'

162

'You mean you haven't travelled much?'

'No, I don't mean that. Let me put it another way. How would you feel if you saw white people living like this – in shacks by the road, in poverty, and white children begging for pencils and sweets? It would be shocking, wouldn't it?'

'But you must have *known* it would be like this. You can't escape knowing about poverty in Africa, even if you live in London.'

'It's seeing it that makes the difference. I tell you, Emily, it pains my heart – and to be on *holiday* here makes it harder. If I'm here at all, it should be to help.'

I hadn't really thought of the impact that Mali would have on Divinity as being any different from the impact it had had on Clemmie and me, but now I saw how she was sure to feel quite differently.

'You help by being here. You are spending money. You're encouraging tourism.'

'Maybe. But it makes me want to do more.'

'Perhaps you'll find a way. I mean, you are keen to source textile suppliers, aren't you?'

'Yeah, I'd love to, but I haven't seen anything I could use yet. Not on those market stalls anyway, but Will says there is a women's craft co-operative in Djenne

– he found it on a French website. I want to go there tomorrow. I'd like to provide employment if I could – an export market.' She looked serious and thoughtful and I felt glad that she was involving herself in the experience that had had such an impact on Clemmie and me.

When we got back to the jeep, Will put his arm round her. 'What was that about?' he asked. 'All the screaming? Are you okay?'

'Yeah, sure, I'm fine. I was attacked by beetles, that's all – as big as my thumb!'

'Do you want some water? You have to remember to drink a lot while you get used to the heat.' He handed her a bottle and she smiled wanly. I really like Divinity, or I wouldn't have suggested that she come on my honeymoon, but one moment I felt sympathetic towards her and the next she annoyed me. I hoped she wasn't going to make a big deal of this discovery of hers that black people in Africa don't have the same living standards as in the West. I mean, from a personal point of view – as if it made her suffer.

'Not far now,' said Hugh to me. 'We have to get a ferry over the Bani tributary and I don't think it runs after dark. Here comes Serufi. He must have shortened his prayers.'

Serufi scuttled across the sand and stowed his mat in the back of the truck. We all piled in and were on the move again in moments. The dry plain went on and on, and then we turned off on to a dirt road through Dogon-like mud villages with their funny little round thatched granaries that look as if they should house a Hobbit. Hugh sat up straight in the front seat. I could see his shoulders twitching with eagerness, like a keen horse. This was the live version of his virtual world. He spent so much time reading and studying that I could understand that to see things for real was tremendously exciting.

What had seemed like a deserted country was now full of life and activity. Finally the road petered out altogether in pools of water, and there was bright green rice on either side, and carts and bicycles accompanied us, going in the same direction, down to the river bank and the ferry.

'Oh my God!' Divinity shrieked. 'Are we crossing in *that*?'

The ferry was a ramshackle affair, clanking, rusty and low in the water. Up the metal ramp went horse-drawn carts and derelict overloaded lorries. Barefoot ragged children swarmed between the vehicles. They gathered like flies round our half-open windows, inserting their stick-thin arms and trying to grab at us, beseeching and shouting and thrusting each other out of the way. Some of the older boys were trying to sell crude little wind-up cars made out of old tins. They knocked them against the windows until Serufi shouted at them to stop. He told Hugh they were made in a co-operative workshop set up by a French charity. Others had trays of tacky-looking jewellery or leather key rings or battered fruit. Serufi shook his head at them all and told us that many tourists came this way to Djenne and the children were a great nuisance. He made us wind up our windows, and for once I did as I was told and avoided eye contact with the beseeching little faces that were pressed against the glass. I felt awful about it, but it was more than I could cope with. I was suffering from begging-child fatigue.

When we showed no interest, they dropped away, searching for another tourist car behind us, although as far as I could see there were no other Westerners in sight.

'I mean, is this boat *safe*?' said Divinity, staring out of the window. 'It's so low in the water, and see how fast the river is running and how wide it is? It makes the Thames look like a stream. I can't even see the other side.' We all looked at the swirling brown water. I have to admit it was a bit alarming, but I wasn't going to show my nerves. It was too late anyway, because ropes were being pulled in and the engine revved and the old vessel started to move away from the bank, crab-like and slow.

'Jesus!' said Divinity, and laid her hand dramatically over her eyes.

The sun was going down magnificently over the brown water, turning it fiery orange, and we got out of the car and took photographs. Divinity remained inside with her eyes shut until eventually we bumped ashore on the far bank. Before long we could just make out the high mud walls of the medieval city. It was dark now, but flares were lit along the way and bright fires burned outside the red mud houses.

It was utterly magical winding along the narrow streets into the heart of the city, where the market was breaking up for the day and carts half filled with unsold produce were going home; melons and potatoes and sacks of rice and yams and tomatoes and maize and chickens in wooden cages all disappearing into the dark.

The mosque was the strangest building I have ever seen – breathtakingly fantastical in the gloom, with its towering windowless walls, turreted and pinnacled and studded with wooden pegs. It was the largest mud building in the world, so Hugh told us, as we tried to take it in, speechless and spellbound.

Our 'encampment' was right next door, through a high gate and into a courtyard. We climbed out of the jeep tired and stiff and Serufi threw our luggage down from the roof. We sorted ourselves out and were shown to rooms on the far side of the garden in a single-storeyed building.

Our room was perfect – a one-windowed concrete cell but with a four-poster bed – a mattress on a wooden base with slender tree trunks holding up a mosquito net. Next door there was a shower room with a table and chair in it. There was air conditioning too, but a moment after Hugh flicked the switch there was a bang and everything went dark. We scrabbled around for torches – and that's another thing Hugh is good at: he always knows exactly where all his stuff is packed and he found his at once.

We showered together in the dark, and the feeling of cool water on our hot, sticky bodies was so good, then we changed into clean loose clothes and went across to the restaurant. The lights had come back on again and little fairy lamps were threaded through the trees to guide our steps. The tables were set under a low thatched roof and the place was entirely empty apart from Will and Divinity, who were sitting at a table drinking beer. Like us, they were in a good mood, refreshed and excited by the strangeness of the place. It seemed amazing that two days ago we had been in London.

'We've ordered for you,' said Will. 'It's a set menu starting with vegetable soup, then chicken and potatoes and then crêpes.'

'Wow! Sounds like the sort of food you would eat in England in January after a morning shovelling snow,' I said, but when it arrived we were all starving and ate everything, and it was all delicious. The crêpes came with a big dollop of solid, bright red jam – like school dinner on a good day.

I don't think I have ever felt happier than that night. I was with the man I loved and who loved me, and this remarkable fact was still new and delightful to me. The night was so beautiful, with stars sprinkling the huge dark sky and the wind rustling the palms of the encampment. The exhausting heat had faded, but the air was very warm and enveloping, and I felt so tired that I couldn't wait to climb into the second four-poster of my short married life.

My sense of peace and satisfaction was heightened because I felt so close to Clemmie. Tomorrow I would see her again, and it was comforting to know that she was not so many miles away. I knew she would be thinking the same and counting the hours until we met.

Clemmie

I N A SPLIT second, I knew that whatever happened
to me, being in possession of my mobile phone
was surely a bonus. As Bazet raised the rifle to his
shoulder to fire, I lunged forward and snatched it from
the cartridge box. The next moment I received a
stunning blow to the side of my head that knocked
me to my knees.

I rolled over, instinctively covering my face, waiting
for the shooting to begin. Nothing happened. I heard
an engine being cut, doors slamming, and then nothing
until men's loud voices filled my ears and I opened
my eyes.

Bazet was standing with his back to me about five
yards away, surrounded by a group of traditionally
dressed men who appeared to be Tuareg. My mouth
and eyes were gritty with sand and I dared to wipe
them with my hand. As far as I could tell, there was

no interest being shown in me where I lay curled up on the ground.

Some of the men remained sitting in the back of the pick-up, and I could now see that what I had thought were rifles in their hands were actually picks and hoes – earth- or sand-moving tools. I sat up and felt the side of my head where I had been hit. It was tender and sore and there was already a lump like an egg forming above my ear. Fuck it, I thought, filled with rage. Bazet had hit me. He'd stolen my telephone and set up this elaborate hoax about me being kidnapped, and then he had hit me. My heart pounded with extreme emotion. What had been terror evolved into white-hot fury.

My first instinct was to get to my feet and rush over to where he stood casually talking with these men, whoever they were, and shout and scream and maybe hit him back. I badly wanted to hurt him and to show him that he couldn't take advantage of me as he had done. He still had the rifle in his hand; in fact he was half leaning on it, the butt resting on the sand. One of the men went to the Land Cruiser and got out a skin of milk and passed it round. They were laughing now, lighting cigarettes, full of bonhomie.

I stood up, and as I did so my mobile dropped to

the ground and it came back to me how I had retrieved it just before I was knocked down. I picked it up and wiped it with my scarf, and switched it on. There was no signal available. Fuck again. I must try and keep calm, that was the important thing. For the moment no one appeared to have any interest in me, and while this was the case I must think through what had happened and try and make sense of it, and work out my options, if I had any.

Moving slowly, I went to where my bag lay on the ground. I picked it up and went to Bazet's truck and climbed into the passenger seat. The men still seated in the pick-up looked over idly. One even raised his hand in greeting.

Sitting in the truck I felt protected to a degree, and I had another look at my phone. There were some new messages from Emily from two days ago. I opened them; they were anxiously asking where I was and if our arrangements to meet still stood as we had planned. There was nothing from Chamba. I tried again to reply to Emily, but with no luck. I thought of the message I had sent from Ibrahim's satellite phone. At least she would have received that and would know that I was on my way.

On my way. I wished I felt confident that I *was* on

my way. I had no idea where we were or why Bazet was behaving like a thug. I imagined how furious Chamba would be when I told him. I touched the egg on my head. It felt vast – more like an orange. Had he hit me with the butt of the gun? I guessed he had. The bastard. What the fucking hell was that about?

I considered the men that he was talking to. They looked nothing out of the ordinary. The one who seemed to be at the centre of things was very tall and his headdress was huge and white – a sign of importance. He wore dark glasses and a deep pink robe. I saw him turn away to answer his mobile phone that he took from a pocket in his robe. An idea was forming in my mind. It was a gamble, but I really didn't see that I had anything to lose.

I found my hairbrush in my bag, then took off my scarf and brushed out my hair, which spread on my shoulders in a sheet of silvery gold. I rubbed the dirt off my face with a corner of my scarf and put on some eyeliner and lipstick. Even in my pocket mirror I could see the dramatic difference a bit of slap made. My face was thinner and browner than before, but this made my eyes appear larger and more blue. I was quite well aware of how exotic I would look to these men. I found the little bottle of Chanel 19 which I was eking out, but this was an occasion when I needed every weapon in my arsenal. I gave myself a squirt and rubbed a little through my hair.

Right, I said to myself. Fuck you, Bazet, and I got out and slammed the door of the pick-up as hard as I could. Every man looked over in my direction as I knew they would, and I walked very straight and slow towards them, my hair blazing in the sun. Ignoring Bazet, I went straight up to the tall man in the pink robe and said in French, 'Excuse me, monsieur, but I am the wife of Chamba ag Baye, and I need your help. May I please use your mobile telephone to make a very important call?'

Emily

IT WAS STIFLING in Djenne that night, but Hugh and I climbed into bed after supper – the electricity had gone again – and went straight to sleep. 'Out like a light' was my last thought, as I felt for Hugh's hot, angular body beside me, and realised that he was already unconscious. The last thing I was aware of was the droning of mosquitoes, an airborne attack, repelled by the swathes of netting.

I had no idea of where I was when I woke with a start some hours later. I lay trying to remember my location and straining my ears for the sound that I thought had awoken me; the slightest movement in the dark of the room. When it came again, I slid my hand across the sheet and found that Hugh was still there beside me.

Hardly daring to breathe, I strained my ears. Silence, and then the faint sensation of something stirring the air a few feet from the bed. It was profoundly dark and I was confused and disorientated. Where was the window, where the door? There was no slit of light to give me my bearings and the mosquito net obscured my view. I could see nothing that made any sense to me.

Could it be an animal? A rat? A snake that had slithered through the thatched roof? The tiny clink of two hard objects coming together convinced me that it was the work of a human hand. There was someone in the room with us.

Even if I had wanted to scream, I don't think I could have managed it. I was as paralysed as in one of those terrifying nightmares when you try to shout out and your voice won't come, and you wake up sobbing with terror and relief.

My instinct was to keep as still as possible. Whoever it was could be armed. Let them take what they wanted and leave us unharmed. If I woke Hugh, he might leap up, and get stabbed, or beaten. I tried to think where we had put our valuables – our money and passports – and with relief remembered that Hugh had hidden them under the mattress. It was a thing he had – he was so used to sleeping out in the rough on field work that anything that really mattered he kept as close as possible to his person.

Our packs were on the floor inside the door and I judged that that was where our robber was located – going through our belongings. With one finger I drew back the netting so that I could see better without moving, and as my eyes became accustomed to the dark, I realised that the door of our room was half open and that the noise had stopped.

I lay still and silent for ages after that, my thoughts ranging from anger that I might have lost the things I was bringing for Clemmie, to thankfulness that we had not been hurt. Eventually I touched Hugh on the shoulder, and as he surfaced from his deep sleep, I put my lips to his ear and whispered, 'There was someone in our room. I think we've been robbed.'

He turned towards me, instantly alert. 'What? Oh shit!' He was up at once, pulling aside the netting, trying to find the light switch, stumbling about, knocking into things. The light came on, and to my huge relief, the room was empty except for us.

'The bathroom!' I mouthed and pointed. 'Check the bathroom!'

He knocked the door open, and rushed in and out. 'No one there.'

'What have they taken?' I climbed out of bed and knelt by our luggage. Hugh's stuff had been disturbed, but there appeared to be nothing gone. It was my things that had been rummaged through more methodically, and it took me a while to realise that it was my old wallet that was missing – not that I had much money in it; it was more a depository for my Oyster card and driving licence and people's addresses, and old photos and stuff that I liked to take around with me for sentimental reasons. The thief, the bastard, had taken the sweets, too, that I had packed to give to children as we travelled.

'Is that all that's missing?' said Hugh. 'Are you sure?'

'Yes, I think so. I had a bit of English money – some notes, not more than thirty pounds. It's the other stuff I mind about – the sentimental bits and pieces and the things that are a pain to replace, like my driving licence. What do we do now? Should we raise the alarm?'

Hugh peered out into the courtyard, which was unlit and utterly still. 'There should be a nightwatchman out there somewhere,' he said, 'but I can't see anyone.'

'What about Will and Divinity? Do you think we

should warn them? How did he get in here anyway? Didn't you lock the door?'

'Yes, I did. The key's still here on the table. The door hasn't been forced. Maybe he picked the lock. It's a fairly basic one.'

'Well, what do we do?'

'Let's see if we can find the nightwatchman and then check on Will and Divinity.'

'I'm coming with you. I'm not staying here on my own. What can we use as a weapon, in case he's still about?'

'My torch? I can't think of anything else. I don't want to use my tripod to hit anyone. It's too valuable to me.'

'I could bring my insect repellent . . . spray it into his eyes.'

'Okay, come on.'

We put on our shoes and set off. It was extremely scary walking in the dark amongst the shifting shadows of the trees and the black lumps of bushes along the path. There was a solitary light by the main gate, which had been closed and locked for the night, and it was there that we found the nightwatchman, flat out on his mattress, fast asleep.

Hugh woke him up with a poke in the ribs, and

he stumbled to his feet clutching a heavy stick. He seemed very surprised, and it took him a long time to take in what Hugh told him. He was tall and thin and weedy-looking and did not appear to have any of the characteristics you might look for in a security guard.

Then he suddenly seemed to remember his role and became very active and excitable, rolling his eyes and rushing about bashing the bushes with his stick. He escorted us back to our room and examined the door and the window latch and then hared around checking other rooms. It seemed that Will and Divinity had escaped and were still asleep, and so after a bit, Hugh and I went back to bed, only to be woken by a banging on the door and the nightwatchman shouting through the window that he was going to stay outside our room until morning.

'No worries!' he cried in a ringing tone that must have woken everybody. 'No worries, *monsieur et madame*! Hassan is here!'

We must have gone back to sleep, because the next thing I saw were the daggers of bright light slanting through the shutters of the window. I sat up and pulled the nets aside. The events of the night came back in a rush and I went to the door and opened it, and found Hassan sleeping peacefully outside.

In the daylight, the terror was just a memory and I began to feel that it was not such a dreadful thing that had happened. We hadn't been harmed and not much had been stolen. It could have been so much worse.

I had another check through my belongings and there didn't seem to have been anything else taken, which was a relief, because I would have hated to lose my camera or my carefully chosen clothing and things for Clemmie. It was odd that whoever had risked breaking in should have snatched only my wallet. It must have just been money they were after, although everything else must have had a market value. I wondered if it could have been a child or teenager because of the missing sweets. It seemed quite possible. I supposed we would have to report it to the management and there would be a hullabaloo and poor old Hassan would be out of a job.

Hugh woke up then and we turned towards each other with relief that we were together and all right. 'Let's not make a big thing of it,' I said. 'I think it might have been a kid who shinned over the gate in the night. They didn't take anything much, and we are so rich by comparison.'

'Yeah, I agree,' said Hugh. 'But I guess the management ought to know. They need to make sure it's not a regular occurrence, or the place will get a bad name with tourists.'

It was still only six thirty when we stepped over Hassan and went to sit at our table, watching bright little birds flitting through the bushes and the gardeners moving about with that African grace and languor. There was no sign of other guests until a middle-aged French couple appeared, the woman with a beach-ball bottom in Lycra cycling shorts, and a strappy top with no bra. I was very disapproving and made a face at Hugh, but he was busy reading about Djenne in some academic paper he had brought with him. There was no air of alarm about the French and I guessed they hadn't been disturbed in the night.

We ate some really good bread and jam and drank a lot of coffee before Will and Divinity appeared. Divinity looked exotic in a long white tunic with a string of huge red beads round her neck. I told them about our break-in and they confirmed that they had slept undisturbed.

'How terrifying!' said Divinity. 'To wake up and find

183

someone in your room! You could have both been murdered in your bed. I'd have been shit scared.'

'I think whoever it was wanted to get in and out as quickly as possible. He didn't take much. He must have just grabbed my wallet and run.'

'All the same.'

'Yeah, well . . .' I shrugged. It was so different in the light of day, and I brushed off the terror I had felt. 'We're okay, and honestly, all I care about is that today's the day we meet Clemmie!'

I went round the table to where Will was sitting and gave him a hug. I knew he would be as excited as me.

'Look, I know how keen you are to see Clementine,' said Hugh, looking up from his book and taking notice for the first time, 'but really we shouldn't hurry Djenne. It's a fascinating city. Incredibly interesting. Serufi said that he will find us an English-speaking guide and that we should be ready to start a guided tour at seven thirty. It will be uncomfortably hot if we leave it any later.' He looked at his watch. 'That gives us fifteen minutes to be ready. Is that okay?'

'Sure,' said Will. 'You're right, of course. We don't want to miss anything. I really want to get a look at the old madrasas if we are allowed in, and there's a women's craft co-operative which Divinity wants to visit. Anyway, Em, we have a fairly loose arrangement with Clemmie. We're aiming to meet any time this afternoon or evening. It can be later rather than sooner.'

He saw my agonised expression. 'Sorry, but it's a shame to miss stuff out. This is a once-and-only chance. We're going to have plenty of time with Clem.'

We met our guide by the gate as Serufi had arranged. He was a very black, turnip-headed young Bozo, a local tribe who lived along the river, according to Hugh, with round eyes and a full white beam of a smile. He was wearing an immaculate shirt and trousers and Italian-looking spiv shoes and he smelled very scented. He spoke English, very fast, and told us he wanted to be a teacher, and he was very, very earnest and enthusiastic.

We set off at a cracking pace. Despite being a World Heritage Site, the city was filthy and crumbling, with open drains and dead rats and shouts the equivalent of '*Gardez l'eau*' as waste water shot out from upper windows. It was like walking round a set from *Star Wars* – just as weird and fantastical. The tall mud houses had ornate and castellated facades adorned with strange pinnacles topped with ostrich eggs. The doors were framed by massively buttressed porches, and there was only one small window above the door, for checking who was knocking, I supposed, and deciding whether you could be arsed to go down and let them in.

The narrow, crooked streets were crammed with children and beautiful women, graceful and immaculate in their turbans and off-the-shoulder dresses. Our Bozo, who said his name was Frankie, which seemed a bit unlikely, took us to a lean-to covered in sacking and showed us a great many mud bricks with explanations of how they were made. Both Will and Hugh found it all fascinating and asked lots of questions, and Hugh wrote things in his notebook and took photographs, while Divinity and I stood in the strip of shade and examined the soles of our shoes to check we had stepped in nothing unspeakable.

We were not permitted to see inside the Great Mosque, but we looked down on it from the rooftops. Frankie demonstrated that we should enter various private homes and climb the stairs to the flat roof, where we were shown different views of the city. It seemed so intrusive to march through living rooms where families were gathered, hunkered down on their haunches round smoky open fires, but I guessed Frankie must have paid them off, because they nodded and smiled and seemed not the slightest bit surprised to have large white Westerners and Divinity trooping in through their front door. Immediately inside was a dark room that opened out on to a courtyard where day-to-day life went on – chickens and donkeys seemed to live there, and I assumed they had to go out through the front room to reach the outside world.

Frankie took the trouble to explain to us that he had worked in Bamako as a shirt seller but that lack of trade had forced him back home to try his luck as a guide. He evidently felt superior to the stick-in-the-mud people gathered round their fires in the houses we visited. He was a man of the world who had taught himself English and was determined to better himself if he could. I wished we could help him, or even give him some encouragement, but I felt disheartened by the hopelessness of it all. In spite of his impeccable turnout and his aftershave, I couldn't see that he would ever get the training he needed to become a teacher. How did Clemmie stand it – this sense of overwhelming odds? I sometimes felt a bit like this at home, teaching in London, but at least there were agencies to help and the possibility of achieving modest goals with sufficient support. Poor Frankie appeared to have no one, and nothing, to weigh in on his side.

Divinity and I complained that it was too hot to be tourists, but Hugh was enthusiastic to see everything. 'This is all so fascinating!' he said. 'Between the eleventh and thirteenth centuries, Arab sources speak of Djenne as the dominant commerical centre of West Africa. It was the major centre for the gold, salt and slave trades of the Trans-Saharan trade route, but later Timbuktu took over and Djenne's fortunes never really recovered – that's why it looks so frozen in time. The first European to get here was René Caillié in 1828. I was reading some of his diaries this morning, and from the descriptions he gives, I would say it hasn't changed much.'

'The slave trade, huh?' said Divinity. 'So for all I know, my ancestors might have come through here?'

'They might have done. Black slaves were captured across Africa and sold on to Arab dealers, then resold and shipped off round the world from West African ports.' We all went quiet imagining the horror of it. I hoped that Divinity hadn't understood that the Tuareg were chief amongst the slave traders. This was a subject best glossed over.

At last Frankie allowed us to stop. I suggested that he took Divinity and me to the women's workshop and the men to see the Islamic schools for which the city was famous and to which women were not admitted. So we left the men at the entrance to a mosque and he led us off down back streets and through an imposing door into a large, dark room presided over by a vast, queenly woman in a scarlet turban and a purple dress.

Divinity and I spent a happy hour poking about amongst carpets and woven bedspreads and brightly printed rolls of cloth. There was a wooden loom in a second room upon which was stretched a half-finished length of cloth, and we watched as two girls about eight years old wove the bright woollen threads back and forth and worked the shuttle with flying fingers. I asked the woman about them, but she spoke little French and couldn't answer my questions as to whether they went to school and how many hours a day they worked. I sat and watched them and took photographs with their permission to show my class at school how bloody lucky they were to lead such idle lives.

The big lady made us tea and invited us to sit with her, but Divinity was too busy holding up textiles and taking photographs and making notes.

'Oh my God!' she cried. 'It's all so wonderful! Far better than I'd hoped. Some of this stuff is inspirational.

189

I need Hugh to translate because I want to know how I can ship cloth back. See the Islamic influence – the repeating patterns – combined with the African colours and raw energy? I love this one with the brilliant birds flying all over it. It's just fabulous.'

The large lady handed us a scuffed sheet of cardboard on which was stuck a blurred photocopy of an article from a French newspaper about the co-operative. It appeared to have been set up with help from a French foundation for the economic emancipation of women in Mali. I translated it roughly for Divinity. At the bottom were contact details and an address in Djenne which Divinity tapped into her iPad.

She made a pile of what she wanted to take back with her and tried to find out if larger pieces could be shipped. The total of what she chose came to nearly five hundred pounds but she brushed that aside and said it was nothing when she considered the quality of the work. She wanted to know about vegetable dyes and cotton and wool mixes, but we didn't get very far with that line of questioning. The woman was very dignified and impassive and showed not the slightest bit of excitement at the prospect of such a large sale. She made me feel as if we were the lucky ones, and as far as she was concerned she could take or leave our money. She would have done well in one of the designer shops on Bond Street.

'Where's that husband of yours when we need him?' Divinity said. 'He could have got all my questions answered.' But we had arranged to meet the guys back at the encampment, and they would no doubt by now be waiting under the vines drinking cold Castel beer.

'Let's go and find them,' I suggested. 'Then Hugh can come back with you and do the negotiations. I expect Frankie would help too.'

The woman indicated that Divinity could use a credit card, which seemed fairly unlikely, but she produced a hand-held machine from the floor beside her.

'Okay,' said Divinity. 'Look, I'll take the smaller stuff with me now, and then we can ask Hugh to come back and work out how I can get the bigger pieces sent to the UK.'

The woman nodded as if she understood, and ten minutes later we were threading our way back through the teeming streets laden with brown-paper-wrapped parcels, with one of the small girls showing us the way. She took my hand and I was shocked to find that her fingers and palm were as hard as stiff leather. It was a proper workman's hand – like my dad's after years of farming.

When we got back to the encampment, the men were there as we had guessed, sitting in the shade of the thatched bar and reunited with a row of Castel beers. They had paid off Frankie, who it turned out was not the guide that Serufi had designated for us. It seemed he was just a quick-witted chap who hung around the gates waiting to offer himself to tourists and had seized the opportunity when he saw us. Serufi had been quite put out and the neat little man, Jimmy, who had been booked as our guide had been most disappointed. So they had paid him as well.

Divinity immediately unwrapped her parcels and spread out her fabric, urging Will and Hugh to go back with her to the co-operative to complete the shipping arrangements for the bigger pieces. 'After we've finished these beers,' said Will. 'I've been hallucinating about sitting in the shade with an ice-cold glass the whole morning. Frankie did a very good job and we weren't allowed any short cuts.'

Hugh examined the blanket cloth Divinity had bought. 'It's beautifully made,' he said. 'The weaving is so even. I expect the patterns are passed down from generation to generation.'

'Like Fair Isle knitting,' I said. 'Will, can you remember those awful itchy jumpers we were made to wear as children? They were sent from some Kingsley relative who lived in the Outer Isles and had gone native. Aren't today's children lucky with everything coming from Gap and not all lumpy, scratchy hand-made stuff?' Divinity shot me a look. Of course this was the opposite of everything she believed in. Oh well, she had to accept that I have a good-taste bypass.

She was getting impatient. 'Come on, guys! Drink up. It's only ten minutes away.'

'Okay, okay!' Hugh and Will drained their glasses.

'I'll go and pack our stuff. Have you spoken to the proprietor, Hugh, about last night?'

'Yes, I did. He finds it unbelievable. He says there have been no thefts here to date – no break-ins, anyway, just the occasional thing disappearing from an unlocked room in the daytime. He wanted to blame it on Hassan, and I had a job explaining that it couldn't possibly have been him because he was asleep throughout, and then I felt bad about landing him in the shit.'

'There was no way round that,' I said. 'Poor Hassan. I hope he doesn't get sacked.'

'The proprietor promised me he wouldn't. It might encourage him to stay awake, though.'

★　★　★

When they left, guided by Serufi, I went back to our room and had a look at the lock on the door, and saw that it was so badly fitted that it would take no more than a hard push to force it open. I found that I could do it myself quite easily and noiselessly by putting my shoulder to it.

I sat on the bed and carefully went through the contents of my day bag. When I'm travelling I get paranoid about losing vital things, and the theft had unnerved me. I like to know that everything is where it should be. When I had done that, I checked my telephone again, more out of habit than anything else, and miraculously I had a signal. Not only that, there was a message sent from yet another unknown number from Clemmie.

'Trip turning into a bit of n mare but I will be there 2 meet u asap.'

I tried to return the call, but the phone was switched off, so I sent a text.

'We'll be there! Can't wait!'

What sort of nightmare? I wondered. It could be anything – a broken-down vehicle, a minor accident, a roadblock. There were so many things that could cause a delay in this country. I checked when the message had been sent – about the time we were enjoying our leisurely breakfast. Well, I was relieved just to have heard from her again. I couldn't expect Hugh or Divinity to feel the same way I did, and it was only fair to accept this delay in Djenne, but I was burning with impatience to get going again.

Will had always been especially close to and protective of Clemmie, but it seemed that he was now so in the thrall of Divinity, it was a case of whatever she wanted, he agreed to. She dominated him because she had the louder voice and her needs were greater and more loudly expressed than his. She was beautiful and fascinating and had a feistiness you had to admire, but when he was with her he was less the Will I loved of old. It made me sad, but it is a fact that childhood relationships change as you grow up, and that to love someone as he did Divinity, and I did Hugh, was to alter the old loyalties and allegiances. When you are in love with someone, it is inevitable you become a different person to your friends.

I thought of home, and how, when my mother went off to work and my father was somewhere on the farm, I would cycle up the lane from our silent house to join Clemmie and her brothers at the next-door farm along the valley. I used to wish that I belonged there, that I was truly one of them and not just a cousin. My life seemed so poor and scant by comparison with the richness and variety and noise of a house full of children.

Of course there were quarrels and feuds, but the sense of tribal loyalty was strong, and if necessary, exclusive. We didn't need anyone else to join us to make a game. We were a side, a team, a gang, just as we were, and Will was always the leader.

I was thinking of this, sitting on the bed in the peace of the cool room, when I heard the others crossing the compound towards the open door. They were talking loudly and Divinity was saying, in an outraged voice, 'I just don't believe it . . .'

'What's happened?' I went to the door to meet them.

'That place we went to – the co-operative. We couldn't find it. It's not the one that Serufi knows of. Nobody seems to have heard of it and we couldn't even find the street. Frankie has disappeared completely and Serufi's guide says he doesn't know him and he's not even a man from Djenne. It's really annoying.'

'How peculiar! What about the stuff you bought? You paid for it, didn't you?'

'Gone! Unless we can trace the shop and that woman. I took down the contact details from off that sheet she showed us.'

'Was it a scam, then? Between Frankie and that woman?'

'We don't know. Serufi is as puzzled as we are. His guide looked at the stuff I brought back here with me and says it is all really good quality – just as good as the co-operative he wanted to take us to. I feel gutted, to be honest, if I've lost it.'

'You'll have to stop the transaction. Telephone your credit card company.'

'I've tried to and I can't get through.'

'Shit! I can't believe it was a con; who would go to all that trouble – setting up a fake shop and that loom and everything?'

'I don't know. It's the weirdest thing.'

'Serufi is making enquiries and then he's going to the tourist police. It will hold us up a bit, I'm afraid,' said Will.

I had guessed as much. I looked at my watch.

'I've just heard from Clemmie. She says she is having a difficult journey too.'

'What's the problem?'

'I don't know. She didn't say.'

'Well, let's go and have a beer while we wait.'

'Help me with the bags, Hugh,' I sighed. 'Let's at

least have everything ready so that we can get on the road as soon as possible.'

'Look, I'm sorry, Emily,' said Divinity in a defensive tone, 'but it's not my fault.'

'I didn't say it was.' But to be honest, I felt resentful that it was her who was holding us up, whether it was fair or not.

Clemmie

WHEN I HAD finished with the telephone, I handed it back to the tall man and smiled at him sweetly.

'Do you speak French, monsieur?'

'*Oui, madame.*' This was a relief.

'Then please would you tell me what is going on?'

He shrugged. 'What do you mean? I do not understand what you are asking.'

I tried again. 'Are you a friend of Bazet?'

'He is cousin. We are Tuareg!'

'Yes, I know that. But who are you? Why did he think you were following us? Why did he tell me you were bad men? Why did he warn me that you might be kidnappers? Why was he prepared to shoot you?'

The man laughed and said something to the others, who joined in. I blushed with anger. This was no fucking joke. He turned back to me and answered gravely, 'Bazet must be prepared. These are difficult times. There is much talk in Kidal of AQIM operating in the desert.'

'Yes, I know,' I said, although I didn't. But maybe it was this that had been the hot topic in Mariam's yard and the talk was nothing to do with me. Maybe it was colossal egotism on my part to think that I and my affairs were more interesting than anything else.

'Where are you going – you and your men?'

'We are building a well not far from here for the government. It is small gesture to help the Tuareg.'

'Where are *we* going, then? This isn't the route to Gao, I'm sure of that.'

The men conferred again and this time Bazet sounded angry. His laughing mood changed abruptly and he cut the air with his hand as he spoke.

'Bazet brings you this way to avoid army roadblocks which may cause delay. There is suspicion between army and Tuareg. If they choose, the soldiers can make your journey difficult.'

I knew this to be true. Chamba took care to avoid ever using a route that would bring him into contact with the army.

'How do we cross the river?' I was trying, in my head, to visualise the map of Mali, huge and empty in the north. The Niger had to be crossed somewhere, and as far as I knew, there was no bridge other than at Gao. Nothing this man said had reassured me. Why hadn't Chamba told me all this before I left? Or was it true that Bazet had picked up information in Kidal that had made him change the route?

'You cross at Bourem. By boat. This way you avoid all main routes. You travel safely with Bazet, be assured.'

I felt tears well in my eyes. I was sick of it all – this horrible journey, not understanding, being unable to contact Chamba, my anxiety to get to Emily. I swallowed hard; I wasn't going to show weakness now. The weak are despised in the desert.

'Thank you,' I said, carefully. 'Thank you for explaining. You speak good French.' It suddenly struck me as strange – this man with a spade, who spoke so fluently.

'I work many years with the government as engineer. I am regional development officer.'

The sun was so hot overhead that I felt sick and light-headed, and I wiped my face with my sleeve. The man indicated we should move to the shade afforded by the rocks where his men were already squatting, sharing cigarettes, talking in the low voices I have noticed the Tuareg adopt in the desert. The vast emptiness seems to demand a quietness in return.

201

'What's your name?' I asked him.

'Mokhtar ibn Zaid.'

'Thank you, Mokhtar. I would like you to do something else for me. Something very important. Please would you try to contact Chamba? Please tell him how you met me and where I am and where Bazet is taking me. Will you do this for me?' I fixed him with a stern and imploring look. 'Look, this is his number. His satellite telephone should be working, but at the moment it is switched off.'

Mokhtar had removed his dark glasses, and I saw that his eyes were red and tired and that he was older than I first thought.

'I will do this for you. I have his number now in my telephone.' He reached out and touched my hair. 'I heard tell of the English woman of Chamba, the Lion of Temesna, and of her beauty; now my eyes see for themselves it is not a lie.'

The Tuareg are very good at these elaborate compliments, and they must be received graciously. You can't protest and say 'Oh, come on! I'm not anything special!' as you would in England. I nodded my head and gave him a big smile and said, 'I will tell Chamba how kind you have been.' I know this sounds a bit princessy and royal, but I've learned that these formal manners are important and appreciated.

I glanced to where Bazet was talking to the other men. I still felt furious with him. He had bloody well *hit me*, I couldn't forget that. I felt the lump on the side of my head. It didn't hurt much, but the blow still made my blood boil. How dare he! 'Tell me, Mokhtar, is it possible, do you *really* think we could have been followed by bad people? Kidnappers or the AQIM?'

Mokhtar looked serious as he contemplated his answer. 'Police, maybe. Bazet tells me he travels without correct papers.'

Oh, fuck again. That would be my fault, of course, for hurrying him out of Kidal. But surely he wouldn't take up a firing position against the police? It was all too complicated for me to sort out a sensible answer, or arrive at an explanation. God, I hated this helplessness, this reliance on people I found it hard to trust.

'Thank you. Let's hope the rest of our journey is uneventful.'

'You will soon be far from police. An hour or two into the desert and they do not venture further.'

I supposed that was a good thing. It was hard to tell. Maybe I should be glad to be in reach of a policeman. For now, I had to deal with Bazet. I got up from the shade and shook Mokhtar's long brown hand, then walked over to where he was sitting with the other men.

'We should go,' I said, standing over him. I knew he could laugh at me or ignore me, but I doubted he would be disrespectful in front of these men. He looked up, his eyes revealing nothing, and then slowly stubbed out his cigarette in the sand. The other men stood up, and he embraced them one by one before walking with me back to the pick-up. When we were inside the cab, I put my hand on his arm and said, 'Don't ever strike me again. Never. Do you understand?' I dug in my nails as hard as I could. 'Chamba would kill you if I told him.'

'I hit you to save your life! You want a bullet through your head?' He shook off my hand and started the engine.

These were scare tactics, I was sure. I turned my mobile phone over in my lap.

'And why,' I said, 'did you steal my telephone? How dare you take it and hide it from me?'

'For your safety,' he said, angrily. 'You are a stupid woman. You know nothing, nothing!' He couldn't look at me, concentrating on steering the pick-up across a dune of soft sand, but I could see the anger contorting his face. 'You think you can be like Tuareg because you ride camels and live in a tent with a Tuareg man, but you are ignorant like a baby. All the time you are using your mobile; and sending messages is dangerous – for you and your friends.'

His words stung me. It was unjust and unkind to say that I thought I was a Tuareg. Of course I didn't, but at least I was trying to learn and understand. And what was this danger? Mariam had spoken of danger too. Who the fuck would be interested in my calls? I was totally insignificant in this country and it was unlikely to be the *News of the World* hacking my cell phone.

'I don't know what you are talking about!' I said furiously in English. 'And how can I, when you never fucking explain what's going on?'

He couldn't understand, but it made me feel better.

We drove on hour after hour. My head started to spin from the constant heaving and lurching of the truck, and a headache throbbed behind my eyes. The fact that we were taking an unusual route was obvious. There was no visible track of any sort – just endless untrammelled desert. Sometimes there were soft rolling waves of sand that were difficult and slow to negotiate. Three or four times we had to dig ourselves out, but there was no one better than Bazet at knowing at a glance which was the best way through. Then the sands gave out into ugly gravelly plains across which we could race. We saw no one, neither man nor beast. Not a tree, nor a bush. We stopped for Bazet to fill the tank from the jerrycans of diesel that we carried and to make tea and eat some cheese and dates. It was the hardest day's driving I had ever experienced, and it filled me with a dread that I had never felt before in this country. Our journey across the vastness seemed so faltering, so fraught with dangers. I imagined looking down from the white-hot sky, watching the tiny moving thread that was the progress of the pick-up through the desolation. That we should arrive anywhere would seem to need a miracle.

The terrible heat and the incessant movement made it hard to think clearly, and I struggled to hang on to some sense of what was happening. I went over and over in my mind what Mokhtar had told me. We were going to Bourem. Bourem? Bourem? Where was it? I had never heard of it, but it was evidently somewhere on the Niger, because it was from there that we were going to cross the river by boat. It occurred to me that I shouldn't have assumed we would cross by the bridge at Gao – the way I had travelled before. Maybe it had always been the plan to come this way. Maybe it had been decided by Bazet and Chamba from the beginning. I had no way of knowing except by asking Bazet, and he wasn't talking to me. God, it was frustrating.

It was midday now and the sun was right above us, and there was nowhere to stop to find a little shade. We banged on, and although it was a horrible journey, I was glad because it meant we were making progress towards Will and Emily.

I closed my eyes to try and doze, but the crashing, rolling motion of the pick-up jolted me awake. Then suddenly, up ahead, I thought I saw two or three wavering dots on the flat horizon. Concentrating on them as hard as I could, I saw them vanish and then reappear, and grow and become more distinct, and then they multiplied and I realised they were camels. As we drew closer, I saw that it was a large herd, a hundred or more dark brown beasts, unlike the mostly white and dun camels of the Tuareg. These were smaller, less magnificent, more like farm animals, and I guessed they were kept for meat and milk and not for riding.

It came as a relief to me to have arrived somewhere,

even if it was only a camel herd, and then I saw the familiar mound and wheel of a well, and then the shapes of a few low mud-brick houses. Bazet brought the pick-up to a stop and got out and slammed the door. He didn't look back or indicate that I should follow, so I stayed where I was, swigged out of my water bottle, and watched him walking over to where two men were working the pulley to draw water for their beasts. They stopped what they were doing to watch him coming, and to me their faces seemed surly and unwelcoming.

With the engine cut, a weight of silence fell, only broken by the roar of a bull camel somewhere in the herd. Sweat trickled down my back and I still felt slightly sick. I watched Bazet, wondering what was going on. Had he gone to ask the way? Then one of the men went off to walk amongst the camels with a goatskin in his hand, and I realised he was looking for a milking female. Bazet was buying milk. He would drink it warm and frothy straight from the strong-smelling skin. The thought made me feel even more sick, but it would put Bazet in a better mood. Tuareg men love camel milk above everything.

The man came back with a full skin and Bazet gave him some money and shook hands.

'Arabs!' he said when he returned to the pick-up. 'This is an Arab village. Bourem is not far. There are no police or army here.' He offered me the skin and I shook my head. He laughed nastily. 'You are no Tuareg!' he said, wiping his mouth. The milk had refreshed him. He got in and slammed the door and started the engine, and we drove through the small, mean village. The houses were blank-faced, windowless, single-storey in the Arab style.

The street was absolutely deserted. We passed an open door with some sacks and oil drums in the sand outside, but nobody stirred in the dark interior. Only a few rangy chickens dashed in front of us. It was a strange, unlovely place, broiling in the sun.

On the other side of the village the beaten sand road gave out and we were nowhere once again. Bazet drove carefully, peering through the windscreen, and it seemed to me we had changed direction – the sun was to our right now and the desert was less empty. A few donkeys and goats scattered in front of us amongst the occasional thorn trees, and we passed two small boys tending some black and white sheep. A few miles on and we seemed to have joined a very definite track, and two vehicles passed us from the opposite direction.

The first was an old minibus crammed with anxious black faces and loaded down with ramshackle luggage tied in rope nets to the roof. I had witnessed before the terrible journey of these illegal economic refugees, travelling with such hope and expectation, believing they could cross the Sahara and reach the promise of a new life. Their clapped-out vehicles would never make it, and if they were very lucky they would break down before they had got too far.

The second vehicle was a black Land Cruiser, dusted with white sand, its smoked-glass windows giving no clue to who sat within. It was travelling slowly, slewing sideways when it hit the deeper drifts. Bazet shook his head at the incompetence of the driver.

Then I saw the river – a slide of silver fringed with green. It was impossible to tell where sky and water met, but to me it looked as wide as the sea stretching into the shimmering distance.

Bourem must be just ahead. There was more traffic now, a donkey cart or two, and a string of camels led by a tribesman, another overburdened lorry, and then, on a bend in the river, I saw it, quite a large place, with many low buildings and a mud mosque, and a large fort down by the river, surrounded by palm trees.

Although it looked ancient, I guessed it would have

been a French fort, built in colonial days, and it made me think of Great-Aunt Mary, who had brought me to this country in the first place and whose father had served as commanding officer in the region before the Second World War. He would have been here sometime in the thirties, patrolling the desert with his camel corps, and Mary might have come here too, as a very young woman, when she visited him from London. Like me, she had fallen in love, just as hopelessly, but her love had ended so sadly in loss and separation.

I knew and understood her loneliness now. I could imagine what it must have been like to be pregnant far out in the desert and to give birth in a goatskin tent. The Tuareg women may have resented her as a stranger who had taken one of their men, and she certainly wouldn't have been able to speak to them as they tended her. It made me sad to think about her now, and I wished so much that she had spoken about it later in her life when she came to live amongst us in Dorset. Instead, she had sealed over that wild adventure and the tragedy that followed as if it had never been, aided and abetted by Miss Timmis, who denied that any of it had ever happened.

I was thinking of this when Bazet came off the track that looked as if it led into the town and followed another that went towards the river and the fort. It was about half a mile away, surrounded by a collection of broken-down mud houses and scattered goats. Some parts of the walls had tumbled down, but it was still an impressive building that must have once dominated the region and the river.

We drove right up to the high walls and then Bazet stopped and turned off the engine and we sat in silence. I knew better than to ask what was happening. In a moment the children appeared from the houses and crowded round the pick-up and Bazet spoke to them through the window. One of the older boys ran off and came back with a tall, stooped man dressed in a dirty blue robe and a black turban. He was not a Tuareg, I guessed – maybe a Songhai tribesman. He came to talk to Bazet and I saw he had a lot of missing teeth and those remaining were brown and stained. He seemed unhurried and unsurprised by our sudden arrival. Bazet said something to him and the man looked across at me with dark eyes, the whites the colour of Cheddar cheese, and then turned and spat into the sand.

He shouted something to the teenage boy, who ran off at once, followed by the other children, and began to swing open the old wooden gates of the fort. Bazet

started the engine and we drove in. The interior courtyard was empty and rubbish-strewn, with barrack-like
buildings around the walls. A mule was tied to a stake
in the corner. I saw it had terrible harness sores, red and
open and covered in black flies, and its knees were broken
and scarred.

Why had we come here, to this mean, ugly place?
I had a sudden horrible fear that I could be imprisoned
and no one in the world would know. I had never
once been frightened in Mali until this trip. Shit, I
was going completely off my head with these random
wild thoughts. I breathed deeply and tried to remain
calm. Bazet got out and told me to do the same, and
to collect my stuff from the back of the truck.

'What happens now?' I asked him.

'Boat,' he said. 'As you were told.'

'Are we leaving the truck here?'

'It does not swim.'

I collected my bag and blanket and all the bottles
of water and followed him out of the courtyard. The
man was sitting on a plastic chair in the shade, staring
into the distance, his hands loose in his lap. I would
have liked to have shouted at him about the condition
of the mule, but I didn't dare.

Bazet entered into some sort of negotiation and

then signalled to me to go down towards the river, where there was a ramshackle pier at the end of which was a pinasse – the long, narrow riverboats used by the fishermen on the Niger. Two men were working over the outboard motor, which was spluttering and fading. The older boy appeared with Bazet's camel bags and the gun, and signalled that I should follow him.

I relaxed again because this was what I had been told would happen; that we would cross the river by boat because it was safer. For some reason I had imagined a ferry that would take the pick-up. I never thought we would be crossing on foot in such a light craft, and I couldn't imagine what would happen on the other side. The boat looked okay, although there was a small pool of water slopping in the bottom. There was a reed canopy in the centre, and when I climbed aboard, I put my stuff on the wooden seat out of the wet, and sat in the shade. The two men took no notice of me at all, but continued their work on the engine.

I took out my mobile and to my delight saw that I had a signal. I rang Emily's number but there was no reply and so I left her a message. Bazet's remarks had made me nervous and I resisted telling her any details; only that I was on my way and that although

I didn't know when we would arrive, I would definitely be there. Will's phone was switched off and so was Chamba's. I would have left him a message had I not seen Bazet coming towards the pier, and so I pocketed my phone and looked innocent. If he saw me using it he would probably throw it into the river. I was starving hungry and I was glad to see he was carrying a large loaf of bread and some little green bananas. The boy was bringing up the rear with a string of fish. They both hopped aboard and the boy lit a little stove and gutted the fish over the side and put them on a grill with a scattering of salt.

The men got the engine going and untied the boat's lines and we were off, gliding through the flat, calm, pale coffee-coloured water. I felt the excitement of moving swiftly, watching the bank recede, the fort growing smaller. From the river I could see Bourem stretching out along the bend, the gaggle of fishing boats on the shore amongst the trees, the lines of brightly coloured washing draped on bushes and the women knee-deep in the water scrubbing clothes.

It was peaceful out there on the river. It was a much more restful way to travel than walloping along in the pick-up. We passed watermelon-slice boats elegantly punted by graceful, cheerful men fishing with silvery nylon nets. The boy kept catching my eye and grinning, and it cheered me up to smile back. He flipped the grilled fish over and then slid one on to a palm leaf and passed it to me with a chunk of bread. It was crisp and salty and delicious, and I ate it at once, hot as it was. The boy laughed. He pointed to himself. 'Brahim!' he said.

'Hi. Brahim,' I said. 'Very good fish! Very good cook!' He grinned back.

After I had eaten, I made myself more comfortable, leaning on my pack, and closed my eyes. The sun flickered through the reeds above my head, and it was pleasantly cool out on the river. Once it had teemed with wildlife – hippos and crocodiles that the early white men came to shoot – but today nothing disturbed the flat water. I could see flocks of tall birds along the shore amongst the mud flats and reeds but I didn't know what they were. I had come unprepared to live in this country, and almost daily regretted my ignorance.

Bazet was sitting with the men in the stern of the boat, and he too seemed relaxed now that we were on the water. He was smoking and laughing and had eaten well. The men talked quietly, exchanging news, I supposed, of what was happening in the north where we had come from and the situation down here in the Sahel. Apart from Brahim, who was friendly and solicitous – pouring me hot sweet tea, and encouraging me to rest my feet on the wooden seat and make myself more comfortable – the men ignored me. Apparently I was of no interest to them, and that suited me fine.

There were many islands in the river where little thatched fishing villages hung just above the waterline, as if they were floating on the water's edge, and naked children bobbed in and out of the water. Some of the islands looked like little private countries, dominated by fortress-like mud mosques.

'Bozo!' said Brahim, pointing. I had heard of the Bozo people, whose business was fishing, and it looked as if their simple lives had not changed for centuries.

I must have slept then, because when I woke the sun had moved from the middle of the sky and the opposite shore was approaching in a flat green stripe. I looked at my watch. We had been travelling for several hours. I had no idea what would happen after we landed, and I was not optimistic that we would make Homberi that night, but with any luck Ems would have got my text and know that I was on my way. The river had lulled me into a state beyond worrying.

I sat up and watched the approaching shore, which looked a featureless stretch of reeds, and then I saw the shape of thatched huts and guessed we were coming into a village of sorts. There was a landing stage and a few boats tied up and a group of men and children waving at us.

We nudged in and the men cut the motor, and eager hands reached out for ropes to make us secure. Brahim leapt nimbly ashore and stretched to take my pack and bag and then held out his hand to me. I felt he had become my friend and was grateful for his kindness.

Bazet climbed ashore and our luggage was piled up on the ground, then he signalled for me to follow him and we set off into the village on foot. It was nothing more than a collection of round mud huts under the trees, which were magnificent, tall and spreading like mighty oaks. I wished that I knew their name and could add it to the list of things I kept in my notebook to find out about when I had the opportunity. This list of things I would like to know more about now covered many pages. Maybe Brahim could tell me.

As usual, the children of the village came galloping out to meet us, all dressed in raggedy, brightly coloured shirts, and I guessed that these too were Bozo people who lived off the river. I seemed to remember that

Hugh got excited about them last time he was here because although they are Muslim, they are also animist on the sly, and believe that natural objects have a spirit. I'm completely with them on this idea and think at heart I am an animist too. Those great trees by the river, for instance. Surely they have a spirit of their own? I certainly felt aware of it as I passed beneath them.

Outside each house was a line of dried and drying fish of various sizes, from whoppers to tiddlers. A group of men got up from the shade of a tree and moved towards us. There was the ritual conflab with Bazet and then we were led to a roundhouse, where we were invited to sit on a mat in the hot dark interior while some women made tea. They wore the usual off-the-shoulder dresses and matching turbans in exploding colours. Their slender black feet slapped the mud floor as they moved. Handsome, graceful and unsmiling, they showed no interest in me and made no attempt to communicate, and I felt too worn out to try to be congenial.

'You stay!' announced Bazet, getting up when he had drunk several cups of tea. 'I return for you!'

'When?'

'I cannot say. But I will come.'

There was nothing for it. I had to do as I was told.

Was he going to try and hire some transport, or get us a ride from someone? This village was far too poor and remote to boast a vehicle. A donkey cart at best. I had to trust him. I had no option. I remembered what Chamba had said to me, that Bazet could travel like a fox, leaving no tracks. He had spent years crossing national boundaries illegally. He must know what he was doing, and Emily and Will would wait for me. I knew that.

When the men went out, I took off my boots and lay down full length on the mat. I noticed that it was woven from strips of coloured plastic bags, and it was lovely − a work of art. Nothing is wasted in this country. Nothing is thrown away.

I felt very tired from lack of sleep and nerves, and I was grateful that the women left me alone and didn't want to talk. A great fat baby at the crawling stage, with bulging cherub cheeks and chubby arms and legs, was set loose on the floor near me, and one of the women pointed at it and said something to me. I guessed that I was supposed to keep an eye on it, but I pretended I didn't understand and firmly closed my eyes and pulled my scarf over my face. After a minute it started to bellow and one of the older girls came and picked it up.

How extraordinary it was for this household to have a white woman step ashore from a boat into their village and then to lie down flat on their living room floor and appear to go to sleep. What would the proper Dorset villagers, where I came from, make of such a thing happening in reverse? First of all they'd have a cup of tea, I expected, just as happened here. My mother would be all right. She'd know what to do, but someone like Betty Parker, who had not been much further than Weymouth all her life, would probably call the police and get her picture on the front page of *The Blackmore Vale Magazine*. 'I couldn't believe what I was seeing!' she'd say. 'The cheek of it. Without so much as a by-your-leave. I've never seen the like.'

Divinity

EMILY WAS PISSED off with me – she made it obvious – but it was hardly my fault that the textiles I'd bought had vanished. We consulted with the owner of the encampment, and on his advice Serufi took us to the police station and there was a lot of pencil-sucking and forms to be filled in, and explanations to be given. It seems police stations are the same the world over. Hugh did all the translating, and basically it turned out that Frankie and the work-shop operated together, and there should be no diffi-culty in tracing them and retrieving my stuff. Tourists offered rich pickings to the impoverished people of Djenne, and occasional scams were inevitable. The police seemed keen to crack down on unlicensed guides, as Frankie appeared to be, and the unofficial traders he took tourists to buy from. No doubt there was something in it for the police officer, because

Hugh told Will it would help if he offered a bit of an incentive, handed over discreetly.

It all took no more than an hour at the most, and then we piled into the truck and were on the road. We had the ferry to do all over again and it was less terrifying than the first time because I guess you get used to these things, and I stood at the rails with the others and watched the brown water slide past. There were a couple of minibuses and a lorry and the rest of the vehicles were mule and donkey carts. Will took loads of photographs, and Hugh and Emily looked cute, leaning on the rail with their arms round each other. They were not what you would call a demonstrative couple, but soon they were going to split, with Emily driving on north with us, and Hugh going off in another direction to do his thing with these wild-looking guys he's so keen on.

Will took a lot of photos of them, too, although they're both quite averse to the camera and kept protesting. Emily was not looking great, to be honest. She looked tired and her hair had gone frizzy in the wet heat and she had it scraped back in a ponytail. I was glad that I had had a Japanese straightening treatment before I left and mine was sleek and smooth. Also, she doesn't care much about what she wears, and today it looked like one of Hugh's shirts she'd got on, over crumpled baggy trousers. Hugh, on the other hand, was kind of cool with a length of deep blue cloth wrapped round his head. He's so tall and thin he looks elegant in an eccentric way.

After the ferry, it still seemed like a hell of a long drive to get to this town where Emily and Clemmie had spent New Year's Eve in a little hostel on their last trip. Emily gave us all the details; it was the place where she had bought her Peul conical hat which now hung on her sitting room wall in her London flat, and where she and Clem had seen a Tuareg for the first time, and how he had turned out to be a friend of their guide who decided to accompany them on their desert trip. I'm sure I'd heard most of it before, but when we eventually arrived she looked round and said that it had all changed, had been done up, and wasn't as atmospheric as it had been.

We had a good lunch there anyway, of capitaine fish and tomato salad and chips, and the owner guy came over and said he remembered Emily and where was her friend with the hair? He lifted his hands to his own head to demonstrate a flowing mane. He meant Clemmie, of course. That set Emily off and I could see we were going to have the whole Clemmie story all over again, so I excused myself and made Will walk up the main drag with me, looking at the shops and stalls, some of which had amazing stuff. Will bought me some fantastic wooden bangles and a woven wall hanging made by Hugh's lot – the Dogons – but this was clearly a tourist place – French tours stopped here – and the prices were quite high and the sellers aggressive and persistent.

By the time we wandered back, Hugh had fixed himself up with a driver to take him into the Dogon country, where he was going to walk into the interior and camp. Serufi and he arranged that we would pick him up at a certain place five days later. I had to respect someone prepared to be that adventurous. I've never been out of contact with the outside world in my life, and the thought of it scares me half to death.

Emily went into her mother hen routine, checking out his bags and going over everything he might have forgotten, and I was quite pleased to see that as far as Hugh was concerned, it was water off a duck's back and he didn't listen to a word. It seemed like quite a good arrangement between hens and ducks that they had. She got her fix, and it didn't wind him up.

He hopped in the hire jeep beside the driver, looking really excited about his adventure, and with no regrets about leaving his new wife. If I'd been Emily I wouldn't have let him go, no way, but she said how it was wonderful for him and didn't seem to take it personally. I guess she has a sort of confidence I'll never have.

'Let's go!' she said to Will and me, as she waved him off. 'Please, let's go! We've still got a long drive from here and . . .'

'Yeah, I know,' said Will, giving her a hug. However, this was our bloody holiday too, and I'd have liked another look at the shops along the main drag and I told Will as much.

'I haven't come all this way,' I said, 'to be told there's no time to do anything I want to do.'

be no hurry then.'

We were just about to leave, with Emily sitting in the front with Serufi, when a Land Cruiser drew up beside us and a black man in jeans and a T-shirt and sunglasses got out and spoke to Serufi and then turned to us.

'Madam,' he said to me. 'It is good I have found you. I have come from the police department in Djenne – the tourist police.' He flicked open his official card. 'We have found your articles purchased, and if you would like to return with me now you can claim them, and arrange shipping.'

'Oh, wow!' I said. 'That's great news.'

'But we can't go all that way back now!' cried Emily.

'Well, I'm not going to leave without that stuff. It cost me a packet and it's what I've come here for.'

Will, ever the peacemaker, interrupted. 'Look, I'll go back and I'll catch you two up later. I'll find a driver somehow in Djenne. I'm sure the tourist police can help.'

'Driver no problem,' said the man. He pointed at me, 'But it is she who must sign the papers.'

'I'm not going back on my own!' I protested.

'No, I wouldn't let you.'

'Then both of you go back,' said Emily, almost stamping her foot. 'But I'm going on.'

We all stood looking at one another.

'I'll be fine with Serufi,' said Emily. 'He'll see me to Homberi safely and you can catch up with me there.'

'Oh, Christ, Ems,' said Will. 'Are you sure? Will you be all right on your own? I guess we won't be more than a day behind you.'

'I'll be fine. Serufi will look after me.'

'Well, if you're sure. I guess we'd better take all our luggage with us – just in case.'

We sorted out our stuff and loaded it in the policeman's Land Cruiser and then we said goodbye to Emily. I gave her a real hug because I felt for her, going on on her own, and I have to hand it to her, she wasn't making a big deal of it. Just at the last moment, though, after we had got in the car and she came to the window for a final goodbye, her attitude suddenly changed and a look of real concern crossed her face. Our driver had pushed the button to close the window and I didn't catch what she was saying to him, and it was too late anyway because we were reversing out into the road

'What was that about?' I said to Will.

'I didn't hear,' he said. 'She seemed to be telling the driver something urgent. We haven't forgotten anything, have we? Perhaps we should go back?' But the cop was driving as if he owned the road, using his horn and swerving round carts and bicycles, and we had already reached the outskirts of the town and it was too late.

Will checked his bag. 'Everything important is here,' he said, 'and if we have left anything, it doesn't much matter. We'll have caught up with her by tomorrow afternoon at the latest, I'd say.'

There seemed to be so much stress on this holiday, but the beer at lunch had made me sleepy and I put my head on Will's shoulder. I could have a little nap before we reached the ferry.

Emily

W HAT I HAD seen inside the Land Cruiser, right there on the huge black plastic dashboard, was an opened bag of sweets. It took only a second for me to realise that they were *my* sweets, stolen from our room at Djenne, that I had bought to give to the kids because they love them so: the little jelly fried eggs and fat red hearts and cola bottles and rings you can slip on to small fingers and miniature sweetie trainers with white chewy soles. They were right there, opened and half eaten, and the guy saw me spot them as he leaned forward to put one in his mouth. 'How did you get those?' I cried, pointing, as he pressed the button to raise the smoked-glass window and backed out into the road.

Shit, I was fuming.

So had they found my wallet, too, and the other bags of sweets, and if so, why hadn't he told me, and what the fuck was he doing eating them himself?

It was no use trying to explain any of this to Serufi – we didn't have the language, unfortunately – but he was looking at me with a puzzled expression.

'No police!' he said, wagging his finger.

'What?'

'Not police,' he repeated. 'He not police.'

'That man? Not a policeman? What was he then?'

'Agent.'

'What's an agent?'

'Government agent.'

'That's okay, isn't it? That sounds all right.'

'Not Tuareg man. Not friend of Tuareg.'

Okay, I thought. Well, not everybody was. I had read enough about the recent history of Mali to know that the Tuareg could be considered a warring, rebellious and ungovernable minority with a bloodthirsty past; a thorn in the side of a modern government. It wasn't what *I* thought, obviously, but I had to concede that such a view existed.

Why had a government agent got involved in what seemed a fairly trivial police matter? Did 'agent' mean some sort of civil servant, or maybe an employee of the tourist bureau? I had no idea, but if it meant we got results, I wasn't complaining. I wanted to know if they had got my wallet back and the whereabouts of the other bags of sweets. Were small cola bottles and miniature trainers being eaten by other unscrupulous agents at this moment? If so, I wanted to make an official complaint, and I would too, because what hope is there for a country if stealing recovered goods by officials is accepted? And if they ripped me off, what did they do to poor people less likely to complain?

But by now we were on the move again and it was restful sitting in the front with Serufi watching the world go by, which it was doing less and less after Sévaré. The road north was much quieter and the traffic more rural – just a few carts and bicycles, and the odd clapped-out lorry tootling along at a few miles an hour.

I looked out of the window at the flat, featureless landscape and thought alternately of Clemmie and Hugh. I wondered how Clemmie would look after eighteen months in the desert, and how she would view her future. Being in Mali for the second time, I couldn't believe you could live in the desert as a Westerner on a permanent basis, unless you were supported by some sort of global organisation that kept you supplied with medicines and toothpaste and sun screen and other basic stuff. I imagined aid agencies would fly people in and out, but no one would just live here, amongst the Tuareg, as Clemmie had done. I also wondered about her relationship with her man and whether it was still the romantic dream that it was at the beginning. I couldn't honestly see how it could be. The gloss would have worn off by now, and the difficulty of everyday living in such a hostile environment would surely chip away at romantic love.

I was uncomfortably aware that I didn't *want* it to have worked out, and I wondered why I felt this when I loved Clem more than anyone. I guessed I wanted her to come home with me, and I was nursing a strong hope that this might happen. In my heart, I thought that it was what she ought to do. I hoped that the whole Chamba thing was no more than an extended holiday romance which would prove not to have staying power. I remembered a friend from university who met a Kazakh horse dealer on an adventure holiday and married him the following year, but was now divorced. When it came to it, she couldn't live with his idleness and noisy eating habits, and steppe mentality. He couldn't live in a London flat, and she couldn't contemplate his primitive village life back home. The difference in backgrounds made their relationship impossible in the long term, and I thought Clemmie and Chamba might be the same.

Aunt Ellen was amazing, because she hadn't once voiced these thoughts to me, although I guessed she must have had them. She never said 'Try and persuade her to come home . . .' It was Uncle Peter, Clem's father, who had given me the money to buy her a return plane ticket. 'Do what you can,' he had said quietly, as he handed over an envelope. 'You know what I mean,' and I had nodded, knowing exactly.

Hugh and I were the sensible ones. I had met him when I thought my heart was broken and I would never find a good man to love me, and we had gone on to have a conventional relationship that had ended in a lovely country wedding. I could sit here in this jeep, bowling through this wild country, and predict the pattern of our married lives. Quite soon we would move to a bigger flat, or even a little house, and have a sensible number of children, and later I'd go back to work part-time and eventually we'd move to the country. We'd never have much money, but Hugh would be highly regarded in his field and we would be contented. And that was all I wanted.

Why couldn't Clemmie be satisfied with the same sort of deal? Given the right man, obviously. It niggled at me that she had turned her back on the safe, expected route to happiness. It was as if she had higher expectations, wanted more, something different, and it made me feel that what I had settled for was less in some way. Oh, it was silly to think like this, and it made me ashamed when I was so happy with Hugh. It felt as if I needed Clemmie's approval, her endorsement of what I wanted, by her wanting the same thing herself – and why should she, when we had always been very different?

Great-Aunt Mary had known that Clemmie was special. I think she saw in Clemmie what she knew to be true of herself, but in her case she had come back to England and married boring old Tim and lived an unrewarding, frustrated life. I couldn't wish that on Clemmie. Not for one moment.

It was jealousy, too, I supposed, that made me want her back in London and our old mutual need for each other revived. I'd have liked things to be the same as they were before; another case of me not being very good at setting free the people I love.

We were in cattle country now, and I remembered how, in January, Clemmie and I had noted how well the animals looked as we passed the herds on their long trek to the Ivory Coast and how our fathers, who both were livestock farmers, would have been amazed at the condition of the beasts. They were just as good as our fatstock reared on the lush grass of our green valley. Now, in April, the herders were waiting for the rains to begin and the animals were bony and their ribs stuck out and their coats looked dusty and matted. They were gathered in listless herds round muddy waterholes, and the tall boys who tended them were gaunt and hollow-eyed but waved cheerfully as we went by.

I slept for a bit, and when I woke, the light was going and we had passed Fatima's Hand, the majestic and peculiar group of sheer limestone rocks that rise eight hundred metres from the plain. If I looked over my shoulder, I could see them behind us, grotesque against the fiery sky.

This meant that we were nearly at Homberi, and I sat up straight and paid attention and my heart beat fast at the thought of meeting Clem. I combed my hair and tied it back again and put on some lip gloss, and wondered what she would think of me, eighteen months down the line, and whether I had changed because I was now a married woman.

The last time I had been here was on my way back from the desert on my own, having left Clemmie behind, and the feelings of desolation and loneliness came back to me. It had been a terrible time and I had been filled with misgivings, and guilt that I hadn't forced her to come home with me. A hot wind had blown through the deserted shacks along the road and balls of tumbleweed had bowled across the empty sand.

It looked exactly the same today, and the chairs set on the shady veranda of the little hostel were all empty as Serufi drew up under the acacia tree. I jumped out. There was no sign of Clemmie, or anyone else come to that. The same exhausted-looking bitch lay flat out under a table, her extended teats flopping to the side.

I ran inside – no one. Clemmie wasn't there.

I had half expected it, but the disappointment made me want to cry. I looked through to the rear, where the simple guest rooms with open fretwork windows and blue-painted doors were ranged round an uneven baked courtyard, and I knew she wasn't there either.

I went to sit at a table, and a listless youth appeared and I ordered a Coke. I checked my phone, but there was no signal and no messages. Serufi had unloaded his mattress and was already lying on it in the shade of the veranda. He was exhausted by the day's driving. Two more young men came to lounge against the walls, watching me, and I felt very alone and sad. Why hadn't I insisted that Hugh accompany me? Wasn't

237

that the whole point of having a husband – that you did things together?

The drink came – deliciously cold, and a little bowl of peanuts, and with them the owner in the same striped yellow and black robe as the last time I was here. 'No friend?' I said looking from side to side.

He shook his head. 'No friend,' he repeated, sadly.

'She comes tomorrow,' I said. 'I would like to stay here, please.'

He laughed and opened his hands wide. 'Plenty rooms. No other guest!'

'Okay, thanks. And Serufi.' I pointed to where he was asleep, and the man nodded. He said something to one of the young men, who disappeared and came back with some cotton sheets and towels. I followed him out into the courtyard and he showed me a little whitewashed cell with a rough wooden bed and a thin mattress and a wooden chair and table. Everything was covered in a film of white sand, but it was all I needed, and I loved the comforting little brown birds that flew in and out through the window.

He returned with a twig broom and swept the sand out of the door. I made up the bed with the sheets, which were clean and smelled of hot sunshine. There was no pillow, so I rolled my clothes into a bolster, and closed the door and took off my trainers and lay down. The red light of the sinking sun made the walls glow pink. I had to be patient. I had to wait. There was nothing else I could do. Tomorrow Will and Divinity would arrive, and Clemmie, too. All the same, I felt as if something unalterable had happened and things would never be carefree again.

Clemmie

W HEN I WOKE, the hut was empty and dark. I could hear the quiet voices of the women from somewhere outside, and dogs barking and the booming of the frogs in the reeds. I sat up and looked at my watch. I had been asleep for two hours. I found my water bottle and had a drink and checked I had still got my bag beside me and that my phone was where I had stored it.

I went outside and found the women gathered round a fire, cooking fish and rice. They signalled that I should join them and gave me a bowl. I was very hungry, and although the food was plain, it was delicious. They laughed when they saw how I wolfed it down, and refilled the bowl.

'Bazet?' I said, looking around me, miming the act of searching for someone. They laughed again and waved their arms into the darkness as if to say – he's out there somewhere. I ate the second bowl almost as fast as the first and demonstrated that I would like to wash. A bowl was produced and hot water slopped out of a pan near the fire. In my pocket, wrapped in a fold of paper, was my last sliver of soap. I washed my hands and face. It was pleasant to feel the warm night air on my damp face. The women watched me, vastly entertained, and wanted to look at the soap. They passed it between them, smelling it and giggling. I would like to have given it to them but wasn't going to – no way, not until I had got a new stock from Emily.

The barking of the dogs grew fierce and I saw men approaching the fire from the dark. They did not look like Tuareg, or Songhai, and I supposed that they must be river men from the village. One of them indicated that I should go with them and I got to my feet.

'Where is Bazet?' I asked in French, but they wagged their heads and became insistent that I should follow them at once. I wasn't leaving without my pack and my bag, and I went to the hut to collect them. I didn't like it that the men pulled at my arms and urged me roughly, as if I was a lazy donkey. I knocked their hands away and shook my finger at them.

'*Ne touchez pas!*' I shouted fiercely. I appealed to the

women round the fire, but they averted their faces. They didn't want to get involved.

Shit, what was going on? Bazet had told me he would come back for me. How did I know whether he had sent these men to get me? I thought quickly of other options, but it seemed to me that I would have to comply and go with them.

One of them picked up my pack and we set off into the dark. On the outskirts of the village we met another man with a small donkey and I was told to get on and ride. My feet nearly touched the ground on each side, but the sturdy little beast walked smartly. We seemed to be following the track out of the village, away from the river. The night was brilliantly lit by the half-moon and I could see stands of maize on either side. This gave out after a while, and the land became scrub. To my ears, the noise of the crickets, and the frogs from the river, was deafening. I had grown used to the silence of the desert nights.

The men talked amongst themselves in hushed, excited voices and it seemed that this was an adventure for them too. Once or twice we stopped and there seemed to be an argument about which way to go, before we set off again. I had lost all sense of direction and felt a sort of nervousness that made me want to stop and pee every half an hour. Since I had shouted at the men, they treated me with more respect, and when I indicated that I needed to get off and go into the bush, they remained by the donkey and did not attempt to follow me. All the time I cursed Bazet for putting me in this situation.

We had been going for nearly two hours when we arrived at another village with huts on either side of the track, but it was deserted and no dogs ran out to meet us. The men pressed on, pointing and shouting, and I saw a tiny prick of light in the distance. As we got closer, I realised that it was the headlights of a vehicle, and my spirits rose. Bazet must have found us transport, and I took back everything I had thought about him.

However, when we got nearer to what I saw was a Land Cruiser, there was no sign of him, just two black men dressed in Western clothes who walked to meet us, and then, to my astonishment, I realised that the man sitting in the passenger seat, with the door open, was white.

I got off the donkey and untied my pack. The village men crowded round the other guys, who counted out wads of banknotes into their eager hands. Bringing me here was some sort of deal that had paid them well. The white man got out.

'Clementine?' he said, holding out his hand. 'Hi! My name is Alvin Brockenhurst. Great to meet you at last. I have to say that your whereabouts has been causing me and your family quite a bit of concern.'

Divinity

I F I HAD wanted a holiday sitting in the back of a vehicle, I couldn't have chosen a better one than this. By the time we got back to Djenne, with the ferry crossing and everything, it was getting dark, and it felt that we had spent the whole day on the road.

The driver guy took us not to the police station where we had reported my missing textiles, but to some other government building in a compound behind high mud walls with guards on the gate. We were ushered inside and told to sit and wait in a room that boasted nothing but four white plastic garden chairs and a slowly moving ceiling fan. Our driver, who had proved to be particularly charmless, disappeared, and we sat looking at each other, our bags at our feet.

'So where is everybody?' I got up and went to the inner door, which I opened. It led to a corridor with further small rooms off, all of which were empty, although one appeared to be home to someone, because there was a mattress on the floor and a pair of broken flip-flops, and further along there was a toilet with a seatless lavatory and a filthy washbasin. It was the most peculiar public building I had ever been in. What was the point of the guards at the gate when there was nothing inside?

We waited half an hour or so and then began to get impatient. It was dark now and we were starving hungry and I needed the bathroom, but no way was I going to use the revolting one I had found. The fan seemed to do little but stir the wet, hot air, and my clothes were sticking to me. I couldn't wait for a shower and a cold drink.

'This is fucking ridiculous,' I said, finally. 'I'm not sitting here any longer. Why don't we just walk out and come back tomorrow, when there's someone about? We can surely find our way back to the Grand Mosque and the encampment where we stayed last night?'

'Yeah,' said Will, getting up wearily and collecting the bags. 'Let's fuck off out of here.'

We went out into the courtyard and walked towards the open double metal gates where the guards leaned against the wall, one on each side. They both moved lazily to stand in our way.

'Hey!' said Will, pointing to the road outside. 'We'd like to go. There's no one here, so we'll come back tomorrow.'

The men shook their heads and one of them pushed Will back with his rifle butt.

'Stop that!' I protested. 'You can't make us stay here.'

The man shouted something back at me and shoved Will again and pointed to the door of the building.

'What the fuck's going on, Will?'

'I've no idea. We'll have to do what they say, I suppose. They seem to mean business.'

'I'm not going to be pushed around by these punks. They're just trying to face us down.'

I turned to the men and barged between them, out into the road beyond. They let me through, making no effort to stop me.

'Come on!' I said to Will. 'Just follow me.' But they wouldn't let him, pushing him back forcibly.

'Let him through!' I yelled, but instead one of them pulled the metal gates shut in my face.

I banged on them with my fists.

'Go back to the hostel!' shouted Will from the other

side. 'The owner speaks some English. Get him to come back here with you.'

'I'm not leaving you!' I cried. 'I don't want to go on my own!'

'Can you see the Grand Mosque?'

'No, it's too dark. I can't see anything.'

'It's somewhere to the right. It's not far away. I saw it on our way here. Walk in that direction and you'll see it. If you can't find it, ask any woman you meet for "*le grand moskay*". You remember the encampment is right next door? Get the owner to come back with you.'

I could hear the sounds of a scuffle on the other side of the gates.

'Leave him alone!' I screamed, banging with my fists again.

'It's okay!' Will called back. 'I'm doing what they want. I'm going back inside.'

I had no option. I was half sobbing and shaking with anger as I stumbled off in the direction Will had told me. Being pushed around, held by the police for no good reason, was not unknown to me. I grew up with it, and I didn't like it. I'd worked bloody hard to get myself into a place where it didn't happen to me any more. I had earned myself some respect. My brother still got pulled in, but I guess he asked for it, hanging round with the dudes he mixed with. What had just happened to me and Will was different, more menacing, more frightening. It felt like there were no boundaries and no rules. There was not a soul about – just a dark, sand-filled street between dark buildings. I stopped and pulled my scarf over my head and walked fast in the shadow of the walls. Eventually the street took a sharp turn and with relief I saw the looming shape of the Great Mosque at the far end.

This street was busier. Soft lights glowed in doorways where groups of men squatted, smoking and talking quietly. I felt their eyes on me but I was less uneasy with people about. Male voices called out to me and someone threw something that landed with a thud behind me. I knew to keep walking and not look round.

I reached the end, but shit, where I had hoped to see the wide market square, I found myself in another dark, narrow street that skirted the soaring walls. I must have walked round three sides of the mosque. This street was empty and spooky with the tall old buildings and eerie blackness on either side. I ran now, my bag thumping against my side. I had my eyes fixed on the corner ahead, and at last I could see the dark market square. Now I knew exactly where I was, and the relief made me angry. What sort of shithole place was this that treated innocent visitors like criminals? As soon as I had got Will freed, I wanted to go home.

I ran along the front of the mosque, dodging through a herd of goats driven by a small boy, and sidestepping heaps of rags and stinking rubbish. I could see the lights of the encampment. The gates were open and a pair of minibuses stood in the parking area with a bunch of white tourists sorting out their luggage. Christ, was I glad to see them. The proprietor was there too, wearing a queenly long gold robe, like for the State Opening of Parliament, and a baseball cap.

'You've got to come!' I shouted at him. The tourists all looked round, startled. 'Come! You've got to come and rescue my partner. He's been locked up!'

The tourists, who were French, gathered round me in concern. 'What has happened?' they asked in English.

It was too complicated a story to start trying to tell them the details. 'The police. They picked us up on the road to . . .' I couldn't even remember the name of the place. 'This man, he brought us back here to get some stuff I had bought, and then when we got here, we were taken to a sort of police station, only there was no one there, and they wouldn't let my partner out. He's there now. Being held against his will.'

The leader of the French group, an older man with grey hair and a silver beard, and wearing a safari jacket, looked concerned. 'This is not, I hope, to do with drugs? These matters are taken very seriously.'

'Of course it's not. We haven't done a thing wrong. I bought some textiles here in Djenne, and then they kind of disappeared . . .' I pointed at the proprietor. 'This man knows what happened. Then we were stopped somewhere on our way north by this police guy, who said we had to come back to Djenne with him to collect the stuff. Please,' I implored the owner. 'Come back with me and get Will out of that place.'

He shrugged in that maddening way they have out here. 'This is not my business,' he said, sticking out his thick, pouting bottom lip. 'I cannot interfere with a police matter.'

'Oh, for fuck's sake! Just come with me and explain to these guys, will you? We were brought back here to collect the stuff I had bought. I was told I had to come back and sign for it. It's as simple as that. There's been some kind of misunderstanding.'

'I cannot leave my guests and come with you. Maybe later.'

The French guy was still looking kind of concerned, but the others had drifted off with their backpacks, all wanting a shower and a drink. I couldn't blame them. They didn't see it was anything to do with them.

I looked the owner straight in the eye. I was taller than him and a lot angrier. 'Now listen to me,' I said, jabbing my finger under his nose. 'If you want to have Western tourists continuing to stay here, you had better bloody well come and sort this out, because I tell you, if you don't help me, I'll have it all over the net that this is a crap place and a dangerous one. I can say that rooms get broken into and stuff nicked, and guests arrested, and nothing is done about it.'

The Frenchman intervened. 'I think this young lady is correct. This is a local issue, and if she and her partner were guests here last night, it is your responsibility to them.' He turned to me. 'I bring parties here three or four times a year,' he said. 'We have never had any trouble. Malu here will help. I am sure of it.'

Malu, who looked about as helpful as a Chanel shop assistant, grunted in reply. 'I make telephone call,' he said to me and took out his mobile. He paced up and down having a shouting sort of conversation in whatever language, while I followed him, right behind, like ready to pounce. Eventually he rang off.

'It is Customs that hold your boyfriend. You must pay custom duties for what you purchase. It is simple matter. You go back and pay and you are let free.'

I poked him in the chest.

'I'm not going back there on my own. No way. You're coming with me, mate.'

'It is right, Malu,' said the Frenchman, who I was beginning to love. Why do people say that the French are rude? This one was to die for. 'This young woman has no language. You must go.'

Very, very grudgingly, Malu agreed, and while I rushed to the loo, he went to the gate to call for a driver, who appeared from the shadows. Malu was evidently too important to walk. 'Please come too,' I pleaded with my new friend. 'To be honest, I don't trust any of them.'

He hesitated. 'I have my own people to care for,' he said. 'But they are all showering now. Maybe I will come.'

He climbed in next to me. 'François,' he said, giving me his hand.

'Divinity,' I said. 'Hey, man, am I grateful to you.'

The drive took no longer than five minutes and we pulled up outside the enclosure. The gate was now open again and there was a Land Cruiser parked inside. I could see Will's head through the lit window of the room where we had been told to stay. He appeared to be drinking a cup of tea. The two guards were lounging on chairs in the yard and did not bother to get up.

We all hopped out and I ran into the building. There were two robed men with Will and I saw a tea party set out on the dusty floor. Will was talking to them in French and waving his arms around. It all looked quite cosy.

'Shit, Will!' I said. 'What's going on? I've been scared to death about you.'

'It's fine, it's fine,' he said, beaming. 'After you'd gone, I had a brainwave. I telephoned that American guy we met at lunch. I had his card in my pocket. I explained that we'd got tangled up in something and he called someone high up, and these guys arrived and said it's all okay. You have to sign some papers and pay Customs, but it's all in order.'

He was so calm, and pleased with everything, that I could have murdered him. I pushed him really hard so that the chair wobbled and he had to clutch at his cup of tea in surprise. 'I've come back for you with the fucking reinforcements,' I said, 'and you're sitting here drinking tea with these two grannies. I'll tell you one thing. I've had enough of this crap place. With or without you, I'm going home tomorrow.'

Emily

AFTER DARKNESS FELL, I sat on for an hour or two, but the road was empty in both directions and there seemed to be nobody left at the little roadhouse. The boys had disappeared and even the old dog had gone. I looked into the kitchen and it was left tidy for the night, the floor swept and an enormous kitchen knife that looked capable of butchering an elephant gleaming on the tabletop. The generator running the fridges hummed.

Outside, one very bright light shone on the veranda, and I felt like a solitary figure on a stage in the middle of nowhere, exposed and vulnerable. I wondered where Serufi had gone. His truck was still parked under the spindly trees, but there was no sign of him. I wished he had stayed around. We could have played cards and kept each other company. Hadn't he promised he would look after me? It felt as if he had deserted me.

There was no electricity in the courtyard, but I felt safer when I retreated to my little room with my torch propped on the table, like a scared animal in its burrow, hidden from the predators of the night.

I sat on my bed and thought about everything that had happened and how our little party had been split up and I didn't know where any of the others were laying their heads that night. I guessed Will and Divinity would stay at the encampment in Djenne and that Divinity would be moaning about something or other, although she would be glad to have Will to herself. It was strange that she hadn't got into enjoying Mali like I thought she would. I understood what she had told me about her mixed feelings at seeing the poverty and squalor, but I thought she could have been more enthusiastic about other things – the beauty of the people, the colour, the drama, the joyfulness of Africa. None of that seemed to have got through to her.

As for Clemmie, my imagination drew a blank. I tried to work out where she might be, but had no clue. All I knew was that if I was lying here thinking of her, she would be doing the same of me, and that between us there was a connection like the silvery thread of a spider, stretching across the empty miles that separated us.

I didn't want to think about what I would do if she didn't arrive tomorrow. It was like looking at a blank sheet of paper upon which I had no words to write. Waiting and hoping seemed to be the only option, but I couldn't do that on my own. I needed the others, Will or Hugh, to support me.

If she didn't come – just say she didn't – what then? Our only friend was Alvin Brockenhurst. Hadn't he said to call him if we needed help, and knowing that was a scrap of comfort to me. Will had his contact number and we could get in touch with him and see what he could do. He said that he knew the army general in charge of this part of the country, and although it seemed a bit dramatic, perhaps they could send soldiers out to look for her.

Now that it was properly dark, the night was no longer quiet. A camel was bellowing from somewhere, answered by another, and I heard the eerie bark of a fox. Something scuffled in the dirt outside my window and I sat, rigid with fear, reliving the terror of the night before. The scuffling went on, and eventually I relaxed. It was only the noise of some little night animal about its business.

God, I missed Hugh. Where was he? Sitting in a village hut, I guessed, recording what went on around him, utterly absorbed in his work, enthralled by the

Dogon people and probably not missing me that much. I wished with all my heart that I had gone with him, that I hadn't let him go off on his own, or that he had said to me, 'Emily, I'll come with you to meet Clemmie. It's important we do things together from now on.'

I thought this, and my heart felt congested with emotion, and I got up and searched for paper and pencil in my bag and sat on my bed resting the paper on my knees and began to write in the light of my torch.

My darling, darling Hugh (I've been trying to dream up a special name for you . . . like Hugs or Huggiebear or Hughsiepooksie — one of those excruciating names people use in Valentine messages to one another, but nothing suits you better than Hugh, just as I can't be anything more whimsical than Ems),

This is a letter you will never get to read because there is no way I can get it to you before I see you, and I'm not sure I could give it to you and watch you reading it. It's easier to write some things than speak them.

I'm writing this on my knees in my little nun's room at Homberi. It was a friendly place in the daylight with lizards running up and down the walls (how do they do it?) and little brown birds flying in and out through the window, but at night it is a very different story, and

I feel lonely and afraid. The reasons for me being on my own are too complicated to tell, but it's a situation I would never have wished upon myself. If you had to think up a form of torture to cause me most suffering, then solitary confinement would be top of the list. I hate being alone and always have, since I was a small child. I think only children, more than others, need to have people about them or they feel too insignificant to matter, and that's how I used to feel – mother out working, father out farming – until I walked up the lane to where Clemmie and the others lived, and it was only when I got there that I felt myself sort of filling out and becoming a person. It was like what my class call 'colouring in'. Their drawings are wishy-washy and unsatisfactory until they've got hold of the can of wax crayons and done some serious colouring. Then their pictures fill out and come alive.

Here at Homberi, I feel entirely alone, although Serufi is here somewhere, and during the day the guy who owns the hostel, who speaks a bit of French, and a gang of younger guys who loaf about, doing a bit of work but generally lying in the shade gazing at the straight empty road. One way you can see it disappear into the eerie shape of Fatima's Hand, and the other into shimmering nothingness. The heat is colossal, but in culinary terms I am now being baked rather than steamed. I can feel my skin drying out and becoming crinkly and papery and my hair is dead straight like a hot brown curtain.

The wind frets all the time, rolling the Coke cans along the road and sending balls of dried weeds skittering across the sand.

Clemmie has not arrived and I have no confidence that she will come. Now that I am here, and have no telephone contact, our arrangement seems too fragile when set against all this emptiness and distance and killing heat. In my heart, I feel that I have lost her to the desert and I can't shake off a sense of hopelessness. Hugh, I so need you to be here with me, to tell me off for being gloomy and that everything will be fine. You see, I believe in you, and trust you, and love you so much.

Christ, I wish you were here with me. Why did we plan this honeymoon apart? I feel quite angry about it now. All this searching for Clemmie has taken over what should have been about you and me. You should have told me as much. I needed telling. You'll be all right with your Dogons but I am fading away without you.

Loving you so much it makes my heart ache,

Your Emily

I found tears welling as I finished, and I wiped them away, sniffing. I read through what I had written and felt better; a good dose of self-pity had helped to shift the weight of sadness in my chest. I put the letter and the pencil on the floor by the bed. I suddenly felt very, very tired, and as if there was a chance that sleep would come to me.

Clemmie

'WHO ARE YOU? Why are you looking for me?
Where's Bazet?'

I sat in the back of the vehicle with the man called
Alvin, my mind spinning. He was the first Westerner
I had seen for many months, and the English words
were strange in my mouth.

'Of course,' he said, patting my knee in a reassuring
way. 'This is all a bit unexpected for you. Can I offer
you a drink? I have chilled fruit juice here, or bourbon?'

'A bourbon, please.' He had a full bottle in a neat
sort of carrier with a compartment for glasses. The
alcohol burned in my throat in a hot stream. I hadn't
had a drink for over a year.

'First of all, let me tell you that you are in good
hands. You're safe. Nothing to worry about now. The
man Bazet was about to pass you on to the bad guys
out here in Mali. They were planning to demand a

263

ransom, use you as a bargaining tool with the government. It would have been an uncomfortable situation for you.'

I stared at him, stunned. 'How do you know? I can't believe it.' Bazet had been against me from the start. I had always known it, but it was a different thing to actively plot to endanger my life.

'I know because my organisation has an interest in security and safety in the southern Sahara. We monitor comings and goings and have had an eye on Bazet for some time. We picked up on your movement from our agents in Kidal. We nearly caught up with you in Bourem, but Bazet evaded us. He is a cunning and ruthless guy who stands to gain a great deal by his trade in kidnap victims. How did a nice English girl like you get mixed up with someone like him?'

'Wait a minute,' I said, my mind racing and my thoughts muddled. 'You're an American, right? Why are you interested in what's going on here in Mali? I don't get it. Who exactly are you?'

Alvin sighed and ran his hand over his face. He wasn't a young guy, and he looked tired. Exhausted, really.

'I'll try and keep it simple,' he said. 'It's a complicated situation up in the north, with a lot to bid for, mineral rights and so on. There are a number of world players, the States and China being the heavyweights. Let's just say it's my business to keep tabs on what's going on from a humanitarian point of view.'

'Humanitarian? What do you mean?'

'In a nutshell, the government here is looking to get the best deal from the highest bidder, but there are other issues to consider – the nomadic people and their rights, for one thing, and security for another. China's record on humanitarian issues is not encouraging, as I guess you know. As far as security goes, the national army hasn't proved very effective up there. The Tuareg have a history of kicking the sand in its face. As you well know.' He looked at me sharply, but I was still mulling over what he had told me about Bazet's intentions.

'So are you really telling me that you've saved me from kidnapping? That Bazet is a sort of terrorist? He's my brother-in-law, you know. My husband would never have entrusted me to him if he thought he was putting me in any danger.'

Alvin made a sad sort of noise and shook his head. 'Love can be blind,' he said quietly.

'What do you mean? What are you saying? Are you suggesting my husband is involved in some way? That's just absurd. He loves me. He's devoted to me.'

'I'm not suggesting anything. I'm just saying that you may well be unaware of what you've got yourself into with some of these radicalised people.'

This was typical of the American suspicion and ignorance of the Tuareg's desire for recognition. Chamba had told me that the Malian government had convinced the United States that the Tuareg were Islamic terrorists rather than a people engaged in a legitimate struggle.

'What's happened to Bazet? Where is he?' My allegiance had shifted again. I was concerned now for his safety.

'He's been taken care of, don't worry. Look, Clementine, we've both had a long day. Why don't we get the hell out of here and to somewhere a bit more comfortable? After a shower and as good a dinner as you can get in this godforsaken country, we'll talk some more.'

'No, I can't do that. I'm on my way to meet my brother and my cousin. They're waiting for me at Homberi. I must go there at once.' Quite how I thought I would do that, I didn't consider. I suppose I thought I had an option, and that he would take me.

Alvin sighed. 'Sorry, Clementine, but that's not the case. Your brother and his girlfriend are on their way back to Bamako. The girl has had enough. Your cousin was the one who alerted me to the danger you are in; she has come on alone. Tomorrow, after we've had a chance to debrief, I will take you to meet her.'

'I don't get any of this. You've met Emily and Will? Where? When?'

'That's quite a long story. Not far from here my organisation has a pilot and a light aircraft from Bourem waiting to fly us to Mopti, where we can make ourselves comfortable in a reasonable hotel. We can talk properly then. Tomorrow I can get you flown down to meet your cousin. Here,' he opened a brief-case at his feet, 'Emily sent you this. I guess she thought you might need a little reassurance.'

He handed me an envelope, and when I opened it, there was a photograph of me and Ems taken when we were about thirteen – I was still wearing braces, and Emily had her hair in bunches. We were leaning over a gate at home. I could see the dairy calves crowding the pen in the yard behind us. We were holding the head collars of our ponies, and looking straight at the camera with his lovely, kind dark eyes, his neat little ears pointed, was my darling Blazer, the pony that I had loved almost more than anything. That did it. I couldn't help it. I cried like a kid while Alvin patted my hand kindly. It was typical of darling Ems. Only she would have known what that picture meant to me, and how it would bring thoughts of home flooding back.

Later, when, amazingly, we were flying over the darkness, I looked out of the window and thought about Bazet again. Was it really possible that he had been tempted to get rid of me once and for all? It would get me neatly out of the way and he could claim all innocence. I just didn't know what to think. I wondered where he was, and what they had done with him. I thought of his wife, my friend Dianni, and his daughter, Amou, singing 'Twinkle, Twinkle, Little Star' in her piping voice, her little hand in mine. Oh God, what had I got myself into? What trouble had I caused?

Divinity

OKAY, MAYBE I overreacted. Things calmed down after my missing textiles arrived in the back of a pick-up truck, all neatly packed ready for air freighting. According to François, the woman I had bought them from was an unlicensed seller from outside the city, but she was not a thief. I signed the papers and paid the tax, and the guys who had seemed so sinister smiled and laughed and shook our hands.

'You take these now to Air France in Bamako, and they will be flown to the UK,' translated François. 'All is arranged.'

'Thank you so much. It was a pretty scary situation back there.'

'Sometimes it can seem threatening if you don't know how they do things, and do not speak the language. Now, I must ask you to allow me to return. My party will wonder why I have deserted them.'

Malu was still hovering about waiting for us, and I thanked him too, and then we piled into his old car and went back to the hostel.

'Christ, Divinity,' said Will later, as we sat sipping our beers under the vines. 'You sure know how to make a scene.'

'I was terrified. I thought you had been arrested. Beaten up. It seemed like that.'

'Yeah, well try and cool it. Overreacting just inflames things.'

This made me mad. It was like some of this had been my fault.

'Don't tell me that those guys treated us right. They were incredibly aggressive. Nobody pushes me about like that.'

'This isn't the UK. You just have to go with it.'

'I don't care where it is, and no way do I go with it. Those men acted like thugs.'

'So, are you going back to Bamako tomorrow?'

'You bet I am. Malu can fix us a driver. That's what the policeman said.'

'What about Clemmie? She's why I'm here, Divinity.'

'Well, I'm not going any further. There'll be plenty we can do in Bamako. There are music clubs and stuff for you, and the market is supposed to be great. I don't want to sit in the back of a boiling jeep for days. There's no point in us trailing all that way for a few hours with your sister. If she wants to see you, she can come on down to Bamako, can't she?'

Will was silent. He stared into the dark. I could see he was getting into a mood. Fair enough. He didn't like having his plans changed.

'So that's it, is it?'

'That's it.'

'And what if I said I was going on without you?'

'I don't think you'll do that. You brought me out here. It's your job to look after me.'

'Shit, Divinity! You don't know what you're asking. For one thing, I've promised my mother that I'm seeing Clem. It's really important to her, and if I don't, it will be letting her down in a big way.'

'That's all the more reason for Clemmie to come to Bamako. It's what we should have arranged in the first place. It's mad to expect us to trek for three days on some crap journey to see her. Let her do the travelling. After all, it's her choice to live out here. She doesn't care how hard that makes it for your mother.'

Will had no answer to that. He could only come up with a question.

271

'What about Emily? She's waiting for us to turn up at Homberi. She'll be frantic if we don't arrive.'

'Look around you. These guys here use mobiles all the time. You can get a message through to that place, can't you? Someone can send a text message, I'm sure. Just give it a try. Get hold of that American guy again. He sorted out the last fiasco.'

Will looked at me, sadly.

'You just don't understand families, do you? You don't get how they work.'

'I don't expect anything from my family, if that's what you mean, but don't you dare suggest I don't care for my mum and Gira. You Kingsleys don't have the monopoly on loyalty. But I'll tell you where we're different. There's never been room to pretend in my family, like you lot do.' I was warming to my theme. 'One thing we are is honest with each other. We've always told it straight. We haven't allowed great unchallenged myths to develop.'

'I don't know what you mean.'

'Well, let me tell you. For a start, your sister would have been left in no doubt of what she was putting her family through by shacking up with a tribesman out here. My mother would have told her over and over again, with a megaphone and from the rooftops. And she would have been right.'

'Clemmie doesn't need to be told. Do you really think she doesn't know? It was a terribly hard decision to make to stay here.'

'Okay. But it all ties in with the family thing that Clemmie's so special. A bit, like, *above* the rest of us. Well, let me tell you, she's *not*. She's just like any other girl, only she's been blessed with good looks and mega-privilege. She's never had to work at anything and she's more or less been able to do whatever she fancies, and that's what she's like – fanciful and airy-fairy. She was practically brought up to do something crazy like this – wafting about the desert with some sort of chieftain. It was what you lot expected of her.' That was as far as I was going. I'd said as much to Will before and I wasn't going to go on to the subject of his dad's drinking and his mother's self-imposed martyrdom, neither of which, as far as I knew, had ever been addressed by anyone.

Will looked pained. 'Why are you so unkind, Div? Clemmie's never said a bad word about you. I won't argue with your opinion about her or my family, because that's your affair. I'm just sorry you feel like that about us.'

I felt awful then. He's like that, Will. He's so reasonable himself, it's almost annoying. He's also a product of the same family I was just tongue-lashing.

'Oh shit, Will, I'm sorry. You know I love you all. It's just so alien to me, right? All this niceness and generosity about one another. You know what we're like at home, my mum, and me and Gira? We shout all the time, bang doors, hit one another, but it's all out in the open. We don't hide stuff and pretend it's not happening.'

'I expect there's something to be said for that,' he said quietly, 'but it's not our way. I'll tell you what I'll do. I'll go back with you to Bamako and help you with the stuff you're sending home, and then we'll change your return ticket and I'll put you on the first available plane for London. I'm sorry, Div, but I'm coming back up here to see Clemmie. That's why I'm here. The holiday part was just an add-on.'

I'd pushed him too far. I knew from the tone of his voice that he meant what he said. It was my turn to go quiet. I didn't want to go home alone – sent back like a naughty child – but neither did I want to go on. I had had it with the heat, and the dirt, and the discomfort of sitting in a boiling vehicle all day long.

'Anyway,' he said, covering my hand with his, 'let's enjoy this evening together at least.'

This was a low moment, us sitting there looking at each other, both wondering, if this holiday ends like this, where do we go from here?

It was François, who had been sitting at the bar talking to Malu, who broke the impasse by appearing at our table and asking if he could join us. I felt we owed him a lot, so I made a bit of a fuss of thanking him all over again.

'It was nothing,' he said, 'but your situation makes me uneasy. I have been talking of it with Malu and I have a suggestion. We are not happy that you travel north again. This is not a safe plan. The people who bring you back today are not regular police. You know this?'

'Who are they, then?' asked Will.

François sighed. 'There is much in this country that is complicated,' he said, 'and relations with the north are bad. Many people are involved to bring peace and prevent war, but as many wish war to continue. The prize is very valuable for both sides. Great wealth lies beneath the sand of the desert, you understand? Your journey was noticed and you were brought back by these government agents – but softly, softly, no trouble. You understand? However, it would be very unwise to try again.'

'Why? What have we got to do with this situation? We are just tourists, travelling completely legitimately.'

'Yes, but foreigners are a big prize for kidnappers, and also they have eyes and ears to tell what is going on. The government prefer tourists to stay where it is safe.'

'Why don't they impose a travel restriction, then? We weren't told we couldn't go north.'

'Few people wish to travel through the desert. Tourists are happy to stay in the south – to sail the Bani in a pinasse, to visit Djenne and the Dogon people. There is much to see and enjoy where you will be safe. The government does not wish to advertise that the north is a dangerous place. They deny always that there is a problem – just a handful of rebellious Tuareg, they prefer to say. They look for foreign investment in their country. Americans, Chinese, they compete for mineral rights, but not in a war zone where they may lose control of their investment.'

'How could our trip have been noticed? I don't get it.'

'Perhaps when you apply for a visa? You did so in Paris? *Voilà!* It is necessary to state why you are visiting Mali and where you are choosing to travel. Your destination will have been noted at the embassy.'

Those bitches, I thought, sniggering behind their hands. They had marked our cards in some way. They had treated us with disdain from the start.

'But my cousin has continued, on her own, and my sister *lives* in the north.'

'Women are considered less important, perhaps.' He saw the look on my face and added, 'Naturally I do not share this view.'

I turned to Will. 'This is exactly what that American guy told us and you wouldn't listen. You argued with him. He *said* it was dangerous to go on.'

Will looked grave. 'I get your point,' he said to François, 'but it makes it all the more important that I go on to see that the girls are okay.'

'You do not understand. This will not be permitted. You will get stopped by the police on some pretext and it will be another uncomfortable situation.'

'I can't just abandon them!'

'They travel with reliable Tuareg drivers, I believe? They will be okay, I am sure. Now, the suggestion I make to you is this. My little party is short of numbers and you are very welcome to join us for our trip – a seven-day tour of safe areas that I guarantee you will find full of interest. I will have to charge you, naturally, but at a reduced rate. What do you say?'

'I'm gutted. That's what I say,' said Will, but I cut in. 'It sounds really cool. Amazing. Thank you so much.'

'Excellent. I leave you with a copy of our itinerary. Have a look at it, and in the morning I will contact the guest houses and hotels where we stay, and reserve your rooms. We leave tomorrow morning at nine thirty.' He stood up and shook our hands. 'I am relieved for your safety. Mali is a wonderful country and the coming of tourism is very important for its people and their future. For this reason, visitors must be responsible and act wisely. Any sort of trouble is widely reported and has an adverse effect on tour companies considering coming here.'

It all made perfect sense to me. François was one of those quiet, thoughtful men who inspire confidence in their judgement – the opposite of a bullshitter. I could see how his gang of middle-aged, mild-looking travellers would follow him anywhere, like a flock of devoted sheep. I was more than happy to join them.

I might have guessed that Will would be less of a sheep than me. The next morning we enjoyed a lazy breakfast – another whole basket of bread. I was getting fat round my middle from the heat, the beer, the bread and all the sitting about. I hate feeling fat, and was complaining about this to Will when he interrupted me and said, 'Div, shut up a minute and listen. I've been thinking this whole thing through and I want you to stay with François' party, but I'm going on as planned. I can't believe it is really as dangerous as they say, and even if it is, I'm prepared to take the risk.'

I stared at him, taken aback. We had spent a happy night together and I felt we were close again. I hadn't expected this.

'Homberi is only a half-day's journey from here – no big deal. What I'm going to do is go as far as Sévaré with you,' he went on. 'That's the town where we split from Emily yesterday. When we get there, I'm going to get a minibus ride up to Homberi. I noticed a sort of bus depot at those big crossroads in the centre of the town. It shouldn't be too difficult to find a ride. It's how local people travel and it'll be completely safe for me on my own.'

'What about me?'

'You'll be fine with François, and you'll love what's on his itinerary. While I'm off seeing Clem, you'll be visiting this wonderful market town on the Bani and Niger rivers. Look, it says . . .' and he began to read, '"One of the most exciting markets in West Africa where the Bambara, Bozo, Bobo, Dogon, Fulani, Tuareg

279

and Songhai people bring their traditional crafts to sell. These include gold and silver jewellery, cotton and woollen cloths, and wood carvings." I'll spend a few days with Clem, and then Emily and I'll come and join you in Dogon country, which is next on your list and is where we're going to meet up with Hugh.'

'For God's sake, Will! What about all the warnings that you'll get picked up by the police?'

'I don't think I will. If I leave here with François' party, whoever it is that's watching us will assume I'm travelling all the way with you. They won't expect me to peel off and take a local bus later on. It's only a few hours on from Sévaré, and I'm going to risk it.'

He saw my face. 'Come on, Div. This way we both get to do what we want.'

'It's not how I wanted it.'

'Well, nor me, for that matter. But it's how it's turned out.' He looked at his watch. 'Come on, we'd better collect our bags. Here are the first of François' party arriving, looking keen to get on their way.'

They were all right, François' group. There were twelve of them in all, three couples and the rest singles, four women and two men — middle-aged or older, apart from a younger woman travelling on her own who I

liked from the start. The impression I had got of the
French from our trip to Paris was misleading. These
people were charm itself – friendly, interesting, cultured.
Juliette, the woman about my age, was a doll, and it
turned out she was a textile buyer from Lille and she
spoke really good English. She had done a year in
London as a student and there must have been times
when our paths had crossed. I ignored Will and sat
next to her in the bus, which was comfortable and
cool with the aircon blasting. I couldn't stop him doing
what he had outlined to me, but I wasn't going to let
him think I was happy with it.

We crossed the river again. This time I hardly noticed.
It was getting like commuting for me, no more scary
than the District Line, and the rest of the journey to
Sévaré was pleasant. Our travelling companions passed
round bottles of water – it was important to drink at
least a litre and a half a day, they said – and produced
dried apricots and raisins and other healthy snacks from
their packs. These people were serious, thoughtful travellers. They consulted books and sheets of information
they had brought with them. They knew about annual
rainfall and high and low temperatures; distances between
towns and the size of the population of Djenne. They
made me feel ignorant and lazy. Why hadn't I made

281

more of this opportunity to travel somewhere extraordinary? Why had I been such a sap, tagging on behind Will? I told myself I needed a kick up the arse and that from now on I was going to learn a bit more about this country for myself.

We were going to stop for lunch in Sévaré, and when we arrived and drew into a shady courtyard outside a restaurant, I felt pretty comfortable with the thought that I was going to be abandoned. I snatched a brief goodbye with Will. We kissed and he held me close and then swung his pack off the roof of the bus and slipped out of the gate into the main road. He had told me not to tell François that he had gone until the last possible moment.

Our party got washed up and reassembled in a pretty garden where a long table had been set for us, and it wasn't until we were all seated and François was counting heads and organising our food orders that he realised Will had gone. He came to me where I sat with Juliette on one side and a pleasant man, Étienne, a retired geologist, on the other. 'Where is Will?' he asked.

'He's gone,' I said as calmly as I could, because to tell the truth, I still felt pretty miserable to see him leave. 'He's decided to go on to meet his sister. Sorry,

François. You did what you could, but he had made his mind up.'

He shrugged. 'This is his decision,' he said.

'Yes, it is.' I managed a smile to show that it was okay with me. 'He's going to join us when we get into Dogon country.'

'Let us hope all will be well.'

'Yeah.'

It was best to leave it at that. There's only so much you can do to keep people you love safe. It was the same with Gira. However much Mum and I warned him of the shit he could get in unless he straightened out his act, we couldn't be out on the streets with him. In the end, it was his decision.

Will's defection caused a bit of talk amongst those with whom we had shared the minibus. The others were mostly unaware of my personal drama and more interested in whether there was any wine available. Juliette was kind and supportive. We talked a bit about men and she said she was having a holiday from a relationship that was 'complicated' and had caused her a lot of pain; an older, married man, it turned out. Same old story. She said that she had watched me and Will and had felt envious. She thought we had an easy and loving relationship and guessed that we had a future planned together.

'Yeah, well, it's a bit complicated too,' I said. 'We come from very different backgrounds.'

'But surely this makes it more piquant?' she said. I smiled. It was a nice idea.

François had managed to order some wine, and we ate kebabs and delicious thin chips followed by a sort of crème caramel. 'France in Africa!' said Juliette. 'It is the best legacy of colonialism.'

By the time we stood up to continue our journey, I felt very full and sleepy. At this rate I would be vast when I got home and would have to resort to wearing the living room curtains, in the manner of the women of Sévaré. I thought of Will again when I saw the many clapped-out minibuses parked up at the crossroads. There was no sign of him, just a jostling crowd of black people weighed down with bundles and crates and nets of live chickens, all trying to get themselves a ride, and I suddenly felt real fear for his safety and anxiety that I would never see him again.

Juliette distracted me. 'Your people are so beautiful,' she said, looking out of the window.

'My people?'

'You are from West Africa, aren't you? Originally?'

'I think of myself as from London via Jamaica, but I guess my mother's great-great-grandparents came from this part. I know my dad came from Senegal, but he walked out on us years ago and I don't know anything about his family. Yeah, these people, especially the women, seem familiar. When I see them talking and laughing together, and the way they move, I recognise certain familiar characteristics, and yet we couldn't be more different. In our lives, I mean. It's quite weird actually, being here as a tourist. I keep thinking how it was slavery – which is so, like, abhorrent – that took my mother's family from Africa, but in the end it set them free from all this poverty and drudgery you see around you.'

'My parents are Belgian Jews. My grandparents survived the camps in the war but my mother and father grew up with the Holocaust as their immediate family history. It's part of what they are, and what I am. I guess it's a bit the same with you.'

'Yeah.' I could see what she was getting at. Terrible cruelty committed against your own people can't be forgotten. But slavery was only half the story. As far as I could tell from what was going on across Africa now, the red earth was still wet with blood and Africans killed each other, given half a chance, in the most dreadful ways they could dream up. I felt uncomfortable with the whole continent. To be honest, I didn't want to belong to it.

'I feel a million times more a Londoner than an African,' I said.

'And I a Frenchwoman! We are writing our own chapters of history, I think.'

As we drove, the other passengers pointed things out to one another and translated for me. I learned what crops were growing on either side of the road, the names of the massive trees, and how the roaming herds of goats and sheep led to the deforestation of the bush lands, which was a bad thing. I knew I had been mean to Emily when I wouldn't listen to her going on about the country. I just hadn't been in the mood to hear it from her.

The hotel we eventually arrived at was comfortable and modern by any standards and all the guests were Westerners – embassy people and businessmen, I guess, and even some youngish white women with children. It was on a road of other similar hotels that ran beside the great river – as wide as the sea, the edge lined with bobbing boats of the long, narrow variety, that were drawn up all along the bank in the black shade of huge trees with white-painted trunks. The boats were laden with goods for sale: great round green striped melons, or rolls of cloth or sacks of rice or fabulous pots that Aladdin could have kept his genie in.

As we piled out of the bus and the hawkers crowded forward to offer stuff for sale, I felt it was on me that their eyes fell: a black woman who thought she was white. One enormous woman pulled at my arm and hissed right into my face, like a cat looking for a fight.

Inside, the hotel lobby was blasted by air conditioning and at one end was a bar, lined with the usual suspects: lonely-looking white men, overweight, sweaty, drinking their way through the evening. Our cases were piled on hotel trolleys and trundled out through the tropical garden to where the hotel rooms were dotted about in low whitewashed buildings. In the absence of Will, and in the interests of economy, Juliette and I had said we would be happy to share.

The room was strange, furnished with dark Indonesian-type carved furniture, thrown together yesterday but made to look old and a bit colonial. Water buffalo horns made from plastic adorned the wall. Two blown-up photographs of a river at sunset hung crookedly above the beds. I checked out the bedspreads – acrylic, made in China. In this country teeming with cotton and craftsmen! Electrical wires looped out of the whitewashed walls and the bathroom plaster looked as if it had been finished off by someone drunk and in a hurry, but everything worked, it was all clean and the shower was heaven. I got dressed in a fresh set of clothes, put on my towering heels, which made me over six foot, and did my face. I felt good, as if I had stepped back into my real self.

'Wow! You look fabulous!' said Juliette, who had exchanged one pair of khaki combat trousers for another. She belonged to the Emily Kingsley school of utility dressing.

That made me think of Will again, and I hoped to God he had reached wherever it was and had found Emily and Clemmie. Because I felt better myself, I wished them well with all my heart. Let them have their family reunion, I prayed, and please God, deliver them safely back to where they belonged.

'Are we ready to go over for dinner?'

'You bet. What is it about this place? I'm starving again.'

It was dark in the garden and the noise of insects or frogs was deafening. The air smelled of wet earth, and the river, and stuff growing – like Mrs Kingsley's greenhouse after it's been watered on a hot night. The uneven paths were lit by little lanterns. If I wasn't careful, I'd fall off my bloody heels.

Because I was watching my feet, I didn't look up when we met a couple coming the other way, who veered off to the left on to another path. When I did glance across, I stopped and looked after them with my mouth open. Seen from behind, the woman was tall and slender and walked very upright, wearing some sort of tunic and longish skirt. Her white-blonde hair gleamed on her shoulders.

'What is it? You look as if you have seen a ghost,' said Juliette.

'It's the weirdest thing. I could swear I know that woman.'

I saw her again at breakfast. Juliette and I had both slept through our alarm calls and we arrived after everyone else in our group was at the long table eating eggs and toast and drinking coffee, under the whirring fans that stirred the air in the dining room.

She was sitting at a table to the side, with her back to us, opposite an older white man in a smart cream shirt, who was talking earnestly to her. She seemed to be saying little in return. Her back looked stiff with tension and her brown hands toyed with whatever was on her plate. Silver bracelets slid up and down her arms as she raised them to lift her loose hair from her neck.

There was something about her that was so familiar, but how could it be Clementine Kingsley? I went to get myself some more coffee from the buffet table – it was poor, weak brown stuff that went no way to satisfying my caffeine habit – and when I turned to go back to my seat I stopped and had a proper look.

It was the man who now caught my attention. I had seen him somewhere before. My mind raced backwards, and then I knew. It was the American guy who had talked to us in Ségou. I could still only see the back of the woman's head, but I put down my cup and approached the table and touched her on the shoulder. She turned round to look up at me, and I saw that it *was* Clemmie. Her face was thinner and lightly tanned, and her eyes were very blue, but what struck me most was her expression of deep unhappiness.

Clemmie

I DON'T KNOW WHO was more astonished, me, Mr Brockenhurst or Divinity. We all three stared at each other with open mouths. Brockenhurst recovered first.

'Well!' he said, half standing and holding out his hand to Divinity. 'This is a surprise! I was led to believe you had returned to Bamako.'

'Bamako?' she said, stupidly, staring at me. I had got up, my hands to my face, taking in her appearance, trying to work out why she was there and what it meant.

'Div? What on earth are you doing here? Where's Will? Where's Em?'

I went to her and we hugged and hugged. She was so tall and broad and her arms felt strong. I smelled her distinctive perfume and took in her clothes and make-up, her rosy lipsticked lips, her straight shiny hair. It was like being catapulted back into an exotic world I had left behind.

'They're not here. They're not here with me. They've gone on to that place to meet you. What are *you* doing here? You don't know what a fuss there's been about them getting to meet you. Will caught a bus up there yesterday from Sévaré.'

'Look, girls,' said Alvin, also rising. 'There's obviously a lot for you two to catch up on. Why don't I just leave you here for the moment?' There was a sort of uneasy urgency about him. He hastened out of the dining room and I saw him go to the reception desk and demand the attention of the manager.

'What's going on?' said Divinity, pointing after him. 'Why are you with that guy? Why haven't you gone to meet the others?'

'Excuse me, but is everything all right?' asked a young Frenchwoman, coming over to the table.

'No! Yes!' cried Divinity. 'Clemmie, this is Juliette. I've joined her tour party for a few days. I'll explain it all to you. Juliette, this is my boyfriend's sister, the one we've come out here to meet.'

The young woman smiled. 'Wonderful! A lucky meeting! But you will have a lot to talk about. If you don't mind, I'll join the others for breakfast.'

'Yeah, yeah,' said Divinity. 'Go ahead.'

We sat down opposite each other, still staring. My

heart was beating very fast and I felt suddenly weak and shaky.

'Clem! Are you okay?' Divinity moved her chair to sit beside me and put her arm round my shoulders.

'No, not really. I'm not really okay at all,' I said. I could feel my face collapsing into the lines of the grief I had felt since Alvin had told me the truth.

'What's wrong? What's happened? I still don't get why you are here with that guy. We met him, you know, when we were having lunch in Ségou. Emily told him all about you. She thought he could help you.'

'In a way he has. He might even have saved my life. I've had the most horrible time, Div. A really shit time. I can't begin to tell you.'

'Hey!' she said, looking about. 'How about I get a tray of breakfast stuff and we go to your room? You can tell me then. Away from all these other people.'

'Just food for you, then. I've eaten all I want.'

'You're so thin, lady,' she said, looking at me. 'What's happened to you? You don't look like that farm girl any more. Where have your tits gone?'

It seemed that there was less of me and more of her since the last time we met.

She followed me back to the room that Mr Brockenhurst

had booked me into last night, and we sat on the bed looking at each other. I still couldn't believe that she had turned up, really, in my darkest hour, and I told her that she must have been sent in some mysterious way to help me. She snorted.

'What, like God's little helper? Some sort of angel?' she said. 'That's not me, baby. I'm here because I'm a stroppy cow and wouldn't go on with your brother. The rest is just coincidence. Now, tell me what's up with you.'

'The American guy, Alvin, picked me up last night, somewhere out in the bush. We'd crossed the Niger, Bazet and me, and he'd left me in this village . . .'

'Who's Bazet when he's at home?'

'Chamba's brother. He came with me as my driver and bodyguard. We've been travelling for days to get here from the north.'

'Yeah, we knew that. Emily knew that.'

'But it all went wrong. He was offhand with me most of the way, but he got worse after Kidal. He was aggressive, really unpleasant, and actually hit me. He kept on about there being danger and kidnapping and stuff like that. We didn't take the normal route. We left the pick-up at the fort at Bourem, and like I told you, we crossed the river on a small fishing boat. Then he disappeared and the village men brought me out of the village on a donkey. I know it sounds bizarre to your ears, Div, and it was. It was like a dream, but I wasn't scared then. I trusted them, I suppose. They didn't seem threatening. Then, out of the dark, suddenly there was this bloody great SUV, and Brockenhurst sitting in it, apparently waiting for me.'

Divinity's face was screwed up in disbelief.

'How had he done that? How did he know where you were? It sounds like you were in the bush somewhere.'

'Exactly, I was. I don't quite get how he knew. I'm still trying to piece it together. He said he had met Emily and he was there to bring me to her. Then he told me that Bazet had made arrangements to sell me on to kidnappers. He said that his plan had been intercepted, or something. That he had been under observation.'

Divinity got up and started to pace round the room, wringing her hands in agitation.

'My God, Clem!' she said. 'This is no fucking joke, you know. This kidnapping threat. We've been warned about it the whole time we've been in this country. Would this Bazet guy have really done that? He's the brother of your man, you said?'

'I wouldn't have thought so, not ever, not in a million years, but now I don't know. I don't know what to believe, but Brockenhurst is sure.'

'How does he know? He'd never even heard of you until we met up with him.'

'He said he knew about it because of the work he does out here. He calls himself a facilitator, an intermediary. His job is to liaise between these kidnappers and the families or employers of the victims. He kind of works quietly, undercover, but he has strong connections with the police He has to be acceptable to both sides, you see.'

Divinity shook her head in denial, 'That's total bullshit!' she cried. 'He works for the United Nations – rescuing children and stuff. That's why Emily thought he could help you with your school.'

I stared at her. She must have got it wrong.

'Don't look at me like that. That's what he told us!' she cried. 'He showed us his business card and everything. Emily told him all about you. He was really interested.'

The muddle and confusion was overwhelming and I held my head in my hands. 'Then I don't understand. I don't understand anything. It all seems so unreal these last few days, and I have been believing one thing one moment, and then something else the next.'

Divinity walked to the window and looked out. 'Let's think this through,' she said. 'He says he saved you from being kidnapped? Well, whoever he is, and whatever he does, I guess that part could be true. He does seem to have a lot of connections. He helped with a problem we had with some stuff I bought in Djenne. Will telephoned him and he got it sorted. And Clemmie,' she wagged a finger at me, 'like I said, kidnapping does happen out here. Everyone has told us it's dangerous.'

'But it's *not*, it's not!' I said. 'That's the point. I've been in Mali for eighteen months and I have never felt in any danger at all. Not once. Chamba and his people look after me so well. They look after me as if I was one of them. In fact, that's not true. They look after me because, unlike them, I *need* looking after. I just can't believe that Chamba, my beloved Chamba, would have let Bazet bring me down south if he suspected for one moment that there might be danger, or that he isn't to be trusted.' I shoved my hand out for her to see my ring. 'Look, I'm his wife, for God's sake. We are man and wife in the deepest possible sense, more so than if I'd walked down the aisle of

Sherborne Abbey with him, wearing a big dress, with eight bridesmaids and four page boys dressed as tiny Guardsmen.'

Divinity did not look impressed. None of that would mean anything to her. How could she understand what Chamba and I felt for one another?

'But there's worse shit to come,' I said, miserably. 'Brockenhurst reckons that Chamba was in on it too.'

'Christ, Clemmie! What have you got yourself into?'

'He says that he is a ruthless rebel leader, and that he would have sold me off to finance his arms deals. He says I have been deceived from the beginning and that I was going to be used as a pawn in a sort of power play.'

Divinity still looked disbelieving. 'Come on! What is this? A George Clooney movie?'

'I know. It sounds like one, and I just can't believe it either. Chamba *loves* me. I know he does. You can't get that wrong, can you? Can you? But Brockenhurst says that all the times he was away from me he was, like, organising attacks on the army. He says he has a huge price on his head.'

'Well, surely you'd *know* if that was true or not? If you are as close as you say? You've been living with him, haven't you?'

I stared at the pattern of the bedspread and pulled at a loose thread. This was the bit I had been turning over and over in my mind. I didn't want to admit doubts to anyone, but I had to be honest. 'When I started to think about what he claimed, it raised questions in my mind, Div. You see, Chamba *is* often away for days at a time, and he'll never really talk to me about where he has been. I guessed it was smuggling or something.'

Divinity blew through her lips and made a noise like a horse. I could tell that she thought I had been a fool, an idiot.

'As much as I don't want to believe any of it, Brockenhurst is so convincing.' I admitted. 'He knows stuff that makes me think he really has been tracking Chamba. But there's even worse.' It took me an effort to say it. 'He says that Chamba has a Tuareg wife and children in Algeria. He has shown me photographs of him with a young Tuareg woman and a bunch of kids. He says that he has just used me, that I fell into his hands like a prize.'

Divinity plonked down heavily beside me and put her arm round my shoulders, and we sat in silence for a moment.

'Shit!' she said eventually.

'Yes, shit!'

'Well, fuck him!' she said, with feeling. 'Could it really be true?'

'If it is,' I said, 'then I don't know anything about love, or trust, or loyalty, or closeness and all that crap. Because I thought I had all that, Div. I thought I had it all, with my whole heart.'

'But why the hell would Brockenhurst make up a story like that? I mean, what's in it for him?'

There was a knock on the door and Divinity got up to answer it. The man himself stood outside holding a brown leather briefcase, looking like a small, neat, grey-haired professor about to take a tutorial.

'May I come in?' he asked politely. I nodded, and he sat down on a carved wooden chair facing us.

'Yeah,' said Divinity, in her tough voice, wagging a red-nailed finger at him. 'I think you've got some explaining to do, Mr Brockenhurst.'

Alvin raised both hands as if in surrender.

'Okay,' he said. 'I haven't been entirely truthful, but if I'm honest, ha ha, truth over minor details isn't the most important thing at stake here.'

'Well, explain.' Divinity glared at him.

'When I met you guys, it was a lucky break for me. I have had a difficult few months trying to open negotiations in the north between my clients and Chamba ag Baye. He's almost impossible to contact and even harder to pin down for a face-to-face meeting. A meeting, I hasten to add, that could prove highly beneficial to both sides.'

'What do you mean "clients"? You told us you worked for the UN. You told us your job was getting aid to children.'

Alvin cleared his throat apologetically. 'Not entirely true, I confess, but let me go on. The picture will become clearer. I saw your cousin, Clementine, outside that restaurant in Ségou, trying to get close to the kids, so when your driver told mine why you were out here, I took a gamble and introduced myself as a UN envoy. I reckoned it made me more, um, acceptable, to you guys. I have learned it's often unwise to reveal the true nature of my business.'

'But how the hell did you know who *we* were?'

'I didn't, until Emily told me. It's amazing how open people are if you ask the right questions. She told me everything except the name of Clementine's Tuareg boyfriend, but I learned enough to guess his identity. We knew ag Baye was in a relationship with a European woman, but we didn't know who.' He turned to me. 'Emily passed on your cell phone number, and given the general concern for your safety, I was able to track your journey.'

So, Bazet had been right about that. I thought of how angry he had been with me. If I was to believe Alvin, it was because anyone tracking my telephone calls might have thwarted his kidnap plans.

'You had official business cards and everything. You took them out of your wallet. You gave us one.' There was anger in Divinity's voice. She didn't like the feeling that they had been duped.

'I have a variety of those. It's helpful to have a number of identities.'

'So who the hell *are* you?' she said. 'What kind of guy goes round with false identities if he isn't a fucking crook?'

Alvin was unruffled. 'As I said, I am what is called a negotiator,' he explained calmly. 'When I retired five years ago from my post as Professor of International Affairs at Princeton, I thought I could put my expertise to some practical use. It's also a darned sight better paid, and a lot more exciting. I am hired to liaise between people in extreme situations exactly like this one we are in right now. It can be very difficult and sensitive work, but it is rewarding. After a lifetime of academe, it feels good to be at the sharp end of things.'

302

'I still don't get it,' I said. 'You'll have to explain the sort of thing you do.'

'Well, to give you an idea, my last operation involved British tourists kidnapped by Somalian pirates. The usual stuff. In this case, after six months the husband and wife were released by the gang that held them. I negotiated that a ransom should be paid privately, and more importantly, advised on the terms of the payment and the release. Neither government was involved, no one lost face, and it was a happy outcome all round.'

All this seemed so far removed from anything that could possibly happen to me that I still couldn't understand why he had involved himself in my journey, and I asked him as much.

'This is a little more complicated,' he said. 'I represent both Malian and French interests, both of which want the northern desert made safe. The French are anxious to get in first with an eye to potentially vast mineral resources, and to keep the Americans and the Chinese out. The rebels – your boyfriend, Miss Kingsley – are set on disrupting the whole thing, and claiming so-called territorial rights for themselves. They are prepared to wage war if necessary. They are ruthless, armed and dangerous. Their exploits have made large tracts of the southern Sahara a no-go area, a haven for bandits and smugglers, and rendered any preliminary exploratory work impossible.'

I couldn't bear it. It was the same old story of the Tuareg having everything taken from them and their way of life destroyed. Of course I had heard talk like this round the campfires. No secret was made of Tuareg resistance to being driven out of their homeland. I could totally believe that Chamba would be involved, and I would support him in fighting for Tuareg rights every step of the way.

'I can see by the look on your face,' said Brockenhurst, 'that you have already got an opinion on this, but if I may go on, I would like to tell you that it would be in Tuareg interests to negotiate. Mineral wealth would come their way – there would be employment, wells would be drilled, there would be improved medical services, schools, clinics; all these things would be right there on the negotiating table. It is pig-headed to resist. Your boyfriend is standing in the way of progress and opportunity. Tuareg warlike behaviour and their overweaning pride are destroying his people's chance of a better life. It's stupid, stupid, stupid.'

I could see Divinity looked impressed by this. She was nodding her head as if it all made sense. It sounded so reasonable and measured, but I knew enough of recent history to say, 'Look, Mr Brockenhurst, the Tuareg people have heard all this before. You must know there have been other negotiating tables set out with tempting goodies on offer, but *none* of them have been delivered – *none*. Where are the schools and clinics? Where are the new wells? Where is the foreign aid that is promised but never materialises? The moderates have done their best to persuade the hotheads to be conciliatory, but when negotiation yields nothing, they are left looking like saps. Fighting and independence seem like a better way.'

'Criminal activity is never an answer. The Tuareg dream for an independent homeland is dead in the water – you know that. This struggle is about money and power, and the Tuareg prefer fighting to negotiating. They have fighting in their blood and bones. The French never conquered them – and the result is that their region has remained backward, underdeveloped and underfunded, racked by poverty, famine and drought. Are you saying they prefer it that way?'

Some of this was true, I knew that. Some of it I had felt myself, but it was to ignore what it meant to be a Tuareg – the warlord of the desert, independent

and proud, tough and resourceful. Were they to become
the drivers and cooks and manual labourers in great
foreign-owned mining camps sprouting across their
desert homelands? It was unthinkable. It wrenched at
my heart that this was offered to them as an alterna-
tive to their traditional nomadic lives. Say Chamba
agreed to all of this – would he spend his days lounging
in a concrete block house at some newly dug well,
watching satellite television – *Strictly Come Dancing,
Lewis, Downton Abbey* – growing fat on easy food and
idleness?

I couldn't find the words to argue with
Mr Brockenhurst about the importance of everything that would be lost by a sell-out: the delicate
balance of man and desert; the silence of the shimmering sands and echoing, empty mountains; the
beauty and solitude. These things were beyond
value and could never be calculated on a balance
sheet.

I found myself brimming with tears again. Just say
everything Brockenhurst had told me was true – that
I had been used by the man I loved with such a passion
– well, even then I still believed in the Tuareg cause.
My heart might be broken, but I could forgive the
man who had thought me worth selling. I remembered

Mariam touching my hair and saying '*Belle! Mais dangereuse!*' and the throat-slitting gesture. Had she known what awaited me? Were they all in on it?

'Look,' said Divinity suddenly, glancing at her watch and getting up. 'I'm supposed to be shipping out of here in ten minutes or so.' Brockenhurst looked momentarily relieved. He obviously felt Divinity was tough to handle. 'But I'm not leaving you, Clem,' she said. 'Not now. No way.'

The relief I felt was overwhelming, and I swallowed back the tears that rushed into my throat. Just her physical presence, her height and strength and hard-edged glamour made me feel less powerless. I didn't want to be on my own again.

She turned to Alvin, 'So what are your plans for getting us to meet the others?'

He cleared his throat. 'I promised I would fly Clementine over to Homberi, and that's what I will do. If you want to stay with her, we can include you in the arrangements, but first I need to have a private debrief session with her. There are things that would be helpful for me to know – tools of negotiation, let's call them – that in the long run will prevent inevitable bloodshed. It won't take long – an hour or so – and then we can be on our way.'

Divinity looked at me and I nodded. There were many things I wanted to ask Brockenhurst myself.

'I'll be back,' she said to me. 'I'll go and pack and settle my bill and say goodbye to my new friends.'

After she had gone, Brockenhurst said, 'It's not ideal, you know, having her turn up. I had wanted time with you alone, with no distractions, but I guess I can't ban her from joining us later.' He breathed deeply and closed his eyes before going on. 'Clementine, I'm not entirely sure you understand how close you were to terrible danger. I can appreciate that you and ag Baye have been in a relationship, and that you love him. I can see that. It's hard for you to rethink your recent history, but it is important that you do.'

I said nothing. Whatever he had to say couldn't change how much I loved Chamba. I couldn't flick a mental switch and shut off my love for him. It would cause me terrible pain to learn more about his treachery, but I would still love him.

Brockenhurst leaned down and opened his brief-case. 'I have some photographs here that I would like you to look at.' I immediately turned my head away. I didn't want to see further proof of Chamba's Tuareg family, but the black-and-white prints he spread out on the bed beside me were almost worse. They showed a burned-out plane and a line of bodies wearing army uniform. There were close-ups of the young black faces, some grinning horribly in death, some burned beyond recognition, the flesh curled back from the skull.

'These were taken three months ago. This army supply plane was shot down. Any survivors were executed. Your lover's handiwork.'

There were further photographs of bodies, and burned-out vehicles.

'Don't you see that this barbarity must stop? That guerrilla fighting does nothing for the Tuareg cause?'

'Of course. I hate fighting. I hate violence. But I can't believe Chamba is responsible for any of this.'

'We don't know as yet, but this is what's happening up there. Be that as it may, if Chamba can be persuaded to bring his people to the negotiating table, there is a way forward out of all of this. There will be an amnesty. There is a strong possibility that he and his men may remain armed, and that they will be employed, extremely usefully, in the battle against AQIM; al-Qaeda in the desert.'

I shrugged. 'That sounds good, obviously, but I can't be his spokesman.'

'Exactly. That is why we need to find him, and open negotiations. If we can stop internal fighting, then the problem of al-Qaeda can be addressed, peace can be restored and the north of the country can be opened for foreign investment and development. All this can only be good for the Tuareg people. You will get your school, Miss Kingsley.'

'Okay, okay. I get the picture, and yes, it makes sense.'

'Then I need your help. I need to know his movements — when and where he crosses into Algeria, his contacts there. I need to know the position of his base in the mountains.' He started to spread out enlarged aerial photographs of nothing very much. I picked one up and looked at it.

'I can't help you. I've no idea of where we were when we went into the desert, or into the mountains. We were often travelling with the herds, moving from well to well. If the wells are marked on these photographs, I expect I could point out the grazing lands.'

Alvin tutted with irritation. 'No, no, I don't want to know where his animals graze, for Christ's sake. I want to know where he has his base — where he operates out of.'

'I don't know! I never went with him on these so-called military exercises. He kept me out of it all.'

'He uses caves in the mountains, we believe. You must have gone there with him?'

'I did, a few times, but I couldn't tell you where they are.'

'How many days' driving from the oasis?'

'Two or three.'

'Does he travel by night?'

'Not with me. We often took longer and went by camel.'

Alvin gathered up the photographs impatiently, and spread out some more. These were of men's faces — mug shots of dark-eyed, bearded men in the traditional Tuareg headgear, but with their eyes and mouths exposed. They all looked desperate and exhausted. I sifted through them and picked out one or two.

'This man came often to talk to Chamba when we were in Tamanrasset. I think he is a cousin. This man is his nephew, I think. I'm not sure about the others. I may have seen them at some time, but I can't be sure.'

'Jesus!' Alvin swore softly.

'The men are veiled most of the time. I'm not being deliberately unhelpful. Who are they, anyway? Why are you interested in them?'

'It doesn't matter. It just would have been helpful to me, that's all, to know that they work with him.'

'Well, I can't tell you. Look, Mr Brockenhurst, I led a peaceful life with Chamba. We didn't talk about the Tuareg struggle much. We didn't talk about fighting. We just . . .' I couldn't say 'made love', but that about summed it up.

He sat in silence, looking downcast. I felt almost sorry for him.

'What *I* want to know is how, if all this good stuff on offer is really true, you can convince Chamba that you will deliver a humanitarian package. Maybe if you put a basic medical programme in place he would believe in you.'

'Jesus, Clementine! You aren't listening, are you? We can't introduce any frigging programme if we can't talk to the man, and we can't send our people into the region without a guarantee of safety.'

I could see what he meant. I believed he was sincere. If only I could talk to Chamba, I could help him understand what was being offered.

'I've got to speak to him,' I said. 'You must let me speak to him. He has a satellite telephone – the best, a Thuraya. I can get a message to him.'

'He's unlikely to take a call from someone he

intended to sell on to kidnappers. I'm afraid you are history, Miss Kingsley, as far as Chamba ag Baye is concerned.'

'Well, let me try.' I needed to hear his voice. I needed to hear in his own words that he had betrayed my love and confidence, that everything that we had shared had been a pretence on his part.

'No chance, I'm afraid. It's not within my power. You won't have any more contact. You are now under the protection of the Malian government and will be seen safely out of the country.'

This was what I had most dreaded. I had already worked out that it was the inevitable outcome of my rescue.

'If I refuse?'

'My dear young woman! Refusing is not an option. You could be charged with aiding terrorism. You are lucky that you are being treated as an innocent victim. You must leave the country with your brother and cousin and take more care in the future with whom you associate. Stay at home in Dorset, for God's sake, and marry a farmer.'

I flared up then. 'Don't you dare tell me what to do! You don't know anything about me – or him! Or Dorset farmers!'

'All right. I apologise. I'm older than your father, I imagine, and it's hard for me not to give you the advice I would a daughter. But the bottom line is that you are lucky to have got out of this, Clementine. Very lucky indeed.'

'What happens to kidnap victims?' I needed to know to what fate Chamba had been willing to deliver me.

'The last two – Italian men, engineers – were taken in Niger and brought to Mali, and when no ransom was forthcoming, they were shot.'

God, how close had I been to a similar end? My parents are not wealthy farmers. They would have had to pass the hat round. I would have been in competition with the Dorset Air Ambulance and Riding for the Disabled and the Dogs' Trust. Did I deserve anyone's charity when I had brought all this on myself? Better, really, to give it to the doggies.

'Another thing. Where's Bazet? What have you done with him? He is okay, isn't he?'

'He's been handed over.'

'What do you mean "handed over"? Has he been arrested?'

'He'll be being held somewhere. He'll have valuable information, no doubt. I hope I will be allowed to interview him later.'

'He won't tell you anything.'

'We'll see.'

I didn't know whose side I was on. That was the trouble. My head and my heart were at war. Oh Chamba, Chamba, how could you do this to me?

Emily

WHEN A DUSTY figure appeared on the long straight road, I didn't take much notice. I was sitting in the shade of the veranda with a bottle of water, watching nothing happening apart from the sun going down like a vast burning ball in a blazing orange sky. Two lizards ran up and down the wall behind me, but nothing else moved. Today there was no wind, just blistering heat. Trickles of sweat ran down my back and my hair stuck wetly to my head.

No vehicles had come along the road from either direction all afternoon, and although Serufi's truck was still parked in the shade of a few thorn trees, I hadn't seen him all day. The little stalls selling handicrafts were unmanned. I could get no signal on my mobile. Although every now and then I heard someone moving inside the little café, I felt totally alone and desolate. Even the birds had deserted me.

Looking towards the south, the fingers of Fatima's Hand rose darkly, weirdly against the flaming sky.

A carbonated water helped pass the time. It was icy cold, the glass misted thickly with delicious condensation. I had been drinking water all day, and now I felt enormously fat and bloated, the waistband of my trousers tight. What I most wanted, and couldn't stop thinking about, was a Mars bar. Chocolate in this terrible heat! But that was what my brain was telling me. I argued between a Mars bar and a family-sized bag of salt and vinegar crisps, and the Mars bar won hands down. That was how I passed my day. Pathetic, really. Comfort food for poor, lonely Emily.

No Clemmie. That was the most important thing. No Clemmie. I had to be patient, but time went by so slowly. I checked my watch after I thought an hour had passed and found it was just ten minutes. At two o'clock I asked for some lunch. One of the boys banged around inside with pots and pans, and a long time later he appeared with a plate of rice and a thick brown sauce in which sat a single large cube of black meat that I couldn't put my fork into. The sauce was spicy and delicious. I gave the lump of meat to the yellow bitch that lay under the table. She ate it in one gulp. I expected to see it, intact, travelling like a little box down her throat. Then the boy brought me a small green banana and an espresso coffee. The coffee was as good as you would get in a café on a piazza in Rome.

After that, I dozed, stupefied, as the sun moved slowly across the enamel-blue sky. I watched dung beetles pull something through the sand at the bottom of the steps to the veranda. It took them ages, but they never gave up, toiling away with some destination firmly fixed in their beetle minds.

At four o'clock I asked for another Coke and a bottle of water, and while I was waiting, I walked up the road a little way and looked at the stuff for sale laid on the sand outside the makeshift stalls. It was the same tourist tat that you saw everywhere – crudely made jewellery and leather belts and purses. There were necklaces strung with carved camel teeth and dusty-looking orange stones. Everything was covered by a thin film of silver sand.

I walked back, battered by the heat, and flopped on to my seat in the shade. I checked my watch. Only twenty minutes had passed. Surely she would be here soon? My drinks arrived with a bowl of unshelled peanuts.

These occupied me for half an hour or so. I made

patterns with the discarded shells and then flicked them off the table one by one. The full force of the sun was waning now. The light had become soft and rosy and a tiny breeze began to flutter the awning. The sky had faded to mauve and the palest green. It would soon be dark

It was then that I noticed the figure coming down the road, and I sat up and paid attention. Not Clemmie, obviously, and not Will and Divinity. God knows what had happened to them. This was a solitary figure, walking out of the sunset with a sort of determination and briskness that was unusual here, where slow to very slow was the preferred pace.

As it drew closer, I saw that it was a tall, slim man with a pack on his back, and then I realised that it was Will. I leapt from my chair and dashed out into the road, calling and waving.

'Will, Will! What are you doing *walking*?' I shouted long before he could hear me. 'Where's Divinity?'

He waved back and called something in return, and I set off at a jog to meet him.

When we reached one another, he stopped and hugged me. He looked very hot. His face was red and dripping, and his shirt was dark with sweat. He had a half-empty water bottle in his hand, and before he could speak, he put it to his lips and finished it off, letting the water spill from the bottle down his chest.

'Jesus!' he said. 'That was a hot walk.' He took off his hat and wiped the sweat from his brow with the back of his hand. 'The bus dropped me at a dirt cross-roads about three miles back. I was nervous about missing this place and wasn't sure exactly where it was.'

'Where's Divinity? Why are you on your own? Clemmie's not here yet, and I can't get a mobile signal so I don't know if she has been trying to send a message through.'

'I've been trying to call you all day to tell you I was on my way. I just get a French woman telling me that your number is not available.'

'Typical! Anyway, I'm so glad you are here. It's been such a slow day, waiting. Tell me what you've done with Divinity. Why on earth did you get a bus? Why didn't you come in a taxi?'

'It's a long story. Can you get a beer here? You can? Fab. Wait till I've had a beer.'

Later, with his second beer in front of him, Will told me what had happened: how he had left Divinity with a French tour party, that she was okay about it, and that he had arranged to meet her on the way home when we went into Dogon country to collect Hugh.

'So here we are, without or Best Beloveds, in the middle of nowhere.' I felt quite cheerful about this, because I loved being with Will and the relief of having him turn up was so huge.

'At least there's beer to soften the pain of separation.'

'Is it all okay between you and Divinity?' I asked cautiously. I suspected it wasn't, but didn't want to make Will talk about it if he would rather not.

'No, not really.' He took a mouthful of beer. 'She doesn't like our family much, to be honest.'

'I looked suitably scandalised, and he went on, 'Nothing personal. Not really. She likes everyone well enough as individuals, but she doesn't like how our family works. She doesn't like the closeness I feel to all of them – and that includes you, of course. She thinks it's unnatural – that as one grows up, one should grow away. She thinks our family has an unhealthy hold on its members and that we close ranks to cover up various issues that ought to be faced in the open.'

'What sort of things?'

Will sighed and leaned back in his chair. 'Dad's drinking and its effect on Mum, mostly. Clemmie, to a certain extent.'

'What about Clemmie?' How dare she? I could feel my hackles rising.

'Her choice to be out here living with a tribesman. She thinks it's selfish and indulgent and attention-seeking. She thinks Clemmie sees herself as having the starring part in a great theatrical work entitled *Clemmie – her Life.*'

I kicked crossly at the chair leg. 'How does that view sit with her argument that we should grow apart from the family? Clem couldn't be much further away than out here.'

'Yeah, but she reckons that because we are close, Clemmie enjoys the impact it has on the rest of us; that she sort of feeds off the drama.'

I felt angry with Will that he appeared to be able to tolerate this view. 'That's ridiculous. Of course she doesn't. You know it's not true, don't you?'

'That's how Divinity sees it.'

'Then why did she come out here?' I cried. This was my honeymoon; how dare she come with me if she felt like that? 'She knew this was a Clemmie-based trip.'

'I wonder that myself. It hasn't been the greatest success so far.'

Will's voice was so sad that it made me see things

from his point of view and feel sorry that he wasn't having a better time.

'What kind of family does she come from?' Perhaps her contrary, hostile views could be explained by her background.

'Strong mother, absent father, semi-delinquent hoodie brother.'

'Ah.'

'Yes. It's easy to see how alien we are . . . extended family, generations born within a radius of ten miles, strong sense of who we are and where we come from. She finds it all suffocating.'

'I see.' That was all I could say, because I did see, but felt, well . . . that's how it is. Like us or lump us.

'She's right about Dad, of course. We ought to haul him off to AA, I suppose, but what's the point? We all know he's an old soak, but a fairly harmless one. He doesn't drive when he's pissed, or get belligerent. He just goes to sleep. It seems like a lifestyle choice to me. If alcohol makes his life easier to bear, why not?'

'Modern life doesn't allow that. Everything has to be "addressed", doesn't it? It's not as if we are unaware that he's an alcoholic. Not dealing with it is a way of dealing with it, if you know what I mean.'

'Exactly! Divinity thinks Mum has martyred herself.

It annoys her. She would like us all to out Dad, and liberate Mum. Can you imagine anything my mother would hate more?'

'And it's her *choice*! Why can't people be allowed to make what they want of the situations they find themselves in? If they don't ask for help, that is.'

'I suppose Divinity comes from a background of standing up in church and publicly renouncing past sins and weaknesses. She wants it all out in the open.'

I had a sudden vision of Uncle Peter standing up in our little church during matins to announce to the Vicarene and the congregation (five at the most) that he was a dipso.

'When my parents' marriage looked rocky and Mum had that affair with the Artificial Insemination man, I hated it that she kept wanting to talk about her and Dad's relationship. It was awful. I just wished she'd shut up and deal with whatever was going on. That seemed to me to be the grown-up option.'

Will nodded sympathetically.

'So is this difference between you insurmountable?' I hoped he would say that it was.

'I don't know, to be honest. It might be, when it comes to a long-term relationship. Getting married, or having children, could only underline the problem.

I'm not sure, in fact, that Divinity wants either of those things. Her mother really struggled to bring her up on her own, and later her brother. There have never been supportive men around, and this colours her view of family life. She's very suspicious of it.'

'But it sounds as if she's never experienced it.'

'No, not like we have. She can't see how our family is a continuum in our lives, not just a starting point.'

We were silent for a moment. Poor Will. I thought how lucky I was to have found Hugh, who fitted so naturally and easily into my background and whose views on marriage and having children so neatly coincided with my own.

'It's one of the things I worry about with Clemmie,' I said. 'I don't see how she can really adapt to such a different culture. It's like you and Divinity magnified a thousand times. However much she loves Chamba, it must be so hard, and she's so far away. Last night, and then sitting waiting today, on my own, has made me understand a bit better what it must feel like to be totally disconnected from everything and everyone. It's made me almost certain that she'll come home with us. I can't believe that she won't want to.'

'You think it hasn't worked out between her and Chamba?'

'I don't know how they feel about each other, but I think that the weight of difference between them will make it impossible to continue, to build a future. I think that's what she meant when she said there had been problems.'

'We'll have to wait and see. Mum didn't want us to put any pressure on her.'

'I know. Your father did, though. He asked me to do my best to bring her home.'

'I've never known Clemmie to be uncertain or wavering about anything. She'll know what's right for her.'

'Yes, but look around you, Will. Look at the endless barren sand and the burning heat and the aloof, strange people. How can she survive here? Clemmie, who grew up in our valley with the sound of running water and the green hills all about. It's alien, Will. It's alien. She doesn't belong here. This country will kill her in the end.'

Even as I spoke, my words reminded me of the psalm that Clemmie and I had sung for Great-Aunt Mary, when we scattered her ashes at her chosen place in the desert hills. All the time we had known her, when she lived in our village, she had hated the country, hated sheep, hated the outdoors. We always felt she was an exile from Knightsbridge and Harrods, and yet she had chosen a hillside miles away from anywhere as her resting place because she had left her heart there sixty years earlier. 'In pastures green he leadeth me, the quiet waters by.'

Did the psalmist mean that love could transform rocky, barren wastes and turn them into meadows of grass? Maybe he did, but my literal nature rebelled. If he had sheep in mind, they certainly wouldn't survive on love alone. I had fiercely loved the lambs I had bottle-fed as a child, but lots of them had died.

'Come on, Em,' said Will. 'Don't look so gloomy. Have a bit more faith in Clem's good sense.'

So we sat and waited, Will and I, as the sky faded, and night fell, and it became clear that Clemmie wasn't coming. We waited all the following day, too, and as the afternoon drew on, so my spirits drooped until I couldn't bear waiting a minute longer and told Will I was going to have a shower. He said he would sit on, and his face looked sad again and I guessed he was thinking about Divinity, who I knew he loved.

Divinity

THE DRIVER WHO met us at the airstrip was the same guy who had come to collect me and Will and take us back to Djenne to collect my missing stuff, and he had been less than charming first time round.

By now, Clemmie looked exhausted, with violet smudges under her eyes, and her face set in an expression of misery. The prospect of seeing Will and Emily didn't seem enough to raise her spirits, although she kept turning to me and saying, 'I can't really believe that we'll soon be there. What a surprise they'll get – us arriving together, and like VIPs!' She was filled with a nervous energy and sat with her mobile phone in her lap, turning it over and over in her hands and constantly checking the screen for messages.

We were both glad that Alvin Brockenhurst had delivered us to the little army airbase and had said goodbye as he handed us over to a polite and respectful captain. 'You don't need me around, ladies,' he said. 'You've waited for this moment for some time, Clementine. I'm glad I was able to facilitate your rendezvous with your family, and I can reassure you that you'll be safe for the rest of your time in Mali.'

'Yeah, well, thanks for that,' I said, and I was grateful, and so should Clemmie have been, but she didn't thank him. I guess it was a case of shoot the messenger.

'Okay,' was all she said, looking away from him as if she couldn't bear to be reminded of some of the unpalatable truths he had told her.

It was just a pilot, a co-pilot and us in the small plane, and we flew quite low over miles and miles of scrubland, lit by afternoon sun and scattered with occasional herds of some sort of animal – sheep or goat, I couldn't tell. The children who tended them ran in circles waving their arms at the plane. Where had they come from, these kids? Where were they going to? I couldn't see any villages or roads. How could they survive in this emptiness? My God, Africa was a terrible place.

'Do you love Will?' Clemmie asked me suddenly.

I didn't know quite how to reply. 'He's the best man I've ever met,' I said, slowly. 'The kindest and best. But I guess I have an issue with loving men.'

'Why?' she demanded, quite fierce. 'Why can't you love him? He loves you, you know.'

'I suppose my mum was a bad example. I grew up with "uncles" who she was mad about until it all went wrong. She was such a sucker for love. She let them walk all over her, she lent them money, looked after them, believed the crap they talked, and then – bang! They let her down and turned into the drinkers, woman beaters, crack-addicted losers they had been from the beginning – although she couldn't see it.'

Clemmie looked at me, her eyes very blue and concerned. 'That's terrible, Divinity,' she said. 'That's a terrible way to have been brought up.'

I had to smile. She didn't know that most of my friends at school came from the same sort of background.

'But you can't let all that stop you loving Will,' she said, urgently. 'You mustn't let it stop you believing in him, because if you stop believing in love, what else is there? I mean, obviously, life can go on, and you can do stuff, but if you can't give your whole heart, what's the point?'

She turned her phone in her hands. 'You know, even though Brockenhurst has told me all these terrible things, it hasn't stopped me loving Chamba. Not one bit. It has made me desperate to see him again, to speak to him, because everything I know tells me he loves me.'

'Yeah, I can see it's hard for you.' That was all I could think of to say, because sooner or later she had got to accept the truth. She was struggling to come to terms with the fact that she had been horribly betrayed and that love had let her down, and she was trying to convince herself that it had all been worth it in some way.

'So, Div, give it a chance with Will. I know he loves you. He's not like your mum's boyfriends – you know that.'

Of course I did. It was the surrender I couldn't deal with; the instinct to keep a bit back in self-preservation was too strong. Anyway, this didn't seem to me to be the moment for Clemmie, of all people, to give me a lecture on how to love someone, but she went on, looking dreamily past me through the scarred plastic window at the dreadful parched land below us. 'You see, Div, if I hadn't had what I've had with Chamba, I would never have known what love is about. And now I do, and Brockenhurst can't take that from me with his horrible photographs and the things he told me. He can't make a difference to how I feel about the last months. They were so much the best in my life.'

I felt for her then, I really did, and I thought about Will and how much I didn't want to lose him, and how maybe I would, if I didn't allow things to move along a little.

'Yeah, I do love him,' I said, finally. 'And I guess we'll work things out.'

She turned to me with her famous blazing smile, and it was kind of touching that despite her misery, she could be glad for us.

'We'll be there soon,' she said. 'It can't be that far, and I want you to tell him. Please, you must. You can't tell him you love him too often, Div, because you see, you just never know. You never know what is waiting for you.'

Emily

T HE SHOWER WAS a simple pipe sticking out of a cemented wall, but it worked quite well, and now that it was cooler, the little brown birds were back, flying in and out through the window, and I was glad to see them. The water felt wonderful on my hot body as I lathered and rinsed my hair.

The sound of the running water drowned out any other noise, and when I turned off the tap, I was suddenly aware of excited voices and that someone was trying to pull open the wooden door.

'Emily! Emily! It's me, Clem!'

Hardly bothering to wrap a towel round me, I flung the door open, and there she was, and I fell into her arms, and we hugged and kissed and laughed and our mingled tears ran down our cheeks.

★　★　★

There was so much talking to be done. I had spent so long waiting for something to happen, and then, suddenly, everything happened all at once. I had to keep stopping and looking at her, needing to take in her appearance. She was thinner, and her face was lightly tanned and her eyes were very blue. She looked more beautiful than ever, but there was a new gravity about her. Her girlishness had gone, and there were fine lines round her eyes and mouth. Her hair was fabulous – almost white and caught on the back of her head in a silver clip. Silver bracelets slid up and down her slim arms and her hands were decorated with silver rings, including a ring on her marriage finger.

She was wearing a long ochre-coloured skirt and a blue tunic bound at the waist by a many-coloured leather rope, and round her neck was a heavy silver necklace shapped like a crescent moon. On her feet were her jodhpur boots, very dusty and battered. She looked wonderful, part nineteenth-century explorer, part hippie, entirely herself. As we talked, she rootled through my make-up bag and put on eyeliner and lipstick, purring with pleasure.

'I've brought you loads of stuff,' I said. 'I'll get it all out of my bag in a minute. But just tell me again about Bazet and Alvin Brockenhurst, and what happened after you crossed the river. It's so amazing that you met Divinity like that, quite by chance.'

'I tell you, Em, having her turn up was a miracle. I was so down, so depressed, and she arrived like my champion, my saviour, taking no shit, like she always does.'

She got up and went to look out of the window. 'I haven't told you the bad stuff,' she said with her back to me. 'I don't want to spoil seeing you again. It can wait till after we've had supper and celebrated a bit. Divinity made Alvin buy us a bottle of champagne from the hotel. It's in the fridge in the café.'

'It was amazing that he found you like that, and was able to help get you here. I suppose he has the whole weight of the UN behind him.'

'No! He deceived you there. He's admitted it. He's nothing to do with the UN. He's a professional nego-tiator, working for some powerful private clients, and he's in with the government in some major way. That's how he can pull strings.'

'What?' I looked at her in astonishment. 'I don't understand. We met him in Ségou where we had lunch.

He talked about the children's programmes he's working on. He asked all about you, because he said that getting projects off the ground in the north was a problem.'

'Yes, of course he did. He was lying to you, gathering information about me. He wanted to get to Chamba; he says that he is the key figure in the development of mining interests in the desert. He needs his co-operation for security reasons and to combat the AQIM – al-Qaeda.' Clemmie's voice sounded dull, as if she didn't want to talk about this any more.

'He was so one hundred per cent believable! I can't take it in that he was lying to us.'

'Yeah, well, he was. He had some pretty horrible things to tell me, but that's for later on. I'm glad he didn't come on with us. I thought he might have brought us here himself, but he got his henchman to drop us off. He seems able to make a few telephone calls and he has planes and cars at his disposal. The plane we came in was Malian army. It was written on the side.'

'But whoever he is, he rescued you from being kidnapped, didn't he? We've got to be thankful for that.'

'So he says. If he hadn't shown me the photo you sent with him, I might have thought I was being kidnapped by *him*.'

'What photo?'

'You know – the one of us at home as kids, with the ponies. With Blazer. It made me cry when I held it in my hand. It was the first time I broke down on the whole horrible journey. It was the sight of Blazer that did it, I'm afraid, Em, not your cheerful freckled face.'

'I never gave him any photo.'

We stared at one another, and then the penny dropped.

'He stole it! Or had it stolen. Someone broke into our room at Djenne and stole my wallet and some sweets. He's a fucking thief. I lost my driving licence and Oyster card and everything. It must have been one of his cars that came to take Divinity and Will back to Djenne. I saw the sweets on the dashboard. Serufi told me that the driver wasn't from the regular police. He called him an "agent".'

I couldn't take it in properly, or make sense of what had happened, and why. We sat and looked at one another, trying to fit the pieces together.

'Well, you're here, and we're together, and that's the main thing,' I said finally. 'You can tell me about all the rest later on.'

'Yes,' said Clemmie sadly, and then her face brightened

and she took my hand. 'There's so much I've got to hear about. Your wedding, Em!' She looked at my ring. 'I thought about you so much on the day, and I felt really miserable not to be there. But look at you! You look so happy. You're the cat that got the cream.'

When we went over to the café to join Will and Divinity, there was one thought uppermost in my mind. I had given Clemmie the things I had brought out to her, and she had been sweet about them all, exclaiming over each one and squirting herself with scent in genuine delight. But I knew, without being told, that these gifts were superfluous, because Clemmie was coming home. It was clear that something awful had happened to her, and that her life with Chamba had gone so horribly wrong, but she was coming home with me, and I was glad.

Clemmie

DESPITE MY ACHING heart, we had a happy evening. Kamil, the owner of the motel, was in high spirits in his lovely yellow and black striped robe, and his jaunty baseball cap and his impressive gold teeth. There was a lot of laughing and back-slapping with Will and cheerful teasing of Emily when he was told that she had just got married. 'But where is the husband?' he asked, looking left and right. 'Already he is missing?'

Emily looked so contented and well, and laughed at the teasing. I had thought so often of the miserable Emily I had left behind when I rode off with Chamba, and now, *voilà*, she was transformed by the love of a good man. I sat next to her and we hung our arms round each other's necks, and it was so good to be close again.

Divinity fetched the champagne from the fridge and Will opened it and we toasted each other. Divinity had also managed to bring some potato crisps from the hotel for the party she knew we would have. Kamil ordered us a slap-up meal of some very chewy meat and potatoes. Nothing was said about the future. No one asked me about Chamba. Divinity must have warned Will to keep off the subject, and Emily was silent. Later, when we lay in the dark, I would tell her how my life had ended, how the gently spoken words of Alvin Brockenhurst had torn my heart in two. It may sound overdramatic, but all the time I was laughing, eating and drinking with the others, I was aware of a dull ache in my chest where my heart was like a stone between my ribs.

'Tomorrow is market,' announced Kamil, coming to our table. 'Many camels. Many men. Very early rise!'

'Well, I'm ready for bed,' said Will, stretching and yawning. 'It's been quite a day for all of us.' He held out his hand to Divinity and she took it and put it to her lips. I was struck by how happy they looked, and I hoped that she had taken my advice.

Emily and I had found a two-bedded room on the little courtyard and moved our stuff into it so that we could talk, as in the old days. We undressed in the dark and climbed into our narrow wooden beds, and I lay staring at the stars shining through the pointed window, and waited for the words to come to me to tell her about Chamba's betrayal.

I knew that she was waiting too. I could hear her gentle breathing and the space between us was alive with her unspoken questions.

'Brockenhurst says that Chamba was involved in the kidnapping plot,' I began quietly. 'He says that he and Bazet had arranged to sell me on, to raise money for the terrorist stuff he's involved in, and that I was a valuable prize that fell into his hands. I really do believe he loves me, but apparently he never lost sight of what I was worth. Recently the stakes have been upped, with more military activity in the north, and Brockenhurst says he used my journey to meet you as a means of getting rid of me. You would have been contacted by the kidnappers and a ransom demanded. It's happened before out here. It's nothing new. If you had failed to raise the money, I would have eventually been bumped off.

'Alvin told me that Chamba has a Tuareg wife and a family in Tamanrasset. He showed me photographs. Now I have had time to think about it, what he said fits in with Chamba's movements. He was often away for days at a time, leaving me with his family in the

341

desert or at the oasis village where he has a house. He took me to caves in the mountains which Alvin says are the headquarters of his "army". He keeps weapons there, and even hostages – soldiers that he has captured from the Malian forces. I thought he was just involved in smuggling over the border, but it seems it's far more serious than that.'

Emily had been silent, but she leaned across and found my hand and held it in hers. 'Oh, Clemmie!'

'It's a bugger, as Grandpa would have said.'

'It *is* a bugger! So what happens next?'

'I want to speak to Chamba more than anything, to hear it all in his own words, but Alvin says I will not be allowed any further contact. I don't dare try to ring him because I don't want the call to be traced, but I'm living in hope that he will contact me. I've left messages for him all along the way. Brockenhurst says that I must leave the country with you, and that's that. Chapter closed. But I can't do that, Emily. I can't leave without speaking to him again. It would kill me. Do you know what Brockenhurst said? He told me I should settle for a Dorset farmer and count myself lucky that he rescued me from kidnapping and a horrible fate.'

I knew that Emily probably thought the same. Any sensible person would.

'But let me tell you, Ems, about when we said goodbye.' I looked through the window at the stars and my voice shrank to a whisper. She was the only person in the world I would share this with. What I was about to tell her was already my most precious memory of when I had been happiest.

'Chamba had been away, and he came to find me with Bazet. I was out at the tents with the women and children. I love the nomadic life much more than when we are at the oasis or in the town. The day begins with the rising sun and ends as it goes down, and everything is very simple, and I help with the goats and the sheep which I am good at, because I can pare a foot or file teeth, and I can milk as well as they can.

'Anyway, Chamba and Bazet arrived and there was a bit of a commotion amongst the women, and a kid was killed, and while it was roasting, Chamba and I took our camels – my beautiful white Orion and his Absau – do you remember Absau, Em? – and rode out into the desert.

'We rode side by side and he drew Absau so close to Orion that we could hold hands, and he pulled my chech from my head and asked me to loosen my hair, so that it whipped behind me when we galloped.

343

'We found a place to stop – a perfect place where there was blue shade from a rocky outcrop, and the sand was almost white and rippled like a sea from the wind. We hobbled the camels and made love, so tenderly, Em, and he told me how much he would miss me while I was away, and how he would think of me on every step of the journey. He showed me the symbols on the bracelets he had given me, the camel train that would bring me back, the moon, the star to guide me, and the funny little symbol that means a Tuareg is never alone.'

I paused, and Emily got out of bed and came to sit beside me and put her arms round me. Her face was wet with tears.

'I can't bear it,' she said. 'I can't bear it for you.'

'Bazet and I left that evening. We drove back to the village and I collected my stuff and we left. Chamba simply held me to him when we said our last goodbyes, but his words were with me. I carried them with me. They are still here in my heart.'

I covered my wet face with my hands. 'Was it all lies, Em? Was it?'

'No, he *loved* you. I know he did. He loved you from the beginning. I was there, remember. It made me fucking jealous. Maybe all that stuff Alvin told you is true, but Chamba loved you. He can't take that away.'

I sniffed and sighed. It was hard not to weep, but if I started, I wasn't sure I could stop. 'I know he did,' I said. 'I know he did. You can't be mistaken about something like that, can you?'

'No. Remember all those silly women who thought my dad was in love with them because he got pissed and flirted with them at dinner parties and tried to kiss them and put his hand up their skirts? Daft women, whose heads were turned by his attention. It was usually all over in a few weeks. Remember me and Ted, how I convinced myself I loved him because I was in the habit of it, and because I thought my life would end if he left me. I was in denial and deluded. If I'd really been prepared to look at the facts, I could have seen he was a worthless bum. What you've described isn't like that. It's the real thing, Clemmie. You know it is.'

'Yes, I know. Even if he was involved in getting me kidnapped, I still believe he loved me. And if he didn't, Em, if it turns out to have all been a pretence and a lie, then I'm lost, I'm done for.'

'No you're not. Don't talk like that! You're fabulous, you're beautiful. You'll come home and make a new life, and . . .'

345

'I can't do it, Em! I can't make a new life after what I've had here. How can I? I keep thinking of Great-Aunt Mary and how, really, she didn't live again. I'll be the same, blocking off what happened to me in order to survive. But there's something else. There's a difference.'

'What do you mean?'

'Can't you guess? Didn't you notice I only sipped the champagne tonight? I'm pregnant, Em. Three months gone, I think. I'm having Chamba's baby. I'll have a part of him for ever. I'll have what was snatched from poor Great-Aunt Mary.'

Emily hugged me closer. 'I'm so glad for you!' she whispered. 'I'm so glad you've told me. Didn't you notice that *I* only sipped the champagne tonight? I'm pregnant too. I found out just before the wedding. I haven't told anyone – not even Hugh. We'll have our babies together, side by side in Dorchester Maternity Unit. Oh Clemmie, how wonderful!'

But she'll have Hugh, I thought, and I'll have no one to sit beside my bed and hold my hand. I'll look through the window and the sky will be heavy and grey and there will be no desert stars to shine on Chamba's baby.

★ ★ ★

346

We talked on, right through the darkness of the night, and slept only an hour or so before a pale light crept through our window. We yawned and looked across at one another. Emily had dark smudges under her eyes, and that grumpy early-morning look I knew so well. She mumbled about needing a pee and stomped off across the yard in her flip-flops. I lay for a while longer, remembering what we had talked about. Sharing my grief with Emily had helped, and my mind felt clearer, even if my heart was still heavy.

'Have you felt sick?' Emily demanded, reappearing in the doorway.

'No, have you?'

'Not until this morning.'

'Have you been sick?'

'No, I just feel it.'

'Do you want a coffee or a cup of tea? Would that make it better?'

'I don't know. I haven't been pregnant before. I feel absolutely starving, though. Shall we see if there's any breakfast?'

There was. Bread and coffee and hard-boiled eggs and dates and bananas. It was a fine breakfast and we ate a lot, and as the sun grew hot we peeled off our layers and watched the business of the day begin. Donkey carts were arriving from both directions and stalls set up all along the road. Little fires were lit and water boiled for tea. Strings of camels appeared out of the desert and came to a halt, standing motionless while the camelmen hunkered down on the sand and shared tea with friends.

Divinity and Will wandered off to see what there was for sale, and to take photographs, while Emily and I sat sleepily in the sun like two farmyard cats.

'Are they Tuareg, these camels?' Emily asked, as another string went by.

'Yes, I think so. Some may be Arabs. I'm going to miss camel riding. Can you remember how I wanted to buy a camel with my credit card when we travelled together last time?'

'It's a shame you can't take one home.'

I wish she hadn't said that. Home. Where was home? If we were talking about stones and bricks, it would always be the old farmhouse in the Dorset valley. That was where I belonged, but my sense of home included anywhere I had been with Chamba. He was my home. 'Houses are the graves of the living' is a Tuareg saying. They don't understand our attachment to bricks and roofs.

'That man seems to be calling us over,' said Emily, shading her eyes.

'Where?'

'The man with those four white camels. Look, he's waving again.'

I stood up, my heart suddenly pounding in my chest.

'Okay, let's go and see what he wants,' I said calmly, at the same time taking Emily's hand and digging my nails into it.

'Ouch! What's that for?'

'I don't know, but I think, I think . . .'

She read the expression on my face. 'Don't go, Clemmie. You've been threatened already. Don't go over. Stay here. You don't know that man. It could be anyone.'

Nobody could have stopped me. I crossed the dusty road and walked towards the camels, Emily trailing behind me, grumbling and trying to get a signal on her mobile so that she could ring Will and summon him back.

'You're mad, you're mad,' she kept saying. 'It could be the kidnappers, for God's sake.'

I reached the man, who stood with his back to me, ignoring me once he had attracted my attention. He was tall and slim, wearing a blue robe and a black chech. He turned when I greeted him, and I did not know him. He was a stranger to me. Without a word he pulled a piece of paper from his robe and handed it to me. I turned it over. There were only three words, clumsily written in pencil on the back of a cigarette packet. 'Bazet. Today evening.'

Emily

I HADN'T FORGOTTEN HOW headstrong Clemmie can be. She set off down the road with me trailing behind her and went straight up to the tall man, who gave her no sign of recognition, merely passed her something and turned away again. She looked at the scrap of paper in her hand, closed her fist on it and came back to loop her arm through mine.

'Keep walking and talking,' she hissed. 'Don't say anything.'

'How can I keep talking and not say anything?'

'Easily. Talk drivel.' She paused by a stall. 'Look at these lovely onions. All for sale.'

'How lovely,' I said, smiling at the Peul woman who stood behind her glistening golden mound. 'What beautiful onions!'

'Just behave normally. We'll make our way back to

the café, order some tea, and I'll tell you what I have in my hand.'

We sauntered along further, admiring sweet potatoes and a pile of strange roots and a lot of bananas, and then crossed back to the other side and walked very slowly back to our table on the veranda.

'*Deux thés, s'il vous plait,*' I called to Kamil, who was lying on a sun lounger with his eyes closed. He relayed the order to a boy inside the kitchen without sitting up or opening his eyes, then trilled two fingers in my direction to show that the message had been received. Market day clearly had no great impact on the number of his customers.

Clemmie opened her fist and put the small rectangle of dirty paper on the table.

'What is it?' I asked.

'Read it,' she said. 'It's a message.' Her face was flushed and her eyes were bright.

'"Bazet. Today evening",' I read. 'What does it mean?'

'Ssshh!' Clemmie looked round nervously at Kamil. 'It means he's coming this evening. It means he's coming for me!'

'How can you read that into it? It could mean anything. He's under arrest, isn't he? It could mean he's going to be taken out and shot today evening.'

352

Clemmie glared at me. 'Don't say things like that, Emily.'

Our teas arrived and Clemmie turned her message over. When the boy had gone, his bare feet shuffling on the wooden floor, she turned it back and stabbed it with her finger. 'It means that he will be here this evening to take me home. To take me back to Chamba. I know it does. I feel it in my heart.'

'It could be another kidnap attempt,' I pointed out. 'That's just as likely.'

'No, it's not. I've never believed the kidnap theory – not really.' Clemmie's face was shining with joy. 'Don't you see, it's all a lie. It's a fabrication of Alvin Fucking Brockenhurst. We know he's lied to us and he's staged robberies and God knows what. Why should I believe him? Why should I trust him and not Chamba? I don't know why I've been so stupid as to not see this before, but he's worked on us all, so that we believed him and didn't question what he told us.'

'Why should he bother? Why should he put on all this . . .' I waved my arms in the air, 'this charade?'

'The stakes are very high. There's enormous untapped wealth in the desert. Chamba knows this – all Tuareg know it. Brockenhurst wants leverage over Chamba. He wants bargaining power. He'll tell Chamba he is holding me, and get him to negotiate. Meanwhile I'll be shipped out of the country, out of the way.'

'This sounds so unlikely, Clem.'

'No more unlikely than what he's been telling us.'

'What about the photos? The evidence?'

'You can doctor photographs, can't you? How do I know it was really Chamba's wife and children? I allowed myself to believe it, because that was what I was told.'

'Well, just say this *is* a message from Bazet and he does turn up tonight. Are you really going to set off with him again, after what you've told me about him? You've told me how he behaved to you on the way here. How horrible he was. He hit you, you said.'

'Don't you see? There *was* danger in the desert. He picked up on that in Kidal. Maybe it was Mariam and her son. Maybe they tipped off the government – I don't know who exactly; government *agents* – that we were travelling south on our own, that I was a valuable prize. Who knows? I kept trying to use my mobile to contact you – it made him mad, but maybe they *were* tracking my calls. How do I know?'

'But you said Bazet told you to leave, to come back with us. How do you explain that?'

'It's very simple. He was furious with me and he

thinks Chamba should have a Tuareg wife. He's a traditionalist. Perhaps he would *prefer* I came home with you, but he would do nothing to make that happen. He respects and loves Chamba and he was made responsible for my safety. He would do everything he could to look after me.'

Emily was silent, taking this in. 'Well, it's an explanation of sorts,' she said finally. 'But in that case, Brockenhurst will come after you. He seems to have cars and planes at his disposal. He'll find you and bring you back.'

'No he won't. He doesn't have a clue about the desert. Bazet's a million times more clever. He knows how to disappear.'

'But do you really want to go back?' I pleaded. 'It sounds so dangerous and you're having a baby, Clemmie. You can't have a baby in a nomad's tent. Look what happened to Great-Aunt Mary.'

'I've thought about all of that. I'll come home to have the baby. I had already decided. I'll stay for a month or two, and when the baby is bigger and stronger, I'll come back here.'

I sighed and took her hand. 'I hate you doing this,' I said, miserably. 'I had made up my mind that you would be returning with us. I imagined the scene in your kitchen when you walked through the door with us. I thought about how overjoyed your mum would be.'

'Stop it, Emily! Don't say any more. Don't make it harder for me.'

'Please speak to Will before you make your mind up. Tell him all that you've told me.'

'Of course. You don't have to ask me to do that.'

'But do you really want to go back to that life? It's hard and lonely. You've told me so.'

'It *is* hard and lonely at times, but I love my man with my whole heart. When the baby arrives I won't be so lonely, and I can be useful. Meeting Brockenhurst has shown me that there is a way to make things better for Chamba's people. He may very well turn out to be a useful contact. It's time that the Tuareg had a negotiator on their side, and that could be me. I really could get the school up and running.' As she spoke, Clemmie turned the cigarette packet over and over in her slender fingers. She was transformed by energy and determination. It almost sparked out of her.

'Your father sent money for your air ticket,' I said, reluctantly. 'He hoped you would be coming home with us.'

'Give it to me, Emily. It can pay for when I come

home to have the baby,' she said, with a bright smile. 'In the summer. It's not so long to wait.'

'You're so thin,' I said. 'You don't eat enough out here to have a healthy baby.' It was a mean thing to say, but I couldn't help it.

'Em.' Clemmie turned to look me in the eye. 'The Tuareg have big, fat, healthy babies. I shall just have to start eating sheep fat and drinking more camel milk. I will, don't worry. I'll turn myself into a brood mare. I'm sorry, Em, I can't do what you want. I love you, you know that, and I love all of them, my whole family, but Chamba is my man. I can't be dragged off home to live a "normal" life. You see that, don't you? Now that you've met Hugh? Try to put yourself in my shoes.'

I was quiet, then. I didn't know how I would feel if Hugh wanted me to go and live in Borneo, or Easter Island, or somewhere. I suppose I knew he wouldn't ask that of me. He would be more understanding – but he'd go himself, I was sure of that. The dynamics of our relationship were so different. Our love was less dramatic, less demanding. Less passionate. I felt a pang of disappointment, but I told myself sternly to stop. I had found what I wanted in Hugh. He was as much my man as Chamba was Clemmie's.

'Look at us!' said Clemmie, and she pointed to how we were both sitting with a hand laid protectively on our stomachs. We smiled at one another. 'It's wonderful, isn't it?' she said. 'Wonderful to think what's happening in here.' She patted her stomach. 'I'm so happy, aren't you?'

'Yes!'

'I'm so glad you're expecting a baby at the same time. We'll be growing fat together. When our babies are born, we can push them up the lane like we did with our dolls. I used to think I wouldn't know what to do with a baby, but I find I'm watching mothers now, how protective they are, how they seem to know what to do quite naturally, and I'm hoping that's what will happen with me.'

'Yes, I know what you mean. I worry that I'll forget mine – leave it by the till in Sainsbury's or something, and I had a nightmare that I'd had the baby but I put it in the garden and forgot to feed it.'

'We'll have Mum to advise us. She'll be the fount of all knowledge. She'll show us the right way up to hold them and all that.'

'I wouldn't rely on *my* mother for advice. I've always felt quite surprised that she managed to rear me at all.'

We both grinned, and I had a vision of Clem and

me sitting on the grass at home like we used to do, with our babies on a rug beside us.

'Be brave for me!' she said quietly. 'Please, Em, be brave. I don't want to leave you and Will when we have only just met again, but you do understand, don't you?'

'Yes,' I said. 'I understand.'

Will and Divinity came back then, Divinity loaded down with various things she had bought which she set out on the table. She had practically stripped the little jewellery stall. The languid boy who looked after it followed behind grinning from ear to ear. He disappeared into the café and came out with a Coke. He squatted on the sand in the strip of shade and waved it happily in our direction. Divinity had made his day. Or year, more likely.

'Will, I need to talk to you,' said Clemmie. 'Will you come for a little walk with me?'

'Sure. It's still only half past seven. Bit early for a beer.'

Divinity sat next to me and looked after them. 'What's that all about? What's going on?' she asked suspiciously.

'There's been a development,' I told her. 'Clemmie

has had a message that she thinks is from Bazet – the guy who brought her down here to meet us.'

'The one who was going to sell her on to kidnappers?'

'Yeah.'

'He's under arrest, according to Alvin.'

'Apparently not. She thinks the message means he's coming for her this evening. To take her back.'

'Bloody hell! Is she going to get him arrested?'

'No, she's going with him.'

'What? You must be joking!'

'Sssshhh! She doesn't want anyone else to know.' Briefly I told her of our conversation, guessing at her outraged reaction. She would think Clemmie was certifiable.

But, 'Good for her!' she said when I had finished. 'Go, girl! I've never been convinced by Alvin Brockenhurst. I don't think he's looking out for her, or us. He's got his own agenda. He'd sell his grandmother if it suited him.'

'That's what Clemmie thinks. She believes in her man, in Chamba.'

'She's changed. I've got time for her now. She's serious, you know what I mean? It's right she should trust what she feels.'

I looked at her, surprised.

'I don't know how dangerous it will be for her, trying to get back. I don't know how trustworthy this Bazet man is. It's a horrible risk,' I said.

'Your lot like risk. It keeps you going.'

'What do you mean?'

'It's in your upbringing. All that fox hunting you were brought up to do. All that being pitched over thorn hedges into ditches. All that shooting and outdoor games. It's in your blood.'

I had to laugh at that, but in a way it was true. Since we were children, we had done things that would terrify us in cold blood. Clemmie and I used to go back after hunting and look with wonder and pride at the enormous hedges our small ponies had jumped.

I don't know what Clemmie said to Will, but they came back arm in arm and I could tell she had been crying and Will looked grave.

'Well, it *is* time for a beer now,' he said, forcing a cheerful voice. 'It's all of half past eight.'

We spent the day lazily, taking hours over lunch and then going to our rooms to lie on our beds in the blasting heat of the afternoon. Clemmie knelt on the floor and packed her bags, exclaiming again over all the things I had brought her. Then she lay on her bed and wrote a letter to her mother.

'Don't let her be sad, Emily,' she said. 'Tell her I'll be home very soon. She'll be happy about the baby, won't she? She'll have that to look forward to.'

When the heat of the sun was fading, we went to sit on the veranda and found Will and Divinity already there.

'How will he come, do you think?' asked Will.

'Horse, carriage, wheelbarrow, cart!' said Clemmie. 'I don't know. Not a clue.'

The market was packing up for the day and the sand road was busy with carts, horses and camels. The man who had passed the message had gone, disappearing with his camels into the empty distance. Clemmie sat on the edge of her seat, tense with watching and waiting, her eyes searching. I sat next to her, and to be honest, I was hoping he wouldn't come.

Then, from amongst the carts, a small, familiar figure appeared and trotted across the road, looking dusty and weary.

'It's Serufi!' I cried. 'His truck has been here all the time, but I haven't seen him since we first arrived.'

Clemmie sprang down the steps and ran to greet him with a hug, then led him over to where we sat.

'Where have you been, Serufi? I missed you,' I said. 'I hoped you would stay here with me.'

He said something to Clemmie and she translated, 'A roof is a prison for a Tuareg. He preferred to go and stay with his "cousins" – he means Tuareg people close by.'

We all sat smiling at one another, but it seemed to me that Serufi looked tired and as if he had walked a long way. The edge of his robe was very dirty, and his feet were dusty. He readily accepted a cold drink and some food that Will ordered for him. I remembered how the Tuareg love painkillers, and I went back to my room and found some paracetamol and offered them to him. He took them happily and swallowed them with his Fanta.

Clemmie sat watching him with an air of intensity, and I guessed that she was longing to ask him what he knew. His home was in Tamanrasset where Chamba was supposed to have his Tuareg wife and family. I remembered what he had told Hugh at the beginning of our journey, and I hoped that he would spare her, if any of it was true.

When he had finished eating, he wiped his mouth carefully and began to talk, with a little English, some French and mostly Tamashek. Clemmie sat beside him, listening, translating, asking him to speak more slowly.

'He's got news of Bazet!' she told us, with shining eyes. 'I can't understand it all, but he says that he *is* coming for me! He says that there was talk amongst the Tuareg he has been with that Bazet had been held for a day and a night by men of a Bozo village, where we crossed the river. They had been paid well, but they are gentle people and they let him go. Then he found a man who has just sold Bazet three good camels. He says Bazet will come this evening and that he will be contacted when the time comes, and he will take me to a place not far from here where I will find him waiting.'

'I'd like to go with you,' said Will. 'I need to see that you are safely on your way.'

'Me too,' I said, although 'safe' was not how I would have described it.

'We must leave very quietly and without drawing attention to my going,' said Clemmie. 'I'm sure old Kamil is trustworthy, but it seems that Brockenhurst is free with his bribes, and you never know.'

Eventually we worked out a plan. When Serufi received the message that Bazet was close by, he would knock on our door and then leave the front of the building with Will, as if they were going to have a stroll and a smoke together. Clemmie and I would find a way out through the back and meet them behind the building.

We got up to go back to our room, and Divinity said she would join us shortly to say goodbye. When she knocked on our door a few minutes later, Clemmie let her in and closed the door behind her.

'Thank you, Divinity,' she said, 'For seeing me through a horrible time.'

They hugged each other, and Divinity said, 'Hey, I've got something for you,' and passed over a plastic bag containing one or two lipsticks and a full bottle of scent. 'They might not be your taste,' she said, 'but it's all I've got to give you, and I guess there's not much choice out here.'

'Oh, Divinity! That's so kind and thoughtful,' said Clemmie. 'A bit of slap and a squirt of scent is like a lifesaver when you are living in a tent and smelling like an old sheep.'

'I wanted you to know,' said Divinity, looking quite bashful, 'that I did tell Will, you know, what we were talking about. It's the first time I've told him, and I guess it's kind of important. To us both.'

'I'm glad!' said Clemmie warmly. 'I'm so glad.'

365

I began to feel a bit left out here. After speaking to Will, I'd never have thought there could be real affection for Clemmie on Divinity's part.

'Yeah, well, good luck, and I guess I'm kind of proud of you. More than that, I think you're fucking amazing!' She gave Clemmie another hug and was gone.

'Bit of a change of heart there,' I said. It was on the tip of my tongue to tell Clemmie what Will had told me, but I refrained because it would have been a spiteful thing to do.

'She's all right, is Divinity,' said Clemmie. 'I can tell you, it feels good to have her on your side.

'I've been thinking,' she added, scanning the view from the window. 'We can go out this way when we get the signal from Serufi.'

'I'll never fit through there.'

'Yes you will. It looks a bit narrow, but you'll be fine.'

'How will Serufi get the message?'

'On his phone? By messenger? I don't know. Somehow.'

She had barely finished speaking when there was a tiny knock on the door. She opened it a crack and I caught a glimpse of the back view of Serufi crossing the yard. We looked at one another for a moment before Clemmie went into action.

'Help me, Emily,' she said, as she squashed her bags through the window and they fell to the filthy, littered ground below.

'You see, it's a good thing I'm thin,' she said as she climbed on the chair. She got one leg out and then the other and hopped down on to the ground.

'Are you coming?' she asked.

'I'm too fat!'

'No you're not. Try!'

'What if I get stuck?'

'Come *on*, Emily! Don't be such a wuss.'

So I tried to squeeze through, and the fancy bits of the frame stuck into me quite painfully, but eventually I did it, and dropped to the ground beside her.

Together we picked up her bags and started to walk to God knows where – just away from the building.

'Where are they?' I said, looking about me. There was a pile of rubbish from the hostel and some roughly dug pits, but otherwise nothing. 'There's no one here.'

'They'll be here somewhere. Just wait.'

Away from the road it was very still and quiet. I could hear just the voices of the last of the market people in the distance, and the sound of a donkey braying. Although it was late afternoon, it was very hot and sweat immediately trickled between my breasts and down my neck.

A stone rattled on the line of low rocks to the right. We both turned our heads to look. It was followed by another.

'There they are,' whispered Clemmie. 'Come on!'

A moment later, I could see Will and Serufi waiting for us, tucked behind some small boulders. Will took Clemmie's bags and she and I walked arm in arm, following Serufi, who trotted in front. He turned to raise ten fingers at us. 'Ten minutes,' said Clemmie. 'Bazet is ten minutes away.'

We walked in silence, following a rough sort of track, towards a line of scraggy thorn trees in the distance. It was now completely quiet and I heard only my heavy breathing and the mewing call of a large bird of prey that wheeled lazily in the darkening sky.

'There they are!' said Will suddenly, pointing, and following the line of his arm I made out three couched camels beneath the trees, and two men. One of them came to meet us, dressed in a blue robe with a dark yellow chech.

'Is that him?' I whispered. 'Is it Bazet?'

'It's him,' said Clemmie.

★　　★　　★

She cried when we reached him, and he put his arm round her and wiped away the tears with the edge of his sleeve. I knew then that she would be all right, because this man was tender towards her. He would do her no harm. They talked together rapidly and then she turned to us and said, 'He *has* come to take me back, Emily, like I said he would. He asks me how I could ever have doubted him.'

'What if you're followed?'

She grinned. 'He's got a rifle. I can shoot the tyres out of any vehicle.'

'You could, too,' said Will proudly. Clemmie had always been the deadliest shot of all the Kingsleys.

Bazet handed her a bundle of cloth and she shook out a long dark blue robe, which she pulled on. I helped her bundle up her hair and she expertly wound a pale blue chech round her head. She took off her boots and stowed them in a saddle bag, then removed her bracelets and her necklace and put them in her bag.

Will went over and talked to Bazet, and there was a lot of arm-clasping in a brotherly way. I guessed he was asking Bazet to look after his sister. I saw that Bazet had a strong face, but that his eyes were kind.

He called something to Clemmie, and she turned

to me. 'We've got to go,' she said. 'He says we've many hours' riding before we can stop.'

We hugged, all three of us, and she hugged Serufi too, and then she turned and mounted one of the camels. It sprang up from its knees as Bazet swung himself up on his own beast.

She looked so slender and fragile, her bare feet resting on the towering neck. 'Take care!' I called, stupidly, my voice thick with the effort of not crying.

'Don't worry, I will!' She indicated her belly. 'I've good reason to look after myself, and so do you.'

'Don't forget the sheep-fat sandwiches!'

'I won't! Tell Mum I'll be home soon. And tell her I love her. Tell them all I love them!'

We stood and watched them go. After five minutes they were just three small figures in the distance. A few minutes more and they had disappeared completely. The horizon lay stretched out and empty. The sky met the sand in a shimmering, unbroken line.

It was over. Clemmie had gone.

Will hooked his arm through mine and we walked back slowly with Serufi, and although we didn't talk, I was grateful to have him there. It made all the difference.

★   ★   ★

The following morning we set off to meet Hugh, as arranged, at Sangha, a village in Dogon country. It was a long day's drive, but as we worked our way south, we left the empty sands behind and found ourselves entering another world, with winding rivers, huge stands of trees, and tidy little patches of onions and maize. Gangs of monkeys raced across the road, and the people we passed seemed gentle and cheerful. Scratching away at their land with stone axes, they straightened up to stare and wave as we went by.

Old men cycled very slowly between the villages of funny little round thatched huts, and laughing children herded cows to wander and graze along the roadside.

It felt a happier country, and we were all affected by the change in mood. We had said goodbye to Clemmie, but at the same time our spirits lifted. Will and Divinity laughed and talked and held hands, and I couldn't wait to see Hugh again.

As we drew into the courtyard of the simple guest house where we were to stay, I could feel my heart thumping with anxiety that he wouldn't be there, that something would have befallen him, but there he was, coming out to meet us, opening the passenger door of the jeep and actually lifting me out and holding me to him in a bear hug.

'Christ, Ems, I've missed you,' he said. 'My work's been fantastic, but I've missed you so much!'

We had a long, leisurely lunch and there was so much to tell each other, and afterwards we lay on our bed in our shady room, both feeling exhausted with the happiness of being together. Hugh was so excited by his field work that he wanted to tell me all about it, and I was glad that he could share it with me. He had found evidence of the Dogon belief that their ancestors could fly and had colonised their escarpment from the air. Belief in this still existed, and it made him very happy. He had also discovered evidence of twenty different Dogon languages, many more than had so far been identified, and had managed to record a good number of them.

'You see, the Muslim Peul people drove the Dogons into the mountians and took their farming land, and the common language is now Peul. These old languages will disappear, Emily. They'll be gone in twenty, thirty years as the old people die out.' I felt proud of him for caring about such a tiny scrap of inconsequential history that would never make him rich or famous.

We had told him all about Clemmie over lunch, but now, feeling so close to him, and able to share the pleasure he got from his work, reminded me of something she had said.

'You know, it was hard saying goodbye to Clemmie all over again,' I told him. 'It was as bad as the first time – or even worse, because she told me how hard the loneliness is to bear, and how little she can share of Chamba's life. But she loves him so much, and from what she told me, he loves her too.'

I could tell from Hugh's voice that he was smiling when he replied. 'You can't organise everything for everybody, Em. However good your intentions. Clemmie knows what she is doing, and the loneliness must be a price she considers worth paying.'

Our wide-open window overlooked the village school yard, and suddenly, in perfect harmony, came a choir of childish voices singing 'Frère Jacques'.

'Listen!' said Hugh. 'It's lovely, isn't it? The sound of children singing.'

I told him about the baby then, and afterwards I lay in his arms and he stroked my hair.

'I can't imagine ever feeling happier than I do at this moment,' he said, and neither could I.

When we got back to England, my proper married life as Hugh's wife began and the new school term started and Hugh began to write up his field notes, and we were pretty busy for a week or two. The memories of Africa began to fade and I got tired of people asking where we had been on honeymoon and when I said Mali, them replying, 'Why on earth Mali?' or, 'Mali, where's that?'

We had a happy weekend staying with my parents in Dorset, and when I told my mother about the baby, she astonished me by bursting into tears of joy and saying she thought that I had just got fatter than usual.

'You've always told me you hated being pregnant,' I told her.

'Yes, but this time I don't have to have the baby!' she said.

We went to celebrate with Aunt Ellen and Uncle Peter and found them in a state of excitement that Clemmie would be coming home before too long. They had managed to speak to her on the telephone and had learned that she had got back to Chamba without incident and was happily settled in village life again. All I could hope was that this was true.

'The photographs you all took are wonderful. They give us such a good idea of what the desert is like,' said Aunt Ellen. 'But Emily, I can't help but think it looks so desolate and lonely. How can Clemmie bear it, after this?' and she raised her hand to the kitchen window, which looked out over the green cow pastures to the grey stone roofs of the village.

I wanted to be truthful but didn't want to alarm her. I remembered what Hugh had said to me.

'She told me that it's hard and lonely at times,' I said. 'But it's a price worth paying, to be with the man she loves.'

Later, when I was back at school, I looked up Alvin Brockenhurst on the internet. There was no record of him ever having been a professor at Princeton University. In fact, there was no evidence that he existed at all.